Born in Hobart, Tasmania, **Sean Rabin** has worked as a dishwasher, cook, script reader, copy-editor and journalist. He has lived in Ireland, Italy, London and New York, and now resides in Sydney, Australia. When not writing, he is reading and listening to music. His short stories have been published in Australia and the United States.

First published in 2016 by Giramondo
This edition first published in Great Britain
by Dodo Ink, an imprint of
Dodo Publishing Co Ltd
Flat 5, 21 Silverlands, Buxton SK17 6QH
www.dodoink.com

Artwork by Tristan Rogers
Design: Sorrel Packham
Typesetter: Ben Ottridge

ISBN 978-0-9935758-1-5 paperback

Printed and bound in Great Britain by Clays Ltd,
1 Tudor Street, Blackfriars, London EC4Y 0AH.

WOOD GREEN

SEAN RABIN

1.

Michael gripped his shins and bent his head towards his knees. The panic in his chest refused to be rationalised or contained, and infiltrated the extremities of his body with every shudder and lurch made by the Boeing 737. He could hear the other passengers laughing, but knew it was just a survival mechanism. If one did not laugh at their impending collision with the coast of Tasmania, and disintegration in a fireball of aviation fuel, then the only other option was to scream with terror.

He tried to curl his body tighter and feared his spine was about to snap; held his breath, swallowed against the pressure inside his ears, and squeezed his eyes closed to avoid glimpsing the rushing approach of land. If only the pilot would turn towards the water where they all had a better chance of survival. A change in direction, however, required time, altitude, and sufficient control over the plane's steering mechanism, all of which he assumed were no longer available or dwindling fast. He felt himself violently shaken sideways and braced for impact; the clamour of the under-carriage scraping along the tarmac; veering suddenly off the runway; a wing snagging on a patch of grass; cries from passengers as legs were broken, arms shredded and bodies cut in two. Michael was ashamed of the way he had grumbled at check-in about the need to pay an additional twenty-five dollars to secure a bulkhead seat. What was such a paltry sum when compared with the good fortune of sitting in one of the strongest sections of the plane, closest to the exit, with the added protection of a nearby wing? Had he been seated behind someone else it would have proved impossible to bend so far forward. The space between the rows was woefully inadequate, and offered no other option than to brace against the seat in front, leaving the top of his head – as the emergency manual illustrations demonstrated – completely unprotected while the roof of the aircraft was torn away.

Catering trolleys clattered and rattled as the cabin suddenly tilted. Michael interpreted the silence spreading amongst the other passengers as a sign that land was near and it would all soon be over. A smell of fear flooded his nostrils. A sour taste rose to the back of his throat. He would probably feel no pain. One minute consciousness, the next...nothing. The comforting voices of his mother and father, dead more than five years, whispered in his ears until drowned out by the whine of engines making a futile attempt at acceleration. The wheels were lowered next, sounding like a pack of barking dogs let loose in the cargo hold. None of it offered any reassurance as he knew the pilots were required to follow landing procedure irrespective of their chances of survival. If only he had caught a different flight then none of this would be happening – well not to him at least. Michael dispatched mental apologies to everyone he had ever wronged, and wondered if Rachel would cry at his funeral. She had every reason not even to show up after the way he had left without saying goodbye. Though their status as a couple had ended more than three weeks ago, he knew their fourteen-month relationship had been serious enough to warrant greater consideration than disappearing to another state without leaving word. But if Rachel did attend, would she wear that little back dress he found so alluring? He guessed it depended on whether the service was held in the warmth of Sydney or the chill of Hobart. Would there be enough of him left even to conduct a funeral?

Michael wanted to hold the hand of the woman sitting next to him in a gesture of solidarity as they faced their demise together. Except his body was rigid with fear. Fixed into a ball. Isolated from all contact with the world aside from the seatbelt buckle pressing painfully into his stomach and the aeroplane shaking beneath his feet. The anticipation was almost too much to bear. Michael's breathing quickened; he could sense a scream mounting in his lungs. What did it matter if he exhibited cowardice in the final moments of his life. No one would live to tell the tale. In a few seconds everyone on board was going to die regardless of whether they had been brave or not.

Excuse me Sir.

He felt a hand pressed gently to the middle of his back, and opened his eyes to a flight attendant with ruthlessly plucked eyebrows and a thick coating of make-up that was beginning to crack. Her hair was tied so tightly behind her head that the concern she attempted to express looked

7

closer to a case of Irritable Bowel Syndrome. Michael then noticed the other passengers glancing in his direction as they retrieved their luggage from the overhead lockers.

The fasten-seatbelt sign has been turned off, said the attendant. It's time to leave the aircraft.

2.

Tiny droplets of rain stung Michael's ears as he descended the mobile steps parked against the rear exit of the plane. Hobart's cold wind made him gasp, smile with relief at having survived another flight, then feel hot shame at yet again failing to control his phobia of flying. On the tarmac he looked back to the aircraft and realised he had never before stood so close to one. All previous air travel had been a clinical, sanitised affair where he was carefully funnelled through ubiquitous terminals and gateways until he stepped through an oval doorway into the pacifying internal organs of a mechanical bird. Now, however, he could observe the decelerating rotations of the turbines, identify the hydraulics of the landing gear, measure himself against the height of the wing, and witness the luggage being unloaded from the far side of the undercarriage. It briefly gave him a childlike sense of wonder, and made the prospect of his return flight home – whenever that might be – marginally less ominous.

Though one of the states in Australia, Tasmania's island locale made its landscape distinct from the mainland. Behind the small terminal building topped with a 'Welcome To Hobart' sign were hills as golden and rolling as a Tuscan postcard. Yet in the opposite direction stretched a windswept plateau populated by short robust trees whose dark foliage had more in common with those inhabiting marshlands. The cold easily cut through Michael's clothes, constricting his skin, quickening his pulse and confirming his long-held belief that he was a warm-weather person. His thin-soled shoes offered scant protection against puddles, and the prospect of wet socks hastened him towards the terminal building.

At its entrance stood a group of Chinese tourists struggling to interpret the concerns of a customs official who had singled out their party and led it to a large yellow garbage bin with a sign mounted above it indicating the laws against carrying fruit and meat into Tasmania, and the fines to be faced should anyone decide to flout them. Inside, the other passengers congregated around a small baggage carousel while watching a life-sized plastic seal – advertising scenic speedboat rides – disappear and reappear from behind the black rubber curtain that concealed the dock where their suitcases were to be loaded. Michael observed families reunite – children hold up toys for uncles to appreciate – while he tried not to consider the solitude that could potentially accompany the job he was about to begin. Lucian Clarke had not hired him for small talk or literary opinions. Besides any questions he posed concerning the forty years of paperwork he had been employed to organise and classify, Michael anticipated there would be little conversation throughout his working day. Lucian Clarke's novels were large works of complex imagination that contained stories within stories and required hours of undistracted concentration just to read. Michael therefore presumed the focus necessary to write one of them would demand even longer periods of sustained, uninterrupted silence. Lucian Clarke was far from famous, but had earned a readership loyal enough to ensure his works were reviewed by most major newspapers, and occasionally included in the contemporary literature syllabus of selected universities. For years he had ignored all interview requests, politely declined invitations to edit short-story anthologies, wilfully insulted faculty heads who had offered him the chance to teach creative writing courses, and flatly refused to scribble endorsements for anyone else's books. In 2002 he had been given long odds to win the Nobel Prize for Literature, but in the years since then the name Lucian Clarke had failed to reappear as a contender.

The passengers who had travelled with Michael emitted a collective sigh of relief as suitcases started to appear upon the carousel. Soon after a small beagle, under the guidance of its trainer, began to scamper across the luggage searching for the scent of illegal apples or T-bone steaks. A full explanation of the dog's role in safeguarding quarantine regulations was printed on the stiff cape tied across her back, along with guidelines not to pat her in case it proved a distraction from her very important work. As he admired the animal's conscientiousness Michael acknowledged that an equivalent level of dedication would be needed if he was to achieve his objectives for this trip.

Else the sacrifices he had made – job, relationship, friends, home – would have all been for nothing. Novels did not write themselves. He needed to work harder than he had ever done before, or risk repeating the two failed attempts that had marred the past four years of his life. Michael felt instinctively that this was his last chance. If not here and now, then when exactly was he going to write the story that was so persistent in his imagination? The realisation flooded Michael with determination, and inspired him to haul his suitcase from the carousel in such a brusque manner that it turned the head of almost every Tasmanian who stood nearby.

3.

Wood Green? No problem. Just throw your case in the back. First time in Hobart? Holiday or work? Thought so, too damn cold for sight-seeing. They reckon it's going to stay this way for the rest of the week. Still, we could use the rain. Whole place is too dry for my liking. Get a bushfire down here and it's hard to stop it. Too much wind. But a few days of rain should green things up a bit. In from Sydney or Melbourne? Went there once. Wanted to see the Opera House and Harbour Bridge. Didn't like much else though. Too many people, and too fast for an old fella like me. Things are a lot slower down here. Quieter too. You'll get used to it after a while. Probably won't want to go back in the end. Just joking. Although there isn't much to do in Wood Green. Just a shop and a pub and a whole lot of trees. Good if you like bushwalking. Bring some boots with you? Might need to buy a pair if you're planning to stay on through the winter. They're not hard to find in town. Wait, wait. There it is. The Derwent River. Not bad eh? Deepest harbour in the Southern Hemisphere. Bit misty today though. They call that fog the Bridgewater Jerry. Don't ask me why. Should be gone in an hour or so. There was a whale and her calf spotted in the river a few weeks ago. First time in years. Some people say the water's not safe because of the zinc works and paper mills, but I reckon a whale would know if it was clean or not, right? I've got friends who eat fish out of it all the time and there's nothing wrong with them. That's Mount Wellington over there in the distance. Bit of snow on her peak so I'd say it's going to be a cold one today. Wood Green is just on her left side, about a third of the way up. Wait, wait. That section of the bridge we just drove over was the part that collapsed in 1975. You're probably too young to remember. Bulk ore carrier hit one of the pylons and four cars fell about one hundred and fifty feet. Five died that way, and seven of the carrier crew went down with the ship. Poor bastards. People around here still don't like to talk about it. Hobart is a small place, so you never know if someone lost someone, or knows someone who lost someone. And this is *our* opera house. They call it modern architecture but it looks like a rusty tin can to me. Bloody awful. Thought I'd take you the scenic route and show you the docks, it's just as quick. Get a good feed down here. Fish straight off the boats. Down that road you've got Australia's oldest pub, been closed for a couple of years though. And over that way is Salamanca. They put on a big market there every weekend. Tourists love it, but between you and me it's mostly the same tat you can buy everywhere else. Take that road into town and you'll find the oldest theatre in Australia, as well as the country's first synagogue. Not that I think you're Jewish. I'm not either. I just thought you might be interested to know. Wait, wait. Coming up on our right is Australia's oldest Royal tennis court. There are only four in the entire country, but ours was the first. Bet you haven't seen one of those before. If we'd kept going straight we'd have reached the Cascade Brewery. You'll get there eventually, everyone does. The tour is pretty interesting, or so I hear. When my father was a boy the brewers used to roll a couple kegs into the street every Friday afternoon and tap them for the local residents. Oldest continually operating brewery in the country. Just north of Hobart we've also got the oldest golf course in the Southern Hemisphere. And in Richmond, about twenty minutes drive north east, there's Australia's oldest bridge; oldest postal building and oldest Catholic church. Lake St Clair, about two hours away, is also said to be Australia's deepest lake. And up in the northwest you can see the world's oldest tree, if you're inclined that way. Bet you didn't know Australia's first circus performance was in Tasmania, did you? Me neither, but who gives a damn, right? Might get a bit of snow in Wood Green if the weather continues like this. It doesn't usually rain so early in autumn. Looks like we're in for a wet winter. Wonder what the greenies will have to say about that? Nothing good I suppose. That tall building you can see down there is Wrest Point Casino. Australia's first legal casino. Keep going in that direction and you'll reach the Taroona Shot Tower. Three hundred and eighteen steps to the top. Built in 1870, it was the tallest building in Australia for four years, and stayed the tallest building in Tasmania for a hundred years. You can walk to the top if you like. It doesn't cost that much. Wait, wait. Here you are. Wood Green. Told you there wasn't much to the place. Nice view though. What road did you say you were after? Brenan Street. Right. Not sure about that one. They don't go in for street signs much up here, do they? Might have to consult the map. Or I could ask this guy. 'Scuse me mate, Brenan Street? Next left? Gotcha. Thanks. See, what did I tell you, friendly people. Here we are. Brenan Street. No house number? All right, well I guess we'll just stop at the first place we see. You look left and I'll look right. Plenty of room for development along here. Hardly a house in sight. Wait, wait. You think that's it? You're sure? Well okay, that'll be sixty-five, forty. No need to tip here mate, this isn't America. Just give me a call next time you need a cab. Dave's my name. Number's on the card. Enjoy your stay. You're sure there's someone home? Okay then, good luck.

4.

On the covered verandah at the front of the house stood a firewood box that Michael hefted his suitcase on top of so he could rummage through his clothes for a coat to keep him dry as he walked down the side of the house. Rapping his knuckles against the front door had drawn no answer, so Michael decided to check if Lucian was working in a shed or writer's room out back. Mud and water filled his shoes as he squeezed past pricking plants, neglected garden tools and the trunks of giant gum trees that were either standing sentry over the old wooden home, or slowly encroaching upon it. Fallen bark and leaves gave a scent of sumptuous earthiness to the cold quiet air, which Michael inhaled deeply as he rounded a rainwater tank and saw that no shed or hut existed. Large panes of glass constituted the right rear corner of the house, and revealed an unoccupied sunroom with no sign of recent habitation. A kitchen garden overrun with weeds extended to the edge of the forest. Michael tried to distinguish a track between the trees, but had already decided that a search for Lucian would be foolhardy. Turning back to the house he noticed the metal roof was new, maybe two years old at most, while the structure underneath, long ago painted avocado, had evidently been built some time in the late nineteen-sixties.

Michael knocked on the back door in case Lucian had been asleep, then succumbed to the fear that his employer was out of town. He rushed back to his belongings to check the letter confirming his appointment as secretary, along with the date he was supposed to arrive. Lucian had refused to correspond via email, fax or telephone, making a two-month exchange of letters, full of surprisingly personal questions, necessary for Michael to secure the position. As the letter began to sag with moisture he noticed the pale lichen growing along the verandah's wooden railing and colonising the cane armchair beside the wood box. He sat down and tightly crossed his arms and legs in an effort to conserve body heat. The coffee cup beside the chair might have offered hope that Lucian had just stepped out, if not for the insects decomposing in its dregs. Hardly the welcome Michael had hoped for from the man he had spent the second half of his twenties writing a PhD about. There had been few personal details to include in his examination of Lucian Clarke's fiction, and now Michael feared that the author's retreat into isolation was more an indication of deficient social skills than a yearning for a tranquil location in which to write. His letters had certainly been curt and matter-of-fact, and offered no assessment of Michael's thesis. Yet Lucian must have read part of it as he had made initial contact through its publisher. He chose to interpret this as Lucian safeguarding against the development of a sycophantic relationship. But it was too late for that. For weeks he had been reminding himself to act professionally when he finally shook the hand that had written *The Bombardier, Foxtrot, Lady Cadaver* and *Dismantling Ivan's Circus*. Last thing he wanted was to appear besotted or fawning. Michael pulled out his cigarettes and lighter, and embraced the warmth of the smoke that filled his throat and lungs. He retrieved the business card from the same pocket and dropped it into the muck at the bottom of the coffee cup. Any cab driver *other* than Dave would do from now on. An early start, with the stress of flying, and not finding Lucian at home, had left him exhausted. He turned up the collar of his coat, used his suitcase as an ottoman, closed his eyes, and must have fallen into an unexpectedly deep sleep because the first sound he heard of Lucian's return was the lid of the wood box slamming shut.

5.

Kitchen and laundry are through there, along with the sunroom. That's the library. Bathroom. And this is the sitting room. The dog's name is Sadie. She doesn't move much these days, but she's never been one for strangers so I'd leave off introducing yourself until she gets used to seeing you around.

Michael was more than willing to follow Lucian's advice. He had always been nervous around dogs, and tried not to make eye contact with the greying beagle scrutinising him from between two large reading chairs.

Lucian corralled his guest back up the hall towards the front door. In there's my bedroom, and this is the junk room. But I suppose from now on we should call it your office.

Michael leaned through the doorway, registering the cardboard boxes and overflowing filing cabinets; binders piled high on a kidney-shaped desk; newspaper clippings teetering towards collapse, and silverfish scurrying from the glare of the dangling ceiling light.

I wouldn't have needed to hire you if it wasn't a mess, said Lucian as he observed a stunned expression spread across Michael's face. He then noticed the trail of wet sock-prints on his floorboards. Anyway, it's too late to get started now. Have you organised yourself a place to stay?

I've booked a week at a bed and breakfast.

Whereabouts?

Michael pulled a slip of paper from his shirt pocket. Battery Point.

Lucian raised an eyebrow. Fancy. I might have to renegotiate your wages.

It's just until I can find a room in a share-house, or maybe a bedsit to rent.

Wait and see policy, eh? Don't want to sign a lease until you're sure the job is right for you.

No, that's not it at all. I definitely want the job. I just wasn't sure if we were going to be doing any late nights, and if it might be better for me to find a place to live that was close by.

I'd say that practically every night is going to be late, so I suppose you could rent a room in Paul's pub if you wanted to. But I hear it's not particularly well heated. If I were you I'd stay in town. Hobart is a pretty small place, so it never takes long to get anywhere. A cab from Wood Green should have you back at Battery Point in about twenty minutes. You can't stay here though.

No, of course not. I wasn't trying to suggest that I should.

Both men stood awkwardly in the hallway. Michael waiting for Lucian to offer him a seat, and Lucian wondering why his new secretary was not pulling his shoes back on.

Well, like I said, it's too late to start work now, so there's no use trying to get you dry. Lucian reached around Michael and opened the front door. You might want to buy yourself a pair of boots before you come back up. It's only going to get wetter at this time of year. There's a public phone down at the local shop. You can call a taxi from there. If it's out of order just tell Tim or Maureen you're working for me and they'll let you use their private line. They sometimes take messages for me as well, so whenever you see them don't forget to ask if there's anything they need to pass on. No phone here I'm sorry. No internet either.

Michael clumsily squeezed on his sodden shoes. I've got my mobile with me.

Won't do you much good up here. Something to do with the density of the trees. Seems to interfere with reception.

Michael unfastened his leather satchel and confirmed his phone was useless.

Lucian escorted him onto the verandah. I'll see you tomorrow. Around 1pm is best. I write in the mornings so I need the place to myself until then. When you see Maureen at the shop tell her to put some rubber gloves in my next delivery. And maybe a can of bug spray as well. I suppose you could just pick up everything on your way back here tomorrow. Save Tim making the trip. I never know when he's going to arrive. Usually just leaves a box outside the front door for me to trip over. Don't worry about food. I'll make dinner tomorrow night. But it'll be your turn the day after, all right? Can you cook?

Michael picked up his suitcase. I'm competent.

I'm sure you are. Wouldn't have hired you otherwise. Well, you'd better get a move on. Looks like this rain is starting to set in.

6.

Lucian jammed an iron poker between two logs and pried them apart to feed oxygen to the coals underneath. As flames flickered up he stepped back, slumping into his favourite chair with its rounded arms, braided upholstery and snug embrace. Sadie's tail thumped against the floor as she exposed her belly to the warmth. Lucian caressed her head and ears and noticed the back of his hand was covered with scratches. That he had no recollection of when or where they had been inflicted deepened his appreciation of how confused he had become in the forest. The signposts that he usually relied upon to point him in the right direction had all of a sudden disappeared. Familiar trees, Gaudí anthills, abandoned nests and rotting logs no longer distinguished themselves amongst the dense foliage. And the arrival of rain only made things worse – so befuddling Lucian's senses that at one point he stood undecided about whether to continue walking down the mountain or to turn around and head back up. Perhaps he had accidentally passed Wood Green and was moving further away from home with every step. The trees in this section of the forest were so tall that he could not see a damn thing. But even without a view of its peak Lucian knew Mount Wellington would be capped with white. The feeling of snow was in the air. And should he have to spend the night outside then it was almost certain he would suffer from exposure. The solitary existence he had so successfully cultivated for himself meant that days could pass before anyone questioned his whereabouts. Maureen and Tim might grow curious, but they had a business to run and domestic injustices to fight. Sadie was no help. She was exhausted from their long walk together and did not seem to comprehend that her master had forgotten how to find his way home. Lucian felt a warm trickle down the inside of his leg and was shocked at the depth of his fear. It sobered and focussed his mind. Keep walking down, he told himself. Something familiar will appear, even if it's the shore of the Derwent. Keep walking down and you'll be inside before nightfall. Just keep walking down and eventually you'll stumble upon your backyard.

Lucian discarded his clothes on the bathroom floor and stood beneath a hot shower waiting impatiently for the chill beneath his skin to stop wriggling. The fresh shirt and trousers he chose were reassuringly comfortable and after raiding the refrigerator for cheese and milk he set about lighting a fire in the sitting room. There was more than enough kindling to get things started, though his supply of thicker branches and split logs needed to be replenished from the wood box on the verandah. When he saw Michael asleep in the cane chair Lucian remembered why he had gone for a walk in the first place. To clear his head in preparation for the young man's arrival. Well clear his head he had. Cleared it of all common sense and memory of what he was supposed to be doing. Lucian sank lower in his chair and wrestled the urge to weep. Shook his head in shame at such feebleness, and the recollection of failing to offer Michael even a cup of tea. His irrational determination to have the young man out of his home as quickly as possible had put at risk all the plans he had been meticulously devising for the past six months. Lucian doubted Michael suspected anything. The letters from the thirty-four-year-old academic revealed he was not particularly overburdened with intellect or curiosity. Yet still Lucian reprimanded himself for being so irresponsible. This was his last chance. Mess this up and everything, his entire life, would be lost.

7.

Maureen knelt on the floor restocking chocolate bars while Tim rotated the freshest milk towards the rear of the refrigerator. The telephone was ringing in the back office, and both were pretending not to hear it as an experiment to see how long it would take the other one to stop what they were doing and answer the bloody phone for once. Tim leaned deeper inside the fridge so he could insist, in all honesty, that he had not heard a thing. Maureen quickly opened a large box of potato chips and rustled their noisy wrappers so she too would have an excuse. Finally the ringing stopped and both were left wondering who had called. Maybe someone had seen their advertisement in *The Mercury* about the store. In the two years it had been listed for sale there had been only three enquiries, resulting in a single, fruitless inspection of the premises. Tim was baffled as to why the business was taking so long to sell. Surprisingly, it made good money. As the only market on the south face of Mount Wellington they serviced not just Wood Green, but also the houses higher up and the hobby farms below. And with fresh eggs daily; a wide selection of groceries; fruit and vegetables; hand-made sausages; basic hardware and pharmacy supplies; newspapers; magazines; a postal service and a library of DVDs to rent, all with free delivery, there were revenue streams coming in from all directions. Maureen had taught herself to bake croissants, which along with the purchase of an espresso machine had helped the store become the focal point of the Wood Green community, at least until Paul opened the doors to his pub at 11am. The work it demanded, however, had caused Tim and Maureen's relationship to fray and unravel. So much so that the moment the store sold their marriage would be over. Though neither had said as much, the absence of any discussion about where they would go next, or how they might reinvest their capital, left little doubt about their respective intentions.

Tim shut the fridge door, checked his watch, then announced he was going to do some paperwork in the office. Midday was porn time. It only took a few minutes, after which he strolled out to the chicken coop to enjoy a cigarette. Maureen rolled her eyes and started on a second box of chips. She knew exactly what Tim was up to, and was more than happy to let him drool over petite Asian women so long as it meant he continued to refrain from all late-night advances. That the porn actresses were so different from her body type made complete sense to Maureen. She already knew she would never again be with a man as hairless as Tim. Maureen had grown too fond of Lucian's furry chest, and the way his beard lightly scratched the inside of her thighs. Even the fuzz on the small of his back had become strangely attractive. At first it had been shocking, especially after so many years with Tim's bald chest and downy limbs. But now she found thick hair masculine. Arousing. Maureen's former lover materialised vividly in her imagination. Made her aware of her solitude, and the quiet of the shop, and the way the corner near the vegetable racks could not be seen from the street. With one foot on a box of aubergines, her back against a shelf of canned goods, and a scenario already playing behind her eyes, Maureen dispatched a hand beneath the hem of her skirt.

The tiny silver bell above the shop door rang just as her foot returned to the floor. The abrupt resumption of reality – after a particularly filthy fantasy – made Maureen feel awkward as she hurried towards the counter. Was her face flushed? Could he tell what she had been doing?

I'm here to pick up Lucian Clarke's groceries, said Michael.

8.

Hello?

Hello, can I speak to Suzanne Pollard please?

Who's calling? If you're trying to sell me something I'm hanging up in two seconds flat.

No, please, I'm not selling anything. My name is Rachel Atler. I'm wondering if you have a brother called Michael.

Yes, I do.

And does he teach English at the University of New South Wales?

That's right. Has something happened to him? Has Michael been in an accident?

No! It's nothing like that. I'm sorry, I should have explained straight away. I didn't mean to frighten you. I'm a friend of Michael's and I'm just trying to track him down.

If you're a friend of his then why don't you have his phone number?

I do, except he's not answering my messages and I'm starting to get a little worried.

You think he might be in trouble?

I don't know...I don't think so.

Then maybe he's just avoiding you.

I suppose that could be it, but I...oh how do I explain this?

Just spit it out dear, I've got about five minutes before I need to leave for work.

Your brother and I were involved for quite a number of...

Adopted brother.

Really? Michael was adopted?

He never told you?

No. He never mentioned it.

Sounds about right. Michael was always secretive as a kid.

Well perhaps that explains it then.

What?

When we broke up we promised to stay in touch with each other, but I dropped by his flat a few days ago and found that someone else was renting it. So I rang his work and discovered he'd taken a leave of absence.

Sounds to me like he's left town for a while.

That's what I thought as well. But he never said a word about it. And I only saw him a few weeks ago.

Well that also sounds a lot like Michael.

Look, I don't need to speak to him directly. If someone else has heard from him recently, that's fine. I just want to know he's all right.

Sorry dear, but I haven't spoken to Michael in over five years. Every Christmas I send a card care of that university where he works, but I never hear back from him. Last time we spoke was when our parents died. He came up to Brisbane for the funeral, then flew back to Sydney the same day. Felt guilty I suppose. They were driving down to see him. Got tired of waiting for Michael to pay them a visit.

Do you have any other relatives who Michael might be staying with?

None that I know of. We're a pretty small family. That's why my parents adopted Michael in the first place. A few cousins scattered about here and there, but none of us are close. Sorry I can't be more help.

No, no, you've been very kind to speak to me. Thank you.

Listen, you seem like a nice girl, so I hope you don't mind me saying this, but if I were you I'd forget about Michael and find someone else. My brother has always been a little weird. Even as a kid he was always on his own. Never wanted to share his toys or join in on games. And if he did decide to take part, he used to cheat so much that no one ever wanted to play with him. But maybe that was his way of making sure he was left alone. Who knows? I could never figure him out. I think deep down he feels as though he doesn't belong anywhere, and it makes it hard for him to commit to anyone. That's just my opinion of course. If you do speak to him tell him that some of his junk is still in my garage, and he can pick it up any time he likes.

I will. And thanks again.

No problem. Hey, just asking. How did you find my number? I don't imagine Michael gave it to you.

He mentioned you a couple of times, and I knew he grew up in Brisbane, so I just started looking through the phone directory.

You called everyone with the surname Pollard?

I got lucky pretty quickly. It didn't take too long.

Wow, you sure are...oh Jesus is that the time? Sorry dear, I've got to go. I'm late for work.

9.

I agree wholeheartedly.

Michael jumped at the sound of Lucian's voice so close to his ear.

The author stepped back, thrilled at how successfully he had snuck out his front door and read over Michael's shoulder. Are you writing something about Wood Green?

Michael closed the pocketbook and returned it to his satchel. No, just an observation.

Well I couldn't have put it better myself. Maureen's face does indeed hold your attention. And it's not even what I'd describe as beautiful. It's just her features are so strong. That nose and chin: they're like picturesque hills and valleys for your eyes to tumble over. And the way her hair appears a little bit out of control. I admit I've often felt the urge to reach over the counter and take her head in my hands just so I could hold it still and stare at it. Writers always get poetic about a woman's eyes, but how often do you see a pair that truly make an impression? Most people don't even notice the colour of another person's eyes. But Maureen's are amazing. Grey flecked with gold. They're almost avian. You can use that if you like. Avian. Not bad. Not bad at all. I suppose you're writing a book, are you?

No. I mean...I haven't started yet. Michael was a little stunned. Lucian had spoken like someone in love. But I have an idea for one.

Well I hear that's how they usually begin. Sorry about not opening the door sooner but I told you about my 1pm rule didn't I? Bring that stuff inside and we'll have a cup of tea before you get started.

Michael hefted the groceries from the top of the wood box, kicked off his muddy shoes inside the front door, and followed Lucian to the rear of the house where he was shown what went where in the kitchen cupboards. The lesson implied he would be putting away more shopping in the future, and a detailed explanation of how Lucian liked his tea prepared furthered Michael's suspicion that his duties were not to be restricted to the realm of manuscripts and letters.

Across from the kitchen was a sunroom with two black leather couches, creased and worn, facing each other over a long coffee table supporting a clean ashtray, cigarette papers, lighter, plastic sandwich bag filled with marijuana, notebook, pen, dictionary, reading glasses, and a catalogue of a Francis Bacon exhibition at The Art Gallery of NSW. The windows were floor to ceiling, offering an expansive view of the forest that stood no more than ten metres from the rear of the house.

Lucian set the teapot down, lowered himself into the corner of a couch that no longer rebounded from the weight of his body, and turned towards the windows in the hope of seeing one of the local wallabies, or the family of pink robins that hunted insects among the remains of his kitchen garden. He would have liked his guest to take up a similar pose, but a sideways glance confirmed that Michael sat like a child witnessing an inebriated parent for the first time.

You can pour the tea if you like.

Michael preferred it with a spoon of sugar, but was too embarrassed to ask. He found his cigarettes and placed one between his lips.

I'd appreciate you not doing that inside the house, said Lucian. A spliff is the only smoke that Sadie can tolerate. Shall I roll one for us?

Michael put away his cigarette and for the first time noticed the dog staring at him with suspicion from the foot of Lucian's couch. Shouldn't I start work first?

Your professionalism is duly noted and commendable, said Lucian as he dangled a cigarette paper from his bottom lip. However, in my vast experience I have often found that being stoned is the optimum state of mind for dusting. He unsealed the sandwich bag and inhaled the aroma of its contents. Don't worry, it's not too strong.

You're the boss.

Lucian flinched. Michael seemed as incapable of resisting clichés in conversation as he was when theorising about Lucian's books. And the thought of how such a mind might eventually portray Maureen in a novel made Lucian pull hard and deep as he lit the spliff.

Michael sank back into the couch with the realisation that he was thoroughly, terribly, stoned. At some point in the past half an hour the pot had undermined his ability to speak, and in the vacuum an album of trippy French folk – *Paix* by Catherine Ribeiro + Alpes – had taken over the room. So like Lucian he turned his attention towards the forest. Its details were infinitely more complex than Michael had first appreciated. The variety of greens and browns was astonishing, and the countless faces that appeared in the clusters of leaves flickering in the breeze seemed to all be competing for his attention. Look, a kangaroo! Michael shouted with a gesture so large and fast that the marsupial immediately disappeared back between the trees.

Lucian scowled at his new secretary. Time for you to start work I think.

10.

Michael rested his feet on a low windowsill and admired the grey clouds advancing towards Hobart. The wide vista from his B&B room took in the Derwent River, its eastern shoreline, along with the rooftops and chimneys of the houses built further down the hillside. Situated on a headland, Battery Point was a historically significant suburb that fostered an atmosphere of white-bread exclusivity, manicured old-world charm, heightened colonialism and prohibitive affluence that Michael's lower-middle-class upbringing instinctively condemned, while his university-educated consciousness revelled in its beauty. The houses were predominantly Georgian in style, with front doors that opened onto generous and spotless footpaths. Along these strolled couples inspecting restaurant menus and estimating real estate prices; European backpackers trying in vain to discover what their guidebook authors had found so exciting about the suburb, and groups of old ladies patronising tea rooms while marvelling at a part of Australia that had remained unchanged since they were girls. Turn a corner and there was an original sandstone wall; a circus surrounded by renovated workers' cottages, or a secret staircase down to Salamanca and the wharfs. No trace of graffiti was visible, and all architectural aberrations appeared to have occurred in the nineteen-sixties, so even the few apartment blocks that had wheedled their way into the area had an old-fashioned quality. It felt like a guilty pleasure to enjoy it so much, and Michael knew he was being marketed to, but no more than the inner-city suburb he had left behind in Sydney that sold ideas of vibrant unconventionality while landlords waited impatiently for gentrification to occur. At least Battery Point was unambiguous in its ambitions, giving Michael a sense of freedom to enjoy all its trappings.

Directly in front of his window the Derwent River ran smooth and bright, but to the south, beneath the advancing clouds, the water had grown dark and fractured by rain. It created a distinct line across the river's surface and revealed exactly how fast the morning storm was advancing towards the city. Michael felt privileged to witness such a spectacle of weather, and vindicated in his recent decision to extend his stay in the B&B for another month.

Of the twelve tables in the dining room on the ground floor only three were occupied for breakfast, so after the proprietor, Andrew Tiller, had served everyone, he took it upon himself to sit with Michael – because no one wanted to eat alone – and recount the highlights of the B&B. All the silver came from England with my great grandmother, he boasted. Some time after the end of the nineteenth century.

Andrew was a thin man of medium height and shallow chest who shaved every day and bought his clothes from discount stores because he was always forgetting to put on an apron in the kitchen. He checked his reflection in most shiny surfaces, and used his immaculately clean and slightly overlong fingernails to comb any recalcitrant strands of hair back into place. There was an eerie lack of scent to Andrew's skin, and a fastidiousness in the way his shirt was always perfectly tucked in. He was aware that spit bubbles sometimes gathered in the corners of his mouth, and would haughtily wipe them away with a thumb and forefinger whenever he sensed a moment of disrespect. Andrew's desire to talk about himself was so overwhelming that he never gave a thought as to whether the people and places he mentioned were familiar to anyone else. The same way he failed to question whether there was a motive behind Michael's queries about the tourist season, and if his room was available for another week. The moment he answered without checking the register Andrew knew, however, that he had forfeited ground in a negotiation masquerading as a conversation.

The price Michael had locked in for the following month, with breakfast still included, was cheaper than what he would have paid for a bedsit. And the room, with its en-suite bathroom, free wi-fi and striking view, was infinitely superior to any share-house accommodation he could have secured.

The storm had finally reached Battery Point, and as heavy rain tattooed Michael's window he decided against going out to shop for boots. The three-and-a-half hours before he was due back up at Wood Green would be better spent by beginning work on his book. Even though the whole point of accepting a job in Tasmania had been so he could write without the distraction of teaching and marking, the novel Michael had been attempting to start for the past week was still just a collection of scenes and random ideas. Cleaning Lucian's junk room of dust dating back to Federation, and organising boxes so he could begin sorting their contents, had so far left him too exhausted to contemplate raising the lid of his laptop. But perhaps if he began transcribing some of his notes it would inspire an opening line for his novel. Michael then realised he should probably give Rachel a call before he settled down to work. She had sent three text messages on the day of his arrival in Hobart, and one every twenty-four hours since then, all of which he was yet to respond to. The effort of breaking up had been too great, and he felt there was nothing more that needed to be said. They had exhausted the possibilities of their bodies. Once or twice things had even gone so far that it had made them feel ashamed. Ideas that seemed erotic in theory, in practice had turned out to be sour and unsatisfying, and led both of them to suspect that their relationship might have reached a dead end. Michael would not deny that he sometimes missed Rachel's wry humour and provocative sense of fashion, but he also knew her cynical eye would have levelled Battery Point to rubble, leaving him with nothing to enjoy. It was why he had left Sydney without saying goodbye, and not answered any of Rachel's messages. He already knew what her estimation of his decision to move to Tasmania would be. Michael understood that what he was doing made no sense, yet as soon as Lucian had offered the job it felt as if he had no alternative but to accept. And though he appreciated what he was giving up, Michael also knew that to become a writer meant making sacrifices, and the loss of Rachel's company was just one of things he was willing to forgo.

11.

Tim unscrewed the bottle cap to let the wine breathe, but on second thoughts decided to take his first drink. Maureen was already reading in bed and unlikely to come downstairs again, so why shouldn't he begin the wine he had set aside to keep him company? Sulphur preservatives immediately assailed his sinuses, and for a moment he questioned the wisdom of his plan to consume the inexpensive bottle over the three hours the shop was to remain open. Tomorrow was a big day for deliveries, and Maureen had little sympathy for his hangovers. She was well acquainted with her husband's undiscerning approach to wine, and refused to take a sinus headache into consideration when there was work to be done. Tim, however, decided to risk it. It was such a cold night, and he was so bored, and maybe someone from the pub would wander over later for a chat. Nothing worse than being sober when speaking with a person who has been drinking all night. At the back of his mind lingered the hope that the woman he had struck up a conversation with in the pub earlier that day might make an appearance. She and her less friendly friend had taken a table near to where he was relaxing with a post-lunch glass of red, and as they discussed what to eat he had leaned across to recommend the fish cakes. Tim knew that women loved things like fish cakes, and continued to chat and wink and charm until their food arrived.

This old man bothering you ladies? Paul said as he set down their plates. It was meant as a joke, and everyone smiled, but the expression on the publican's face left Tim in no doubt that he was being told to stop harassing the customers.

He couldn't understand what the problem was. He was just being friendly. Making Wood Green more inviting. Oh well, he said as he stood up, better get to work. Enjoy your lunch. If either of you ladies need anything just pop across the street, we're open till late.

Tim took another drink straight from the bottle before hiding it behind a nearby stack of paper towels. He then wiped down the serving counter, prepared the cash float for the morning, straightened the magazines, touched the breasts of every cover girl, and fed another split log into the potbelly stove. The cucumbers and tomatoes were pestering him. Three times that month he had forgotten to store them in the fridge so they stayed fresh overnight, and each morning after, his breakfast had consisted of cereal, toast, coffee and Maureen's reprimands about wasting food and throwing away hard-earned money. Although Tim knew that most people only wanted chocolate and DVDs at this time of night, he still felt that putting away the vegetables early sent the wrong message. That it looked like the shop was getting ready to close. With a whiff of defiance for Maureen's procedures he decided to let the cucumbers and tomatoes sit a while longer. It wasn't as if there wouldn't be time to put them away later in the night. But for the present he preferred to imagine the friendlier of the two women he had met in the pub earlier that day walking into the shop looking for a little romance. Tim was all for romance. It was Maureen who never wanted to go out to eat, or have sex in the bathroom. She was always too busy reading her books. In fact Tim loved romance. He remembered buying Maureen chocolates once, but they had sat in the fridge so long that he eaten most of them himself. And just because he liked action films didn't mean that going to the movies wasn't romantic. Films with subtitles gave him a headache.

12.

Michael stepped back to inspect his effort. The kidney-shaped desk looked much more attractive beneath the window, and now he could glance over the verandah and down the mountainside while he worked. The sight of the windowpanes cleaned of their layers of dirt continued to give him pleasure, and with the flyspecked roller blind banished to the garbage he could imagine morning light pouring across the wooden desktop that he had carefully cleared of dust, mildew and mouse droppings. A manual typewriter sat on its right side, for aesthetic effect, while opposite was an electric lamp – the only one of four in the room that still worked. Under the desk stood a captain's chair with a broken swivel mechanism that caused it to tilt suddenly and dramatically to one side. Twice it had tried to tip Michael onto the floor, but Lucian had given strict instructions that nothing in the room was to be thrown away unless it was particularly foul.

Along the adjacent wall were suitcases and boxes containing manuscripts, letters – professional and personal

– birthday cards, reviews of Lucian's books, the few efforts of journalism he had not bothered to publish, tax returns, essays he had grown bored with, as well as hundreds of notebooks containing ideas jotted down while composing his novels. Access to such an abundance of information made Michael giddy with the prospect of becoming the world authority on Lucian Clarke's life and work, and kept distracting him with dreams of writing a definitive biography the moment his own novel was complete.

On the opposite side of the room were three cupboard doors that concertinaed open to reveal a long row of tightly packed plastic suit covers containing clothing from what appeared to be every stage of Lucian's adult life. Below them were thirty-nine shoeboxes of corresponding historical relevance, while at the back of the cupboard had been stacked foreign-language editions of Lucian's books.

Against the fourth wall of the room stood a daybed that Michael had emptied an entire can of bug spray over to kill the colonies of insects infesting its wood and cane panels. The floor underneath had turned black with their tiny carcasses, but fear that some survivors might still be lurking in a protective crevice meant Michael remained hesitant to sit on the divan's mattress and cushions.

Lucian appeared at the doorway, leaned through, apparently reluctant to enter the room, and nodded approvingly at Michael's work. I seem to recall it being this neat once before, but it must have been twenty years ago. Typewriter looks good there.

Yeah, I thought you'd like it. I found two others in the cupboard, but that was the only one that still was working. Looks to me as if it's never been used.

You're probably right. I remember buying it years ago off the back of a truck on Portobello Road in London. Thought it might be wise to have a back up in case my machine broke down. Feel free to give it a spin if you like.

That's ok, I have my laptop.

Oh right, of course, I've heard of those. Could never bring myself to use one though. Always scared I'd hit it too hard and break it. I prefer the way you can be physical with a typewriter, as if you're actually building something. And it's noisy, so you can hear the rhythm of what you're writing. Best way I can tell a sentence is working is if it sings when I type it. Computers are designed to be quiet, aren't they? And don't all the keys sound the same? Did you know that Flaubert would tap out the rhythm of his sentences on a piano to check their melody was right. Can you play? Me neither. But I reckon a typewriter is pretty close to a percussion instrument. Hard on your fingers though. Got to keep your nails short. And I won't deny I make a hell of a lot of typos. But I think that's where the best accidents occur. Missed words or punctuation as a page is retyped for the tenth time can take an idea in a completely unexpected direction. Computers automatically correct mistakes, don't they? Well now you know why so many writers sound the same these days. And I suppose they've done away with handwriting as well. Seems a shame to me. Nothing more beautiful than a page covered with crossed out words and alternatives inserted. The only way I know a page is ready is when there are no more pen marks on it. Lucian felt his stomach rumble. But enough of my proselytising. Dinner is ready. And now this place is cleaned up we can get you started on the work I've actually hired you to do.

At the end of each day I want you to write a summary of what you've learned about my life while you've sorted through my papers.

Michael looked up from the flecks of parsley lingering at the bottom of his bowl. Lucian's beef cheek stew, served with gremolata, had been so delicious that it was difficult to accept the meal was over.

You're writing an autobiography?

Thinking about it.

But I thought you didn't believe in them. Aren't you quoted as saying that autobiographies are the greatest dishonesty a writer can commit. Not only to his readers but also himself?

Lucian shrugged. That's what comes from not giving interviews for thirty years. The things you let slip as a young man tend to follow you around for the rest of your life.

You mean you don't believe it anymore?

Let's just say I'm an old man and I'm allowed to change my mind. That's why I've hired you. I need someone who's familiar enough with my books to be able to recognise the parts of my life that were relevant to my work. Don't worry, I'm not expecting Proust. Just take it down in note form if you like, then hand it to me at the end of each day.

Michael returned his bowl to the coffee table as his own biography of Lucian Clarke vanished before his eyes.

Sure. No problem.

Marvellous. Well then, want to make a start on the washing up? That way you can have an early night and be fresh for tomorrow. Lots of work to do, said Lucian as he stood up. I'm quite excited. Aren't you?

13.

You should buy yourself a car if you're going to go up and down the mountain every day. Hobart taxis charge like the Light Brigade.

Michael picked up his satchel from beside the public telephone and joined Tim at the counter. You're probably right. Only problem is I don't drive.

Tim's round, fleshy face, rosy with alcohol, furrowed with confusion. What do you mean? Why not? You an epileptic?

No, just never learned to drive.

A cranky dad? Is that why you gave up?

Sorry?

Your father yell at you while he was teaching you to drive? Can't tell you how many times I've heard *that* story.

I don't think so. You know, I can't remember if he ever tried to teach me. Some friends got me behind the wheel a couple of times when I was at university, but driving always seemed like such a dangerous thing to do.

So how do you get around? Besides taxis I mean.

In Sydney I used to ride a bike to work. And the rest of the time I just used public transport.

Not much of that down here.

So I've noticed. Michael patted his jacket pockets in search of cigarettes; it usually took ten minutes for a taxi to arrive.

Tim pulled an ashtray out from under the counter. Here. It's too cold to smoke outside. Don't worry, I'll have one with you. Just don't tell Maureen. She hates it when I smoke inside. Want a drink?

Sure, why not.

Tim reached behind the stack of paper towels for his bottle of red, tore open a packet of plastic cups, poured a generous measure for each of them, and swallowed his in a single gulp. Michael's nose immediately recognised the pungent chemicals of cheap wine and let the liquid just touch his lips.

Not a bad drop this, said Tim as he refilled his cup. Bought a case with the intention of storing some away, but I think I've only got two bottles left. So how's it working out with Lucian?

Pretty good so far.

Not surprised he's finally got someone in to help. What is he? Sixty? Sixty-five? Once people get past forty I'm hopeless at guessing how old they are.

Sixty-one I think.

Well I suppose you're entitled to be a little grumpy when you're as old as that. Certainly lets me have it when I forget something in his order. He doesn't drive either, you know. Decent enough bloke though. Told us all about the area when we first moved up here. And pays his bill on time. Not a bad writer either, or so I hear. Tried to read one of his books once but only got through about twenty pages. Maureen finished it, but she reads everything. Not much else to do up here. Tim stubbed out his cigarette with the determination of a fire fighter. So how are you finding Hobart? Bit of a change from Sydney I'd expect.

A lot colder than I thought it would be.

Wait till it snows. Your balls will freeze off.

Tim's heavy-handed attempt to cultivate male camaraderie made Michael impatient for the lights of his taxi.

Discovered any of Hobart's hot spots yet?

Not exactly. I haven't had much opportunity to go out. Anywhere you'd recommend?

Tim massaged his left ear and tried to suppress a smirk. You single men aren't after exactly the same type of excitement as us married blokes. Try the Court House Hotel on Clarence Street, I hear it gets pretty busy in there. But watch out for the Orion on Elizabeth, that's where all the timber men drink when they come in from the bush. Looks like your cab is here. You should ask your driver where to go. Those guys know things about Hobart that people like me will never discover.

The moment the shop door closed Tim downed Michael's unfinished wine, then re-hid the bottle behind the paper towels, emptied the ashtray into the plastic cups, and hurried them out back to the garbage bin where the incriminating evidence could be concealed beneath a thick layer of kitchen scraps. On his return Tim locked the office safe and turned off the computer, beginning the long process of closing up for the night that culminated with bolting the front door and inspecting the cucumbers and tomatoes. Their skins were cool to touch, and when the stove died down the room would be even colder. So how much difference would the inside of a refrigerator make? Very little was Tim's conclusion as he switched off the last light and walked upstairs.

14.

Lucian sat at his desk refusing to be intimidated by the blank page scrolled into his typewriter. He had faced thousands of them in his life. Perhaps even millions. Only to see every one eventually fill with words and ideas that had miraculously advanced from the back of his head to the consciousness behind his eyes. And today would be no different. There was no reason to fret. He would just sit and wait until the familiar leaps of imagination intrinsic to his writing began again, as they always did.

The small pile of completed pages at his elbow certainly did not help. Though Lucian was confident in the premise for his new novel, here was tangible proof that its story was not emerging half as quickly as his previous books had. His brain seemed slower, less able to devise fresh scenarios, and there was a constant internal nagging to free things up. Approach ideas from a different direction. An unfamiliar angle. His books had always been admired for their expansive language and quiet structural complexity, yet all of a sudden Lucian felt frustrated by the restrictions of prose. He had no ambition to share a blind alley with Joyce and his posse of imitators. He was just tired of hearing his own voice inside his head. No matter how deeply he inhabited his characters, or displaced them in unfamiliar surroundings, the sound of his voice was always lurking below the surface. And he wanted to hear something different. Look through another person's eyes. Not see the same damn blank page he had been staring at his entire life. Why was it still such a struggle after so many years? Had he ever managed to write a single sentence that did not demand repeated revising? What on earth had ever given him the idea that he was a writer? Lucian suspected that there were some authors who just sat down and typed the first thing that came into their head, then sent it out into the world without a second thought. But he had always felt compelled to fine-tune a book until he could no longer stand the sight of it. An exhausting and demanding process that he was now thoroughly tired of, and frustrated by its devaluing rewards. What was he persisting for? He knew how little time he had left. Why did he not just sit back and enjoy the show? What was another book going to prove? Why this incessant need to torture himself day after day with a stupid blank page?

Lucian heard Michael's footsteps on the verandah and checked his wristwatch. One o'clock already and still nothing done. Lucian could not recall a single day in the past twenty years when he had failed to write a sentence, and committed himself to staying in his chair until he had a paragraph, or at least the beginning of one. The prospect of returning to his desk the following morning and staring at the same blank page was too dangerous. Lucian had never suffered from writer's block because he had never given it the chance to take hold. Let a day go by without getting something down and the same might happen again tomorrow, and the day after that. Too bad if it was chilly outside. Michael would just have to wait. I bet he's been writing all morning on that prissy little computer of his. Tap tap tap. Cliché cliché. The idea made Lucian even more angry, and without thinking he stood up, rushed into the hall and opened the front door to find his secretary pacing the verandah while puffing on a cigarette to fend off the cold.

If you're going to smoke out here then put your butts in the garbage and not into one of my coffee cups, okay? This is my home, not your personal ashtray.

Right. Sorry.

Lucian noticed that Michael had no groceries with him. And where's the food you're cooking for tonight's dinner?

Michael picked up his satchel. I thought we could give ourselves a night off and maybe order a pizza, or get some Thai sent up.

Really, you thought that did you? Well done. Brilliant work. You must have a headache after such a burst of inspiration. But most places don't deliver this far up the mountain. And anyway, I only eat real food. Like the type I prepared for you last night. And now it's your turn to return the favour. So fuck off back down that road and find something for dinner, or don't bother coming back at all.

15.

Maureen watched Michael walk up and down the aisles of her store, drop random groceries into the basket hooked over his forearm, then moments later reconsider their suitability and return them to the shelves. He huffed, and intermittently hitched up his trousers to stop them catching the heels of his shoes. Maureen remembered seeing him wear the same clothes a few days ago, and again thought how odd it was for someone so young to dress as if he were already an old man. Michael's black hair bore a loose curl, and obviously needed a cut as he kept twitching his head towards the ceiling to keep it out of his brown eyes. The skin below them was swollen with dark crescents that seemed incongruous with Michael's otherwise fine features. In a year or two, Maureen surmised, when his jowls relaxed and a little grey salted his whiskers, he might have that rough appeal she had fallen for on a few occasions before marrying Tim. But then Michael tugged at one of his small earlobes and revealed fingernails bitten to the quick. Sore, with shredded cuticles, red enough to have just been dipped in boiling water, the ends of his fingers instantly smothered any spark of attraction that Maureen may have felt, and alerted her to other evidence of compulsive behaviour. Michael's insistence on wearing shoes wholly inappropriate for Mount Wellington might be included, along with the way he kept muttering to himself, as if debating the validity of every idea that occurred to him. His tall body – six, six-one? – bent towards the freezer so suddenly that Maureen gasped in fear he was about to butt his forehead against its lid. Instead, Michael slid open the plastic door and roughly pushed aside cuts of frozen meat, seemingly unable to find what he was looking for. The racks of vegetables provoked further shaking of his head, and at last Maureen realised that Michael's frustration was more with himself than the products in her store.

Can I help you with something? she asked from the far side of the vegetable stand.

Michael rolled his eyes. I seem to have forgotten it was my turn to cook dinner.

I see. Any idea what you're after?

That's the problem. I usually find a recipe online, but now I'm just trying to come up with something that's quick and impressive enough to put Lucian back in a good mood.

The old man of the mountain giving you trouble?

You could say that.

Well I know he prefers savoury over sweet so I'd put that cream back in the fridge if I were you. And chilli sometimes gives him hiccups, so avoid heat if you can. What about you?

Me? I'll eat anything. I just need an idea that's not going to take half a day to prepare. I'm already running late.

Can I offer a suggestion?

No. You can please just tell me what to do.

All right then, hand over your basket. I know the best meal you can get ready in less than fifteen minutes, and I guarantee that Lucian will love it.

As Maureen rang up the groceries she repeated the recipe to Michael for a second time. His concentration on every detail, and obvious excitement at the prospect of pleasing Lucian, reminded her of when she had first read *Foxtrot*. For Maureen, the closer an author's proximity the less value she attached to their work. So when she learned a writer called Lucian Clarke lived only a few streets away from the general store, her assumption was that he must be nothing more than a hack. Writers of significance lived in England, Europe and America, or even Japan and Norway...countries where people read. Not halfway up a mountain at the bottom of Australia. The previous owners of the general store had displayed copies of Lucian's books in a corner dedicated to Wood Green tourism, and passed them on with the rest of the stock they had failed to sell prior to handing over the business. *Foxtrot* was the shortest of the three novels Lucian had published by that time, so Maureen begrudgingly began to read it while she waited for the boxes of her own books to arrive from Melbourne. The low expectations with which she approached the opening chapter were quickly confirmed as she wrestled with the awkward style pressed so deeply into every page, and recoiled against its graphic description of an old man shooting himself at the conclusion of a party. But by the end of the second chapter Maureen had grown intrigued with the mechanics of the backward-moving narrative. And by the end of the third she was much less perturbed by the way the point of view slipped between party guests and family members. Until eventually the opulent English country manor at the centre of the narrative stood perfectly clear inside her imagination, while its past and present inhabitants intermingled behind the blur of an alcoholic lens. And though sometimes it was difficult to observe consecutive generations repeat the same mistakes, and characters commit pitiless deceits to ensure the estate remained within the family, Maureen found herself so emotionally and intellectually engaged that she effortlessly devoured the remaining chapters to emerge out the other end of the novel with an entirely altered view of Wood Green. Her new home now appeared like a secret Eden, full of natural splendour so majestic and mystical that it could not help but inspire such a wondrous piece of writing. Even when she later learned that *Foxtrot* had been written in Europe she refused to change her mind and simply qualified her incorrect assumptions by insisting that for an author of such a powerfully concentrated novel Mount Wellington was an ideal location to write. Perhaps she and Tim had not made a mistake moving to Tasmania after all. Lucian had been so kind the first time they met. Welcoming them to the community, offering advice about what to do when it snowed, subtle warnings about certain locals. And he was thoroughly gracious when Maureen clumsily blurted out how much she adored *Foxtrot.* More than a decade had passed since he had last received praise for the book, and Lucian insisted that her kind words had made his month, if not his year.

Yes, Maureen could understand Michael's desire to please. And as she handed over his change she thought that his hands were not so ugly. If only he did not smell so strongly of cigarettes.

16.

Small chunks of melted chèvre floated on top of hot olive oil cupped in the recesses of four capsicum halves that also held finely minced garlic and anchovies. With a spatula Michael carefully served two halves to each plate then sprinkled fresh parsley on top.

Meanwhile, Lucian stood before a wall of CDs trying to decide what music to play during dinner. There were more than two thousand to choose from, along with approximately eleven hundred records shelved against an adjacent wall. In the corner between them stood a stereo of old and new components, including an amplifier Lucian had found in a Brixton alley in the early nineteen-eighties and had never felt the need to replace. Perfect, he said, plucking a CD from the shelves.

Michael waited nervously for Lucian to join him at the coffee table and taste the meal that Maureen had taught him to prepare. It looked impressive and smelled delicious, but Michael would not relax until Lucian had taken a bite and offered some indication of approval. He sipped the powerful vodka tonic that accompanied the meal – Michael had forgotten to buy wine – and felt the alcohol hit his stomach at the same moment a raw exotic music filled the room.

Lucian handed Michael the CD cover as he sat down. Mmm, what have we got here?

Salah Ragab and the Cairo Jazz Band present *Egyptian Jazz*, Michael read before he put the CD cover to one side so he could demonstrate how the meal was to be eaten. With a bold cut across one of the capsicum halves the plate filled with warm, fragrant oil and the dissolved remnants of anchovies and garlic. He then continued to cut the capsicum into portions small enough to be easily gathered up with a piece of bread that had first been sopped in the chèvre and oil. Michael tried to contain his surprise at the pleasures of the dish, but quickly found himself so involved with the meal that it was half over before he thought to look up to check if Lucian was following the same technique. His dining companion, however, was happily nodding his head to the rhythmic swing of Middle-Eastern jazz as he also greedily devoured the moreish meal.

After the plates were cleared, Lucian selected a different album – Sheriff Lindo and The Hammer, *Ten Dubs That Shook The World* – and began to roll an after-dinner spliff. So how did you get on today? Make any progress?

Michael drained the last of his vodka tonic but tasted only melted ice and lemon. The glass of fine crystal, cut in an elaborate design, felt so attractive beneath his fingers that he was hesitant to put it down. I think so. I came across some of the notes you made when you were beginning *Lady Cadaver*.

That should have been entertaining. I hope your interest extended beyond just the smutty bits.

They weren't salacious at all. They were about your sister, Ursula. She was one of your inspirations for that book wasn't she?

It's certainly the theory your academic brethren have perpetuated, so who am I to contradict it. Let's have a look at what you've found.

Michael surrendered the glass so his hands were free to gather together scraps of paper from various pockets and smooth their creases against the top of his thigh. In exchange for his notes he accepted the joint, from which he took two deep tokes before returning it on the far side of the ashtray.

As Lucian read he could not recall encouraging his six-year-old sister to accompany him down the blowhole at Blackmans Bay. Nor of Ursula ever falling off a path of wooden planks that had been laid across the top of a giant blackberry thicket. He imagined her sitting at the bottom of the brambles, poked by jagged thorns whenever she moved, and the relief of her rescue by their father forever associated with the torture of being pulled back up. Lucian noticed his hands were trembling as he relit the joint.

Your penmanship is atrocious, he said. I can barely read what you've written. Maybe from now on you should type them up for me.

I could buy a small printer for my laptop if you'd like.

Lucian shook his head. I think I'd prefer your handwriting. Just give the typewriter a go. It won't kill you.

17.

Battery Point? No problem. You that guy working for Lucian Clarke? Word gets around. Cab drivers love to gossip. So what's he like? Besides being a good tipper. Really? Thought as much. You can tell from his books. Yeah, of course I've read them. You think I don't read just because I drive a taxi? Just teasing. I bet there aren't many people down here who even know who Lucian Clarke is, let alone own his books. Yeah, but Tasmanian literature is an interest of mine. Bigger than you think. Tasmania has more musicians, writers and artists per head of population than any other state in the country. I reckon it's the climate. Most of the time it's so bloody cold that there's nothing else to do except stay inside and create. I wouldn't say I have a favourite exactly...it's just a hobby that I try to keep up. Well of course there are your notables like Richard Flanagan and Christopher Koch and Amanda Lohrey, but I bet you've never heard of Joan Wise or Nan Chauncy, have you? What about Roy and Hilda Bridges? Brother and sister, both writing around the early twentieth century. I think Robert Dessaix is still here, but Nicholas Shakespeare has moved back to England. Of course we get a lot of blow-ins. Caroline Leaky was here only five years, and sick for most of it. You know *The Broad Arrow*? Don't worry, not many people do these days. But supposedly Marcus Clarke used it as a reference for *The Term of His Natural Life*. He's another one. Only ever visited Tasmania. Never lived here. But most people assume he was Tasmanian because he wrote about the place. At least Gwen Harwood had the decency to move here. So did Katherine Scholes. Ever heard of Arthur James Oglivy or James McQueen? Maybe they're too much before your time. But like I said there's a healthy community of contemporary writers here as well. Carmel Bird, she's sold a few books, and Geoff Dean. Oh, sorry, he died a few years ago. I keep forgetting that. What about Philomena van Rijswijk? Read any of her poetry? Who else is there? Heather Rose. Gina Mercer. Kathryn Lomer. Adrienne Eberhard. No? Well you've got some homework to do, haven't you? Not much use coming to Tasmania and learning nothing about the place. I assume you do a spot of writing yourself? You just look like the type. There's a writers' centre down here you know. I'm a member so I can put in a good word for you if you'd like. Yeah I dabble. Not really poems, more flash fiction. Something short I can get down while I'm waiting for my next fare. Shame I haven't got one here to show you. I've had a couple published. Just in small magazines. What about you? Oh, right, good on you. I'm considering having a go at a novel soon. Don't worry, it won't be about escaped convicts or hunting Tasmanian's tigers. I'd like to think my work is a little more original than that. No, it's about the whaling community that used to be in Hobart. Supposedly, at one time, there were hundreds of whales in the Derwent River. People said you could walk on their backs from one shore to the other. The Governor used to get letters from people complaining that they couldn't sleep because the whales were singing all night. Imagine that! Course they killed them all, but I reckon it would make a pretty interesting story, don't you? Here we are. That'll be twenty-one, fifty. Make it twenty, we writers have to stick together, don't we. Let me give you my card. Just call the number and ask for Phil. I'll come and get you straight away.

18.

By his fourth day in Hobart Carl was thinking he might have to resort to Grindr. Wasn't anyone in this town interested in a little lunchtime action? Back in Jozi the hour between 1pm and 2pm had been so much fun that Carl had almost preferred it to going out at night. Almost. But so far every Hobart cruising spot he had read about online had turned up either nothing, or nothing worth his time. Carl wondered if all the men in Hobart wore fleece, or just the ones who had families to go back to. Curious had never interested him. Carl was more inclined to play that role. Maybe he'd find someone in the Botanical Gardens. With a name like Queen's Domain it certainly sounded promising.

As he followed the paths to the Japanese Garden, the Epacrid Garden, the Historic Walls and the Fuchsia House, Carl told himself that he had always preferred the old school ways. That unlike finding someone with his phone, cruising involved more risk, more adventure, and satisfaction when something eventuated. But after he had removed his jacket to better show off his arms Carl began to reassess such thinking. He had not expected Hobart to be *this* cold. Chilly yes, it was autumn after all, but that wind felt like it had ice behind it.

Until a few weeks ago Carl had been unaware that Tasmania even existed. Of course he had seen the small triangular island when he had looked at a map of Australia. But he must have assumed it was part of New Zealand or a Pacific island, because he had never given it a moment's thought in his plans to make a getaway to Australia. Why would he? His sights were set on Queensland, or maybe Adelaide. Sydney was too obvious. Anyone from Johannesburg looking for their money would almost certainly go to Sydney first. And probably Melbourne next. And Perth already had enough South Africans. The last thing Carl needed was to accidentally run into someone from home. He knew he had to find a place where he could disappear, make a fresh start, even do a little business, and maybe begin a new life for himself while he waited for the old one to blow over. If he was going to avoid being caught Carl knew he had to think beyond the obvious, so when a guy he met in a Sydney bar had told him how the scene in Hobart was small but fun, it sounded like the perfect place. Carl had never heard of Tasmania before, so no one would think to look for him there.

They had found each other in a section of the Botanical Gardens where the trees were so tall and wide and cast such dark shadows that once they left the path no one would have any idea where they were, or what they were doing. Being in the open in the middle of the day was thrilling. It made their skin tight – nipples painfully hard. Not a word had passed between them. Just looks. Embraces. Kisses.

Carl felt whiskers rub against his face and inhaled deeply. The other man was younger, fitter, prettier, but Carl knew he was the stronger of the two. He blew inside his fist to warm his fingers before thrusting them down the front of his new friend's tight fitting jeans. The disappointments of the previous days seemed to heighten his anticipation, because suddenly Carl would no longer be satisfied with anything less than a hot fuck. He perhaps used too much strength as he pushed his companion against the tree, but Carl's desire was too urgent to care about crybabies. He unbuckled his belt, found the condom in his shirt pocket, but could not get it on. In the few seconds he had exposed himself to the cold wind, he had shrivelled to an embarrassing size. He didn't know what to do. Nothing like this had ever happened to him before. His new friend tried to help but his hands were freezing and only made matters worse. This was a nightmare, he thought. How did anyone in this place ever manage to have sex?

19.

Maureen eased open the kitchen door and hurried into the dark of her backyard with no intention of abiding by the rules of separation laid down by Lucian. She wanted to feel his whiskers against her face, tongue in her mouth.

Maureen tasted anchovies and garlic and guided Lucian's hand below the small of her back. But when nothing firm appeared at the front of his trousers the pair awkwardly stepped apart.

Sorry.

I told you before, it doesn't matter. I just like being with you.

I wanted to say thank you for the dinner. He doesn't make it as well as you do though.

Of course he doesn't, but the poor kid couldn't think of anything to cook, and I know it's one of your favourites.

The conversation suddenly faltered, allowing the nocturnal movements of the mountainside to grow louder.

How is everything? How's the book coming along?

Lucian shook his head. Don't ask. What's been happening around here?

Nothing much. More of the same. What are you reading?

The Good Soldier.

Again?

You know the rules.

Has it been two years already?

Probably not, but I felt the need to go back one final time.

What do you mean by that? Is something the matter? Are you sick? Is that why you're having trouble...

Everything is fine. It was just an expression. No need to jump to conclusions. I'm probably not thinking or speaking straight. Too much pot after dinner.

Sorry. I didn't mean to annoy you.

You didn't. I worry about you too, you know.

Really? Because that makes it even more confusing as to why we're no longer together.

Lucian pointed to the upstairs window with a light on. You have a husband in there, remember?

It was never enough of a reason before.

I should be getting back.

If there *was* something wrong you'd tell me, wouldn't you? You wouldn't try to hide it from me?

Lucian kissed Maureen goodnight and smelled roast chicken and coffee on her skin. Nothing is wrong. And yes, I would hide it from you. I don't want you to ever think of me as anything other than a healthy, dirty old man with his hand up your skirt. Now please go back inside where it's warm.

Just over three months had passed since Lucian had ended his affair with Maureen, and as he trudged through the dark scrub that led back to Brenan Street he could not deny a certain thrill at still being able to excite her. He recalled their afternoons together in hotel rooms all over Hobart: his fascination with the wrinkled skin between her breasts, the elegance of her shoulders as she stood in the shower; the way she wore her underpants to bed so he could enjoy taking them off. Maureen was considerate like that. So charming she could diffuse any bad mood Lucian found himself caught up in, and calm enough to lie beside him in bed reading for hours without saying a single word. She was uninhibited, fundamentally sensual, with a face of such atypical beauty that there were moments when it appeared rather plain, even unattractive. Her intellect was steady and pointed, and the times she outwitted him – of which there were many – made Lucian feel unworthy. Maureen was a prize, and always would be. Whereas he was difficult and intense, with a greedy, ungentlemanly imagination. And hardly in his physical prime. Short – five-ten. Hair more grey than black, with a deep line down the centre of his brow. His teeth were okay, and Maureen said he had the hands of a prince, but he smoked too much pot and at times imagined things that weren't real, leading to jealous outbursts. Even a simple love message, such as the dinner he had eaten that night, could still trigger a sharp pain in his chest. Heart attack, heartache or heartburn, either way it forced Lucian to sit down in the middle of a dark country road and rub his sternum, fretfully awaiting the discomfort to subside.

20.

Only when he was halfway down the Blackmans Bay blowhole did Michael finally concede he was doing something stupid. His intention to recreate an experience from Lucian's childhood in the hope of better understanding the author and his books was proving much more difficult than anticipated, especially with the unforecast rain making the ten-metre vertical rock face slippery beneath his fingers and shoes. There was no shortage of reliable footholds, and plenty of vines to grab hold of, but Michael lacked the upper-body strength to control his descent, and was burdened with a low-pain threshold that made every graze on his knees and elbows sting to distraction. At the top of the cliff, attached to a fence waist high and partially collapsing, had been a sign warning of potential danger. And now Michael regretfully realised it applied to adults as well as children.

As his bus passed the Blackmans Bay Primary School Michael had seen the clear cool day begin to disappear behind a sky of grey clouds. The fourteen-kilometre ride from Hobart had taken thirty minutes and ended on a suburban street that despite its two-storey bright veneer, tidy lawns, double garages and tightly closed curtains, still felt like the frontline of the development belt. The beach ten minutes' walk away boasted sands white enough to rival a tropical island, with seaweed and driftwood strewn along the high-tide mark to confirm inhospitable swimming conditions once the afternoon wind picked up. All the local businesses faced the ocean, and the butcher was only too happy to step out the front door of his shop to give Michael directions to the northern headland with its famous blowhole.

Michael jumped the last few feet of his descent and landed on a beach of dark grey rocks that had been pummelled smooth. Everywhere about him he saw evidence that water frequently covered where he now stood. Technically it was more of a sea arch than blowhole, though Michael doubted the differentiation would matter much if he did not get out of there soon. The tide had changed and the rain heralded the approach of a storm. Unfortunately his body was exhausted. The energy Lucian had possessed as an over-adventurous child was not something Michael could replicate, and his lack of preparation – no food or water – sparked a measure of panic. He checked his mobile phone for reception in case the situation turned desperate, and scolded himself the moment he confirmed there was no signal. The grinding rumble of the stone beach turning under the encroaching waves grew louder, echoing back and forth up the walls of the blowhole. For a moment Michael considered swimming out into the ocean and around the headland back to the beach. But his arms were already aching, and the prospect of icy water, avoiding jagged rocks, fighting the tide and suffering the humiliation of riding the bus home in wet clothes, confirmed he had no other option than to climb up again with the hope his body contained an as yet untapped reserve of strength.

Michael was two metres off the ground when he lost his footing and fell. He landed on his bottom, on rocks, sending a searing pain up his coccyx, followed by a terror that he had broken his back. The chill of seawater filling his shoes confirmed he was not a paraplegic, and the sense that he had narrowly escaped serious injury offered valuable perspective when Michael realised his phone had been crushed in the fall. Now he did not even know what time is was. He wiped rain from his eyes and tried to identify the path that Lucian might have taken while piggybacking Ursula up to safety. When their father learned of how much danger the two children had put themselves in he gave them both the belt. Lucian had mentioned the incident in a letter to a friend about the counter-productive effects of corporal punishment, and as Michael recalled reading the correspondence a scene from *Lady Cadaver* suddenly appeared in his head – of a brothel madam being brutally flogged by the women working under her protection. Each one of them lining up to thrash the proprietor with the leather straps and buckled belts that had been made available to the clientele. Perhaps Ursula's influence upon the book was not such a stretch after all? Michael certainly intended to check the novel the moment he returned to his room. If only he could get out of this bloody hole. He looked up for a new course. Safer, with more footholds and vines. It was time to stop being so weak. What would Lucian do in such a situation? The same as he had done with his sister on his back. Climb, damn it. Climb.

21.

The bell above the shop door rang and Maureen coughed across the kitchen table at the front page of *The Mercury*.

Mmm?

Your turn.

Tim held his gaze to the woman modelling S&M-styled footwear in a feature article about how tall boots were set to be the fashion for the approaching winter. What?

Maureen refused to acknowledge her husband's feigned obliviousness and returned to the scene in John Williams' *Butcher's Crossing* where a cowboy was being shown the technique for skinning a buffalo. The action was so well drawn that she could almost hear the flesh being torn off the dead animal's back, and so did not notice Tim sighing, draining his teacup, walking along the hall, past the stairs and into the shop.

The longer she read about eating buffalo over an open fire the stronger Maureen felt dissatisfied with her breakfast of toast and jam. A meal of rare beef now preoccupied her mind, and with it the certainty that a fresh cut from one of

Hobart's butchers would be superior to anything she had stocked in the shop freezer.

That was Paul, said Tim as he returned to the kitchen and lit the gas burner beneath the kettle. Says he's going to the doctor so he'll be opening up the pub late today. Reckons his feet are too swollen to stand.

Maureen thought she might look for a new dress at the same time, then swing by Fullers in case any of the books she had ordered had come in.

I told him to put a stool behind the counter months ago, but he seems to think people don't like to see a bartender sitting down. The kettle spluttered a shrill whistle and Tim realised there was no water in it.

Maureen knew that Fullers would have called if anything had arrived, but the pleasure of wandering around the bookstore was too great to resist. Everyone knew her there. It felt like home.

Oww! Tim dropped the kettle and shook his fingers. He always forgot that the wooden handle grew hot and needed to be gripped with a tea towel.

Maureen rolled her eyes and marked her page with a scrap of paper. I'm going to need the car this morning.

Coward.

Sorry?

Come on, you know what Wobbly Bob and the others are like when their routine is interrupted. They'll be in here all morning complaining about how the pub was better before Paul took it over.

Nope. Still have no idea what you're talking about.

Paul's swollen feet?

He hasn't put a stool behind the counter?

Tim set about filling the kettle to hide his anger and frustration at Maureen not listening to a word he had said.

Uninterested in playing her husband's silent game, Maureen walked into the small office below the stairs where the car keys were kept. The room lacked a window, and she could smell the remains of yesterday's porn date on the tissues in the wastepaper basket. Maureen sprayed air freshener directly on top of them and sat down to check her email. In times past Tim had made an effort to cover his tracks by deleting his search history or using a different browser. But he had either forgotten, grown too lazy or simply stopped caring, because there it was, yesterday's midday entertainment, XXX blah blah blah. Out of curiosity Maureen opened the page and watched the two naked bodies bump against each other in an unimpressively mechanical fashion. The camera had cut off the man's head, leaving visible only his gym body – customised with the same tattoos she saw on most young men these days – against the peroxide blonde who was obviously more concerned with preserving her long fingernails through the experience than appreciating its ecstatic eroticism. Her silicon lips and breasts were as convincing as her acting, and Maureen despaired at how sad and moronic it all was. She closed the page and loaded her emails in the hope of flushing the images from her mind.

Tim heard the office phone ring and grabbed his jacket before Maureen could delay his morning cigarette.

She opened the back door and found him leaning over the fence, talking to the chickens. Hey, hot sluts, I'm leaving. I'll be back in a couple of hours.

Tim choked on his smoke and waved.

Don't forget to bring in those cans of soft drinks that were delivered yesterday.

I thought we were doing that job together.

You can manage on your own. It's not that many. Just think of it as an opportunity to do some exercise. You need to stay buff for all those horny young ladies out there.

22.

Rachel inserted her keys into the car's ignition and sat back to catch her breath. Closed her eyes to calm her mind, then reopened them again to check all the doors were locked. Being chased around the couch by one of Michael's old school friends had left her more frightened than she had felt in years. An introduction to Steve nine months prior had given no hint he would act that way. His invitation to drop by his house to discuss Michael's whereabouts made sense as it was on her way home. And although his reassurances about Michael eventually turning up had sounded blithe, and his topping up her wine glass had been a little over insistent, Rachel had only realised that her time was being wasted once she felt Steve's hand on her knee.

Exactly why she could not let Michael go was becoming as much of a mystery to Rachel as it was for her colleagues at Australia's leading business magazine. They were bored with her obsessive line of conversation, and a little embarrassed on her behalf at the way she refused to accept the blatant signals that Michael was sending. Rachel noticed their dwindling empathy and refrained from sharing her latest theories about where Michael had disappeared to. All urges to check if he had responded to her phone messages she now satisfied in the bathroom stalls. And any direct investigations were conducted in the privacy of the mall across the street. No one from her office ate there, and the rowdy background noise ensured her conversations were kept to the point. The two lecturers from the University of New South Wales that she had spoken with had no idea where their colleague was, and seemed to suspect he had received a private research grant that more than likely should have gone to them. While two of Michael's school friends said he had always been a bit of a flake, and had a habit of doing exactly what he wanted to do without thinking of how it affected anyone else. The third friend, however, saw Michael's absence as nothing more than an opportunity to offer Rachel an evening of consoling sex, so in the end it was no surprise that Michael had failed to inform any of them of where he was going.

If only he would reply to one of her texts or emails then Rachel could stop worrying. But with each day that passed without word she grew increasingly concerned about his welfare. Though they had agreed to have a break from one another, she had not expected him to vanish and sever all communication. Who does that after fourteen months together? Rachel knew that Michael could be a little self-involved. Often unreliable. Not to mention frustratingly neurotic and somewhat emotionally retarded. But what did it take to pick up a phone to reassure her that he was okay? Rachel checked the rear-vision mirror and saw how her eyes looked tired. She needed to go home and get a good night's rest and stop worrying so much about him. If he did not want to be found, then he could stay lost. Searching was too much effort. He was far from the most attractive man she had slept with. And certainly not the wealthiest. There were thousands of other options in Sydney. Rachel then remembered Michael's insistence on reading every article she had published; the in-jokes they had shared at tiresome work functions, and the attention he had given to the smallest details of her body, as if she were a gift and no part could be wasted. Had she taken Michael for granted? Was that why the gulf of their separation felt so deep? But he could not have gone very far. Michael was terrified of flying. And when he showed up again she would simply suggest they give their relationship another go. In the meantime, she needed to get on with her life. Take better care of herself. Not put herself in situations like the one she had just narrowly escaped from. She was smarter than that. As she steered her car away from the kerb she insisted that she was a million times smarter than that. But by the time she had driven three-hundred metres to the next set of traffic lights, Rachel was already thinking of where next she might search for Michael.

23.

Jesus, what happened to you?

It's nothing...I just tripped down some steps.

Looks more like you fell down a cliff. Now I know why you didn't turn up yesterday. Were you drunk?

No, I mean, well not *that* drunk. And the steps were wet.

Didn't I tell you to buy some boots?

Michael nodded as he checked his new wristwatch. It had been one of the cheapest in the store and was already losing time. The hands said 12.45, but Lucian never opened his front door before 1pm. Then Michael noticed the jacket, the ironed shirt. Are you going out?

I have an appointment in town. He indicated to the plastic bag hanging from Michael's fingers. Is that dinner?

Lamb shoulder and tabouli.

Will it keep until tomorrow? I was planning to visit the docks and buy some fish. Do you eat fish?

Sure. No problem.

Sadie's asleep in the library. I took her for a long walk this morning so she probably won't wake up until I come home. See you this evening some time. I've left a CD playing on the stereo that I thought you might like, but if you're not into it just turn it off.

Michael stood on the verandah until Lucian had disappeared down the road, then slipped off his wet shoes, dropped his briefcase inside his office and walked towards the music playing at the rear of the house. He poured a glass of water, raided Lucian's biscuit tin and finally inspected the album artwork on top of the turntable lid. He had never heard of Pärson Sound, but their music was rapidly winning him over, as if he had been waiting all his life to hear such a precarious teeter between rhythm and noise. Michael only realised how engrossed he had become when the hypnotic composition came to an end and he found himself sitting on one of the couches with the CD jewel case still in his hand. He pressed play to restart the album, upped the volume so the music would follow him around the house, then walked into the bathroom to check the state of his cuts and scratches. Sadie opened an eye and gave a growl of warning as he entered the library, but remained in her basket while Michael lost an hour familiarising himself with authors he had not read and erecting a pile of novels he would ask permission to borrow as soon as Lucian returned home. He opened hall cupboards, peeked inside bureau drawers, squinted at signatures scrawled along the bottom of paintings and lithographs, until eventually he stood outside the closed door to Lucian's bedroom weighing the benefits of invading the writer's private space against the likelihood that it would lose him his job. Lucian had given no restrictions or guidelines as to where Michael could or could not go in his house. And if there was something inside he was not supposed to see then surely the door would be locked.

The room was larger and brighter than Michael had expected, and he would never have imagined Lucian's bed with a crocheted blanket on top. A sagging reading chair stood beside the window, accompanied by a weathered green ottoman and a small coffee table. Three glasses of water were next to the bed, along with a copy of Muriel Spark's *Memento Mori*. Michael mentally added the title to his list of books to ask Lucian about, then turned to the wall opposite the window with its photographs of people at parties, in canoes, sunbaking beside a pool, in bed, or enjoying a picnic. Each picture was individually framed but hung so closely to its neighbour that it created the impression of a collage almost two metres long and about half as tall. Michael searched for famous faces or familial resemblance to Lucian, but found only strangers staring back at what he assumed was the author holding the camera. Tucked behind the door was a modest, tidy writing desk topped with a small pile of typed pages. No, Michael would not pry so deep. Instead he examined the few keepsakes placed about the desk, and reverently touched the keys of Lucian's typewriter. He thought about sitting in the chair until a shiver suddenly crossed his back. A suspicion that somehow Lucian was watching him, or had left home for the sole purpose of allowing Michael to explore his room. The feeling persisted even after he had returned to the hall, so Michael grabbed his cigarettes and stepped onto the verandah in the hope that a blast of cold air would shake the sensation from his skin.

24.

1970 – Conscripted into the army and commence training.

1971 – Sent to Vietnam where you serve in the supply division for eleven months before returning home wounded.

1972 – (Nothing found for this year. I assume it involved recuperation from your wound. Cannot uncover any clues as to where this occurred.)

1973 – Find work as a maintenance welder for the Tasmanian Hydro. Begin to write *The Bombardier*.

1974 – Ursula marries and moves to Launceston. You travel to England by cargo ship. Stop in Egypt and meet Patricia Wren for the first time.

1975 – Arrested in London for lewd behaviour and public drunken-ness. The article you write about prison conditions results in a job offer from *The Times*.

1976 – During a boozy lunch you disagree with *The Times'* literary editor about Ruth Prawer Jhabvala's *Heat and Dust*. Argument ends in a fight and you are sacked the following day. Move to Sicily.

1977 – The first draft of *The Bombardier* is complete. Your father dies of a heart attack. Two days later you are wounded in a knife fight and infection sets in. After being flown to London you temporarily lose your vision and spend two months recuperating in The Royal Brompton Hospital.

1978 – Take a job at The Royal Brompton Hospital distributing pharmaceuticals throughout the wards. At night you rewrite *The Bombardier*. Sacked from The Royal Brompton Hospital for stealing amphetamines. Narrowly avoid legal prosecution. Move to Ireland.

1979 – Travel in France, Germany and parts of eastern Europe. Settle in Turkey but return to London when *The Bombardier* is accepted for publication. Re-introduced to Patricia Wren at a party hosted by Harold Pinter.

1980 – Marry Patricia Wren at the Chelsea Registry Office then move to Surrey.

25.

This is good work, said Lucian as he folded the sheet of paper until it was small enough to fit inside his shirt pocket. But I need you to go a lot deeper. Dates and names are fine, but more important are the tiny details that glue the big events together. You need to change the way you think. Rather than pick my life apart, I want you to try and put it back together...so to speak.

Michael leaned forward to accept the spliff Lucian had just set alight. I was trying to find out what happened to you in Sicily but all I could come up with were medical records.

Then go back through my books. Look for scenes that include violence, or threats of violence, and I bet you'll find something to give you an idea of what happened. Hospitals, doctors, how I write about nurses, pain, it's all bound to be in there somewhere. I'm relying on you to read between the lines.

Michael recalled *The Bombardier*'s story of a US pilot being shot down in a Vietnamese jungle and found by a lost and wandering unit of Australian soldiers. Of the men substituting the pilot for their dead superior officer, and making him confront the horrors of a war he had only ever observed from twenty thousand feet. As part of his thesis Michael had researched Australia's role in the conflict and found equal measures of accurate and erroneous historical facts within the novel, though the extent to which the events were based on Lucian's own experiences as a nineteen-year-old soldier was something he had never been able to determine.

But how am I supposed to distinguish between what's real and what's fiction?

Lucian turned to the sunroom windows. He was exhausted from his afternoon of walking the streets of Hobart and wished he could switch off the lights to silently observe the night-time dramas unfolding amongst the trees outside. At present all he could see was a blurry reflection of Michael and him sitting on the couches. Everything is real, he whispered to himself.

Pardon?

Lucian exhaled his exasperation. You think the things that have occurred in my life are more real to me than the events I've imagined for my books?

I...

If a story doesn't live for an author then it sure as hell won't live for a reader.

I...I...

You need to be alert to everything you find in that room. I don't care what I called it when you first arrived. Nothing in there is junk. It's all relevant. And it's been kept for a reason. A purpose. Your job is to find out what that purpose is.

The marijuana hit Michael's bloodstream the moment he stood up, and made his exit from the sunroom unusually clumsy. Lucian suspected his secretary was heading for the bathroom to throw up his dinner, and scanned his vinyl collection for a record to mask the sounds of heaving and retching.

All right, said Michael as he dropped heavily back into his seat. Explain to me the relevance of this.

Lucian lowered the stylus onto Charalambides' *Market Square,* then accepted the faded clipping from a local newspaper that told the story of a woodchopper who had taken second place in the national championships. The article was dated 11 April 1977, and Lucian was surprised that he still recalled why he had cut it out.

Well, what do you think? he asked.

Inspiration for the groundskeeper in *Foxtrot?*

Lucian shook his head. Try again.

Wasn't there a scene in *Lady Cadaver* that involved a couple who liked to feel the cold steel of an axe between them while they had sex?

You're being too literal, said Lucian as he drew deeply on his spliff. Remember, I need you to read between the lines.

I just grabbed it off the top of the pile. I haven't even read *the lines* yet.

Lucian handed back the fragile piece of paper. Just skip to the third-last paragraph.

Michael focussed his addled brain and read how after the award ceremonies were complete the woodchopper had stepped down from his podium and given away his second-place ribbon to a young boy in the audience. The description, however, failed to prompt any memory of a comparable scene in Lucian's novels...and Michael admitted so.

Look at the picture again, Lucian insisted. At the man's face. Don't you see it? That's the face of a man who doesn't know his own worth. Even when life has placed him second only to a champion, he still cannot recognise his own value. Now do you know what the clipping is for?

Dismantling Ivan's Circus?

Lucian raised his glass of wine in salute.

26.

Like a bat, Andrew Tiller used the sound of his own voice to navigate and understand the world he lived in. Just walking upstairs to the room Michael rented required at least a hum, if not a whistle. And should a member of staff have crossed his path then all manner of longwinded instructions would have issued forth irrespective of whether they were necessary or not. The times he changed bed sheets Andrew spoke out loud the mantra for tucking hospital corners that his mother had taught him as a boy. During breakfast he liked to repeat everyone's order verbatim as he delivered dishes to their tables. And checking in a new guest sparked an entire routine about Battery Point: the history of the house; how long it had been in Andrew's family; the day's weather forecast; the likelihood of it coming true; tourism services; when breakfast was served; the rules against smoking, having parties, smoking, leaning out windows, smoking, slamming doors; water conservation; wiping your feet, and how it was not necessary to tip for service as everything had been factored into the price of the room.

But all this came second to walking and talking, hands free, on his mobile phone. Regardless of appearing like a madman – gesturing and conversing with no one in sight – Andrew enjoyed nothing better than strolling into the city while communicating with friends, family, suppliers and even tradesmen. It did not matter what the topic was, just so long as his arms and legs were working at the same time as his lips and tongue. It gave Andrew a sense of moving forward and sorting things out, fixing problems and avoiding mistakes. He felt powerful and in charge: ready to take on the world; make money; exceed expectations; prove the doubters wrong; buck the system; turn a corner, rise to the top and take a bow. At night, alone in his room, when the staff had gone home and all the guests were tucked in, and it was too late to call anyone, Andrew talked to his TV. Told game show contestants to choose number three if they wanted to win a million dollars; castigated politicians for avoiding the question, and warned movie stars that the serial killer was about to jump out and grab them. His favourites, however, were reality TV shows. Because the people were not actors it seemed more like a genuine conversation. So when they failed to prepare food the way he suggested, or chose a tasteless renovation, voted the wrong person off an island, or ignored someone's obvious musical talent, Andrew could feel even more superior. At bedtime he tuned his clock radio to a local talkback station, then effortlessly drifted off to sleep while the low hum of conservative vitriol floated about his room. When the alarm went off at 5.30am Andrew sometimes did think of when his wife had been around to help. But Betty was not much of a talker, and could never fall asleep if the radio was on, so it was probably wise they had decided to divorce. She remarried soon after and moved to Howrah on the Eastern Shore. The last time they had seen one another was across a crowd in the Cat and Fiddle Arcade. Both had waved without stopping to avoid discussing the swollen stomach so obvious beneath Betty's clothes. Her baby must be a year old by now, assumed Andrew as he stood outside Michael's room.

He knocked, just in case, looked left and right, then took out his master keys. Everything was as Andrew had suspected, including the stale scent of cigarette smoke that permeated the room even with a window left open. The carpet just below was damp with rain, and Andrew felt an internal conflict between his desire to avoid further damage and the risk of Michael noticing that someone had entered his room during his absence. The B&B proprietor sneered at the chocolate wrappers in the waste paper basket, and shook his head at the soiled underpants on the bathroom floor. This was no way for a guest to behave. There were marks on furniture that were never supposed to have hot cups placed on top of them, and all the doilies his grandmother had crocheted were curiously missing. He found them stuffed into a drawer with the ornaments that usually stood along the mantelpiece; then registered how the three watercolours had all been turned towards the wall. It was as if Michael had rejected everything in the room that was beautiful. Still, Andrew had what he needed. More than enough evidence to deny a continuation of the discount rate should Michael ask to stay another month. In light of the repairs the carpet and furniture would require, Andrew thought he was well within his rights to charge peak season rates. No smoking meant no smoking.

27.

Lucian carefully lowered himself into his bedroom chair and switched on the lamp that stood behind it. He found his spare glasses on the windowsill, then began to reread Michael's summary of his life between 1970 and 1980. Lucian remembered nothing about the article on prison conditions, nor stealing amphetamines from the Brompton Hospital. And the idea that he had ever been in a room with Harold Pinter came as a complete surprise. He wondered who else might have been present. Experience had taught Lucian that the anticipation of meeting a writer was invariably more pleasurable than its fulfilment, but he was amused by the idea that at one time he might have shaken hands with Simon Gray or Antonia Fraser, or even John Fowles. Lucian redirected the light towards the wall of photographs, hoping for a clue as to what else might have occurred during those ten years. Some of the fashions certainly corresponded with the era, however most of the people and places remained infuriatingly unfamiliar. The fact that Lucian *knew* he had forgotten their names only made it worse. If he would just forget the desire to remember as well, then he could finally be at peace. Until then, everything he failed to recall felt like a black hole in his brain. Of course he recognised Patricia with her fair complexion, small lips, sharp jaw, long neck and petulant expression that a simple smile could transform into miraculous beauty. It was a shame she had asked for a divorce after only nine years, but life in Surrey had not suited Lucian. And moving about the Continent, staying in hotels that quickly declined in prestige once *The Bombardier* was replaced by the next literary sensation, was far from the life Patricia had been bred for. The fact that *Foxtrot* was taking so long to write also did not help. Patricia had experienced only the end results of a writer's work – the newspaper reviews, nominations for prizes, window displays and parties full of frightfully clever people. The years of quiet, isolated research and rewriting, with false starts and angry outbursts fuelled by self-doubt consequently came as a rude awakening and were hardly her idea of fun. No children had arrived to provide distraction, and though Patricia appeared more attractive with each consecutive birthday, her daily view of Lucian's loosening jowls, yellowing toenails, thickening ear hair and wrinkling elbows made her panic. The divorce papers were somewhere in the other room. Michael would come across them soon enough. Another piece of the puzzle for him to put together. Lucian then realised he could not recall the sound of Patricia's voice, or what it felt like to kiss her lips. How sad, he thought, that after being so close to someone such intimate details could be forgotten. Yet the longer he dwelled on it the more he discovered what else had vanished from his memory. Such as Patricia's taste in music, or whether she liked to dance. Did she ever eat chicken with her fingers? Or allow herself to get drunk? He assumed she had done both in his company, except Lucian had no recollection of it. Nor did he remember what she looked like naked. He had no idea of where Patricia had attended school, or how many siblings she had grown up with. Did she cook? Could she ride a bike? And which side of the bed had she preferred to sleep on? No matter how hard he stared at the photograph of his first wife, such details refused to reappear. It almost felt as if the two of them had never actually been married. Well of course it does you old fool, he shouted as he crushed the notes and threw them against the wall of pictures. Lucian waited for his anger to abate, then retrieved the ball of paper from the floor, smoothed its creases against his chest, and inserted it into the filing cabinet drawer that had been cleared for everything Michael wrote. Such documents were too precious to throw away. It reminded Lucian that he needed to leave himself a message somewhere nearby. A physical instruction to look in the bottom drawer should he ever become confused about who or where he was. Otherwise he might forget the information was even in there.

28.

Michael lowered his nose into the boot and inhaled the sweet scent of pristine leather and virgin innersole. The aroma returned him to the Sunday afternoon shoe store expeditions made with Rachel, and the erotic pleasure he had discovered by being surrounded by so many women.

Have you got these in brown? he asked the approaching shop assistant.

Phil wore a khaki shirt with the name of his store printed on its pocket, and sported a goatee to balance the short crop of hair growing in a semi circle around the back of his head. He saw people sniffing shoes every day and thought nothing of it.

No, just black.

And they're waterproof?

That's what it says on the label.

Where's that?

Phil pressed his finger to the product description stapled to the wall. Just there.

Oh, right. Of course. Okay, can I try a pair on?

No problem. Have a seat. What size do you take?

Ten. Sometimes ten and a half.

Maybe I should measure your feet first?

No, a ten should be fine.

As Phil searched the stockroom Michael leaned back in his chair and admired the charm of the store's built-in shelving, wooden serving counter and glass display cabinets. The layout had obviously remained the same for the past thirty or forty years, and though catering for the needs of tradesmen, had a quiet dignity that most modern shops had forsaken for prefabricated fittings and muzak. It was old without feeling stuffy, and Michael detected a surprising comfort in being served by a person who had actual knowledge about the product they were selling.

Thought I should buy a pair now winter has arrived.

Phil carefully folded back the tissue paper surrounding the new boots. Sounds wise. Although it's not here quite yet.

Well not officially no, but it doesn't get much colder does it?

Phil looked up from the three-legged stool at Michael's feet. Just moved to Tasmania have you?

About a month ago.

Working for MONA are you?

No. Who's Mona?

Museum...out past Glenorchy. You'll get there eventually. Everyone does.

You say these are a ten?

That's what the number says on the bottom of the boot. They feel a little loose.

Maybe you've got thin socks on today. Take a walk around the shop. Phil watched Michael pace back and forth. So what are you doing down here if you're not working at MONA?

I'm helping Lucian Clarke to organise his papers.

Who?

He's an author. A pretty famous one actually. Lives in Wood Green. Up on the mountain.

I know where Wood Green is.

Of course you do. Sorry.

Sounds interesting. Good job is it?

So far so good.

And there's no one here in Hobart who could do that work?

Pardon?

I mean you're an expert on this writer? That's why you're down here?

Well he was the subject of my PhD, if that's what you mean. But I don't know if that qualifies me as an expert or not.

Should get a bit of snow up in Wood Green soon.

So I hear.

Got a good jacket? You'll need one to keep out cold like that. We've got a few on sale over there.

I'm fine for a jacket. Thanks. Are those flannel shirts on sale as well?

Everything in the store is on sale.

You're not closing as well are you? There seem to be shops closing down all along this street.

Not yet thankfully. Have to wait and see how the next six months play out.

So these boots are on sale as well?

Reduced to ninety-nine dollars.

You know, I think they're a little too big for me. Maybe I should try a nine and a half.

Why don't you let me measure your foot first.

I suppose you should. Are they an overseas brand? Maybe they're using the American size system. Or the European one.

No, it's an Australian boot, but like everything else these days they're made in China. Used to have a factory right here in Tasmania. Everyone in the state owned a pair.

Are Chinese shoe sizes different?

Couldn't say, never been there. Looks like you're a nine.

You're sure?

Phil pointed to the Brannock Device. Hard to get something like that wrong.

But I've been a ten since I was eighteen. Sometimes even a ten and a half. Look, see, even my shoes say ten and a half. And I bought these in Sydney.

They've seen better days.

The rain got to them. And then I had to walk through some bush.

Let me get you a nine and see how we go.

Phil returned to the stockroom while Michael double-checked the measurement of his foot.

Here, try these on.

Michael stood up in the new boots and walked across the store. Well that's much better. How strange. Feet don't usually shrink do they? Maybe my shoe size has been wrong all my life.

Happens more often than you'd think.

What's that?

People thinking their feet are bigger than they actually are. Men especially.

Really. I never knew. I guess I might as well start wearing them right away. Is there a bin I can put my old shoes in?

Just drop them behind the counter here.

29.

Tim replaced the phone receiver and leaned back in his chair with a queasy stomach and humming in his ears. He squeezed his eyes closed, breathed deeply and swallowed against the wave of panic billowing about his body. Minutes passed this way until his grip of the chair gradually relaxed, and he reopened his eyes to an office transformed. Where every item had suddenly become more distinct. Not glowing brighter, but sharper with meaning – miraculously thrusting postcards, long ago tacked onto the notice board, back into view. Emphasising the appeal of the wooden walls painted white, and the snugness of the staircase intruding overhead. At once everything had developed a reassuring familiarity. Even the synthetic fragrance of the air freshener that had been so pungent all week now seemed to evoke a sense of belonging and home. The hallway was the same – beautiful with its wooden skirting boards, picture rails and old-fashioned floral carpet. The frosted glass in the door through to the kitchen further complemented its charm, and the metallic doorknob that had been broken since the day they moved in suddenly held a direct connection to Tim's heart. He peered into the kitchen to check for Maureen, not intending to stop, yet found himself captivated by the formica tabletop he had eaten so many meals upon; the two chairs at either end; the salt and pepper shakers in the shape of penguins, and the sports section of *The Mercury* he had been reading that morning. Tim realised that he loved it all. Everything in the kitchen. The stained bench tops; archaic stove; taps that dripped unless you turned them off with both hands; the kettle that burned his fingers nearly every day. He loved the smell of last night's lamb shanks, and the cosiness that seemed to grow thicker with each day the cold of winter encroached. He looked to the trees flouncing in the wind and rain. Even the weather felt significant. Back in the hall, past the office, Tim peered up the staircase to the residence and found himself wishing that things with Maureen had turned out differently. Somehow they had lost sight of one another, and in a moment or two everything would change forever. He ran his fingers along the grooves in the banister then sniffed his hand. The polish Maureen used was honeyed and deep and made Tim's eyes brim with water. He remembered the first time they had seen the place, and the dreams they had brought along with their furniture. But no children had arrived, and the effort of running the business had caused them to drift apart. He knew some of it was his fault. But it was hard not to gain weight when work was just downstairs. And he enjoyed wandering over to Paul's pub in the afternoon. It had begun as a tactic to gain acceptance in the local community, but the habit had stuck long after Tim knew everyone well enough to realise they were never going to become best friends. Before moving to Wood Green he had been reasonably fit, and maybe after he left he would be again. Tim had no idea of where he was going to go or what Maureen was planning to do. And for a moment he considered trying to save his marriage rather than face the rigmarole of setting up a new life for himself. But as he walked into the shop he knew the opportunity for reconciliation had passed. Over recent years his connection with Maureen had grown more fractured, and he understood that what he was about to say was going to make it finally snap.

I just had a call from the real estate agent.

Maureen held her eyes to the newspaper spread over the serving counter.

Mmm?

Looks like she's found us a buyer.

30.

Come on.

What?

Time to give those new boots of yours a proper workout.

Michael was halfway through sorting a pile of letters from Grace, Lucian's second wife. Give me a minute. I'll be right there.

Lucian paced the far edge of the yard until Michael appeared at the back door. Hurry up. The sun is already starting to dip.

Sadie isn't coming with us?

She's had her walk for the day. She can stay and guard the house.

So where exactly are we going?

Just up the mountain a bit. Thought it was about time I showed you the forest. Here, you can carry the bag. It's just water and some nuts in case we get hungry.

Michael shouldered the knapsack and followed Lucian through the trees. For the first hour he stayed close behind, stepping where Lucian stepped while trying to ignore all fears of snakes, spiders, getting lost, and widow-making branches silently falling on top of his head. But during the second hour the distance between the two ramblers widened, as Michael felt himself relax and became accustomed to the dank organic reek of decomposing leaves and bark that had fallen during the summer. Some trees were so tall that he almost lost his balance as he leaned back to appreciate their height. And so wide that whenever Lucian's red shirt disappeared behind one he would listen for the old man's footsteps amongst the rustle of marsupials scurrying in the thick undergrowth, and the squawk of birds warning of approaching intruders.

Though Michael had been wearing his new boots for more than a week their stiff leather began to cut into the back of his ankles. His thighs also ached, his breath was proving difficult to catch, and after he had looked down the mountainside to estimate how far they had walked, he turned around and realised that Lucian had vanished. His legs refused all entreaties to run and catch up, and shouting Lucian's name only resulted in hundreds of startled birds flapping noisily into the air. Michael forced himself forward as fast as his stamina would permit, and kept his eyes peeled for any glimpse of a red shirt in the dense and dimming landscape.

Lucian sat among the remains of three fallen trees that had made a small opening in the forest's canopy and allowed for a bed of long grass and native flowers to grow. The warmth of the sun felt delicious against his back, and thoughts of his secretary panicking about being lost kept him pleasantly amused until Michael finally emerged from between the trees with a face covered in sweat and obvious relief.

You made it! Pass the water will you.

Michael handed over the knapsack then lay along the trunk of one of the fallen trees with his face in the sun. It quickly dried his perspiration and made his eyelids heavy.

Beautiful spot, don't you think?

Michael was not yet able to speak.

I don't know whether anyone else knows it's here. I never see evidence of other people visiting it.

He passed a hand across his face.

Thought I'd lost you there for a while. You make an old man like me feel fit.

Michael forced himself to sit up and accepted the bottle of water. Not much of a bushwalker.

Well living in Tasmania should change that.

How far up the mountain are we?

Not too far. It'd probably take another four or five hours to reach the top. Maybe even longer for you. People used to walk up and down here all the time, you know. Long before they made a road. There are tracks right through this forest.

Bet they lost a few along the way.

I'm sure they did. There were a lot more trees in those days. Fire burnt right through here in sixty-seven and thinned things out. That's how I got the house. No one wanted to live in Wood Green after that. Lucian stood up.

I might need a few more minutes to catch my breath.

Take your time. I'm just having a wander around.

Michael appreciated the opportunity to lie back down. His heart was still thumping inside his chest, and forcing him to seriously reconsider the wisdom of cigarettes.

You little beauty, Lucian shouted in the distance. A few minutes later he returned to the clearing with a handful of mushrooms. Can I tempt you to an interesting afternoon?

Michael sat up too quickly and his head flooded with dizziness. How interesting?

About as interesting as it gets on this fucking mountain.

How do you know they're the right ones?

Don't they look right to you?

Couldn't say. Never had them before.

Really? My goodness, well that's even more of a reason to take them.

So what do we do? Cook them up in a stew or something?

Raw, my boy. Fresh and raw.

Now? Up here? But what if we get lost?

How can you get lost on a mountain? Just walk downhill and you'll either hit Wood Green or Hobart.

Michael winced.

All right how about this? We take them now and start walking back straight away. That way we'll almost be home before they kick in.

It was an invitation Michael felt obliged to accept. As he broke through the edge of the forest and saw the faint outline of Lucian's house he almost wept with thanks. They had been wandering the forest in the dark for what seemed like hours, completely lost, laughing and screaming in equal measure, remembering their predicament then forgetting it again the moment a fresh distraction appeared. The bottle of water had run out hours ago, and the lingering taste of vomit in Michael's mouth was the first thing he attended to upon re-entering the house. His new boots were caked with mud, and as he carried them to the front door he heard Lucian break open ice trays and rummage the freezer for vodka. Booze was the last thing Michael thought he wanted, though he soon found himself gulping down the spectacularly refreshing drink as both men sat on opposite couches, grinning.

Fucking strong ones, insisted Lucian. Must have come up just today.

Now safely home Michael realised the experience had not been all bad. Once the nausea and stomach cramps had died down a deeper appreciation for the forest and its role in the world had definitely manifested. There were patterns in the trees that he had never noticed before. And he could not deny the emergence of a palpable, textural connection between himself and all living creatures. Michael wanted to write down his revelations, yet strangely lacked the energy to stand up and find a piece of paper. He convinced himself that he would remember everything in the morning. How could anyone forget such revelatory concepts and ideas? Michael then noticed Lucian staring at him with a quizzical expression.

Jesus you're pulsating at the moment, said the author as he stood up and leaned across the coffee table.

Michael offered a weak smile in reply just as Lucian raised a hand and struck the side of his head with an open palm.

What the hell are you doing? shouted Michael as he fell to one side and watched Lucian prepare for a second attack.

There's something in your hair. I was trying to kill it for you.

You're hallucinating, you idiot. There's nothing in my hair. Go back to your seat. That fucking hurt.

Oh. Did it? Sorry.

Michael's face was throbbing, and he scowled at Lucian while telling himself that there was nothing in his hair, there was nothing in his hair. But the more he tried to convince himself, the more concrete the idea became. He rushed to the bathroom and spent the next twenty-five minutes checking and rechecking his reflection in the medicine cabinet mirror. Only the appearance of music could distract him from his panic. On returning to the sunroom he found Lucian lying along a couch, smoking a spliff, and tapping his foot to the kaleidoscopic rhythms of a low-toned organ music that immediately commandeered Michael's attention. He picked up the record sleeve from the coffee table – Terry Riley's *Persian Surgery Dervishes* – and accepted the joint without a second thought as to what had happened. He then noticed that Lucian had changed his shirt to one of the exact same green as his own.

31.

Despite having the internet café to himself, Carl selected the computer in the farthest corner of the room so his screen would be hidden from the street as well as the somnolent attendant who had taken his money. It was obviously a popular position as there were crumbs all over the keyboard, and the desk felt sticky with what Carl hoped was only spilled soft drink. He considered changing to another terminal, but decided not to draw attention to himself. If the attendant thought he was just another office worker enjoying an early lunch of hard-core porn then that was fine by Carl. He wanted to be nondescript. A quick check of the browser's search history confirmed his suspicions regarding the computer's usage, and augmented his growing appreciation that just because Hobart was a quiet city did not mean its residents were.

Carl, however, was not interested in exposing himself to the lusts of lonely men...well not the straight ones at least. He instead typed in the URLs for Johannesburg's major newspapers and began searching for reports about himself or the money he had stolen. When he found no mention of either, he typed in the name of the bank he had worked for, and began a search of regional publications for stories about pending investigations into account irregularities, or customers complaining about missing funds. When he still found no mention of the crime he had committed, Carl wondered if it had even been discovered yet. Had he covered his tracks so effectively that no one had detected the missing money? Carl knew it was too early to make that assumption. It had only been a couple of months since he had flown out of Jozi. Maybe his theft would show up in the September quarterly reports. Or maybe he simply hadn't stolen enough for them even to notice. Carl prided himself on being too smart to be too greedy. He had seen countless people get caught that way. So when he had finally decided to leave South Africa, he had also resolved that he would take only enough to hide comfortably for a few years, and start up a business of his own later down the track. He knew how to invest. And once everyone had forgotten about him he could probably move somewhere else and build on his capital to make even more money. All the same, Carl could not deny a certain disappointment that his crime had not yet made the news. He knew how clever he had been, and wanted other people to appreciate it as well. Especially his old boss. And those idiots in Human Resources who were always miscalculating the number of holidays he was due. For a moment he considered typing his former name into a search engine, but then told himself not to be foolish. The last thing he wanted to do was lead the police to Tasmania. If anyone did manage to follow the false bank accounts he had set up – and Carl seriously doubted that was possible – then the trail would turn cold in Sydney where he had withdrawn all his cash in large denominations. He knew how easy it was to track people via credit cards and mobile phones. Which was why he had bought a prepay in the airport giftshop. So there could be no way for anyone to ever find him here in Hobart.

Carl leaned back in his chair and pressed both palms to his eyes to soothe the strain of staring at a screen for too long. When the ache subsided he saw there were four other people in the café, and from his position it was obvious what they were all looking at. He felt a sudden need for fresh air, and to wash his hands. Have something to eat, and a glance through the paper. He might go for a walk along the shoreline, see a movie, do some shopping, look for a restaurant, or a club to go dancing. It seemed like a lot for one afternoon, and he knew that to achieve half of it he would have to get moving. He just wanted to have one final check of his hometown news sites to make sure he had not missed anything.

32.

Paul sat begrudgingly on the stool his doctor had recommended he install behind the bar if he did not want his feet and legs to grow any more swollen. It seemed wrong not to stand, like he wasn't working, though the delight of taking weight off his feet did much to appease his conscience. The locals on the other side of the bar were still not talking to him. Opening the pub late was a crime they judged deserving of at least two weeks' silent treatment. The fact he had needed to go to the doctor was irrelevant. Their drinking routine was Paul's responsibility as much as their own, and any interruption would not be forgiven easily. Paul watched Wobbly Bob open his throat like a snake and gulp down the first half of his ninth beer. It was an impressive spectacle that required a lifetime of drinking to perfect, and could not be bettered by any of the other alcoholics perched upon the stools. Paul scanned the scene. Was it any wonder his efforts to turn his business into an out-of-the-way destination had failed. He could paint the walls, update the jukebox, hang framed movie posters and stock all manner of exotic liquors behind the bar...nothing was going to displace those fourteen old timers who drank here every day. Visitors might see the new furniture, smell the delicious lunches that Penny cooked, even stay for a drink or two, but all they would ever take away would be the memory of stained tracksuit pants stretched over beer bellies, and unbridled farting.

Paul wondered how he could have been naïve enough to expect anything different. Did Tim and Maureen see it as well? The uselessness of his situation? Were they laughing behind his back? No, they understood that change was good for Wood Green. Hadn't they managed to transform their own business into something new and successful? Before they bought the general store it had been a dump that everyone in the community complained about. Now it was the heart of Wood Green where people lingered and gossiped and...did not throw up in the toilets. Sure their marriage was a little rocky, but it never got in the way of them making good commercial decisions. Tim and Maureen were smart. Both had told him more than a year ago to put a stool behind the bar, and as usual they had been right. It probably came from being a couple. Having a partner to bounce ideas off. Somebody whose opinion you could trust. Paul doubted he would ever find someone to spend the rest of his life with if all he had to offer was a dud pub and a bad case of water retention. Sure there were lots of men who visited Hobart for the weekend. But none of them wanted to stay. It was too slow and cold, and who wanted to live on the side of Mount Wellington? Paul did, that's who. He loved Wood Green with its cool climate and quiet nights. Buying the pub had been the best mistake he had ever made. But if it did not start to earn more he would have to consider putting it on the market and writing off the past ten years of his life. Wobbly Bob and his crew drank a lot, but not enough to keep open a whole pub. And they would start to die off soon enough. Alcohol consumption at those levels could not be maintained without consequences.

As if on cue, Wobbly Bob slid slowly from his seat, pulling the remainder of his beer with him. Though plenty of heads turned at the sound of the dead weight hitting the floor, followed by the shatter of glass, not a single person moved to help. Paul sighed at the limits of Australian mateship, then gingerly lowered himself from his stool to fetch the mop and raise the old man back to his feet.

33.

Dear Ms Atler

Thank you for your email regarding the whereabouts of Michael Pollard. Although we do have a contact telephone number and postal address for Mr Pollard, it is the policy of this publishing firm not to give out the personal details of its authors. However, if you wish to write a letter to Mr Pollard care of Handel Books we would be happy to forward it to him. I can say that the details we have for Mr Pollard remain unchanged from when we published his book more than four years ago, and were still effective when we last contacted him six months ago in relation to an inquiry similar to your own. As you are an old friend of his, perhaps this will help.

Kind regards

Frank Prescott

Publicist

Dear Mr Prescott

Thank you so much for you prompt reply, and I completely understand your position regarding the privacy of your authors. If, however, it does not contravene the policies of Handel Publishing, would it be possible for you to share the name of the person who sought to make contact with Michael six months ago?

Many thanks

Rachel Atler

Dear Ms Atler

After consulting with the publisher, I can tell you that six months ago we received a letter from the novelist Lucian Clarke, requesting Mr Pollard's details. As we have received no further communication from either man, our assumption is that they have begun corresponding directly with one another.

Regards

Frank

Dear Frank

Thank you so much for your help. Any leads are greatly appreciated. Could I possibly impose upon your kindness for just one more thing? Would it at all be possible for you to forward a letter from me to Mr Clarke? Of course I could contact his publisher or agent, but I fear how long this process might take. I hope you can help.

Many thanks

Rachel

Dear Rachel

Yes, we have a postal address for Mr Clarke. If you would care to send him a letter via this office, I will ensure it is forwarded to him.

Regards

Frank

34.

As Michael admired the fourteen sheets of paper covered with his handwriting, he shook his head in disbelief at how just hours ago they had been completely blank. No characters, setting, dialogue or narrative had existed, and yet now, miraculously, out of nothing, something had been created. Michael had not expected such a bounty as he put aside his laptop in frustration and picked up a pen. It was more a final resort in his effort to cure a persistent and frightening lack of production. But something about removing the barrier between himself and the page had enabled his ideas to flow more freely, and now he felt an irrefutable sense that a novel was finally underway.

Michael's only regret was that the story concerned a writer. He had read enough debut fiction to appreciate how typical the subject was for a first time novelist. And had he been given the choice he would never have embarked upon such a topic. But free will, it seemed, played no part in the process. The story had appeared fully formed in Michael's imagination, and now demanded that the shabby ideas he had been trying to bring to life for the past four years be put to one side.

To a point he knew it was wishful thinking – the idea of an established writer assisting an aspiring one. But that was where the similarities with his trip to Hobart ended. The story he had started to write would be more subtle than his own relationship with Lucian, and he intended on having a woman at the centre of the narrative. Michael wanted to undermine the cliché of an older writer taking advantage of an aspiring one. It had been written too many times, and few had improved upon *The Lesson of the Master* by Henry James. Although he would allow his readers to believe something sinister existed behind the established author's encouragement towards marriage and children, Michael's objective was for the aspiring writer to achieve all his ambitions. Maybe he was missing Rachel more than he realised, but Michael was sick of the idea that closing a heart to life, be it love or the responsibility of children, was conducive to being an artist. It was nothing more than a Hollywood cliché. Most of the authors he admired had either large families or long-term partners, and he wanted to demonstrate that if art was legitimately present it could emerge in a domestic setting as effectively as it could in a cold-water garret.

Michael understood that the writing process would be neither quick nor easy, but also knew the work he had travelled to Hobart for was far from complete. The quantity of papers Lucian had accumulated over his lifetime was daunting, and Michael envisioned at least four or five more months of sorting, filing and making notes. Enough time, hopefully, to have a first draft ready to take back to

Sydney. The idea of writing a biography about Lucian now seemed a dreary and obvious pursuit when compared with working on his book. He could not understand why the famous author was bothering to do it. Unless of course his ideas had dried up. Was that even possible with a mind like Lucian Clarke's? Michael doubted it. The day's productivity had given him a rush of self-confidence, and with it a belief that he now had a better understanding of his employer and his work. An insight deeper than anything he had gained from writing a PhD or climbing down the blowhole at Blackmans Bay. Michael checked his watch and saw he had less than an hour before he was due back at Wood Green. Continuing his work would have been his preference, however Lucian had asked him to pick up a special type of sausage for their dinner. As Michael descended the stairs of the B&B he met Andrew walking up.

I was just coming to see you.

Sorry, I can't stop, I'm running late for work.

Yes, yes, of course. What time do you think you'll be back? Perhaps we could have a chat later tonight?

I don't usually get in until after midnight. Why don't we have breakfast together instead?

The idea instantly appealed to Andrew. All right. That sounds lovely. I'll see you at eight, shall I?

Michael hurried outside as Andrew continued up the stairs. There was now no reason for him to keep climbing, but the idea of a breakfast date made Andrew feel light on his feet. And more than a little pleased with himself. It was so nice to have friends to stay rather than just guests, he thought. Friends made the place feel less like a business and more like a home. Of course there were still bills to pay. Everyone has to eat. But there was no need to be always so concerned with counting pennies. Andrew suddenly realised that he did not care whether Michael smoked in his room or left a window open so rain wet the carpet. What was a little water damage amongst friends? And really, if Michael had not been renting the room it would have stood empty. At this time of year Andrew usually closed up half the house until spring arrived. So what did it matter if he was giving Michael a discount rate? A little money was better than none, and after all, he was a friend, not just a customer. The prospect of a long chat over breakfast thrilled him. Maybe he would cook something special for the occasion. No, better not. There were still other guests in the house and the last thing he needed were jealous complaints about favouritism. Andrew reached the top of the stairs and stood at a hallway window watching waves being blown across the Derwent River. It was such a pleasure to have a permanent guest at the B&B. It almost felt like family. Just without the noise and mess. Andrew wiped a layer of dust from the windowsill. Well, without the noise at least.

35.

Lucian opened the front door but did not step onto the verandah. He had onions, celery and garlic sweating in a pot on the stove and was unwilling to leave them unattended.

Michael kicked off his boots, dropped his briefcase in the office and carried a bag of groceries to the kitchen.

Here are the sausages you asked me to pick up.

What's that?

Sage and mushroom, right?

Lucian frowned. I didn't ask you to buy those.

Of course you did. Last night. Just before I left.

Why would I ask you to buy sausages when I've been planning to make a vegetable pie all week?

Who knows? But you definitely asked me to do it. Why on earth would I make up something like that?

Lucian lifted the lid of the pot and stirred. You must have dreamt it. I had no intention of eating meat for dinner two nights in a row.

Michael placed the sausages in the refrigerator then searched his pockets for the receipt. With it he found the scrap of paper on which Lucian had written his preferred sausage type, as well as the deli's address on O'Connell Street. Michael put both on the kitchen counter and walked back down the hall.

After he heard the office door close, Lucian turned off the heat beneath his pot and inspected the note. He had no doubt that Michael was right, and threw both pieces of paper into the garbage. Destroy all evidence he thought to himself. Then set the kettle to boil.

Michael swivelled warily in his chair and watched Lucian carry a cup of tea towards his desk.

Sorry about the mix up, he said. Must have smoked too much weed last night. I'm already making a vegetable pie for dinner, so why don't you cook those sausages tomorrow night.

When Lucian left the room Michael shivered, unnerved not only by the uncharacteristic hospitality of being brought a cup of tea, but also Lucian's willingness to concede he was in the wrong. Neither had happened before and it left an odd atmosphere inside the room. As if Michael was dreaming and something similarly unexpected was about to occur. When all remained still and silent, he returned to a large yellow envelope mailed to Lucian by his London agent. Inside were reviews of *Dismantling Ivan's Circus* that had appeared in the British press, and from their pristine condition Michael judged they had been completely ignored. Carefully he unfolded each sheet of three-year-old newspaper and read how Lucian's most recent book had been received by the critics of the day. Half-heartedly was his conclusion, as each review broadly summarised the narrative, identified a few distinguishing features, and arrived at the same judgement – reclusive Tasmanian author writes strange book that fails to live up to the promise of his first two novels. Michael was shocked at how much the journalists had plagiarised one another. Though the earliest critic had clearly misinterpreted a key element of the plot, all the ensuing reviewers had perpetuated the mistake like a Chinese whisper. Few had bothered to discuss the novel's structure, voice or context in contemporary literature. And all had failed to detect the references to Alfred Jarry's Ubu plays that Lucian had included at the beginning of each chapter. It was as if the reviewers had skim-read the novel. Or grown too impatient and not bothered to read to the end. Michael had encountered a similar quality of reviewing in North American and Australian papers. A dividend, he believed, of the spare clean style of prose that was currently in vogue with publishers and universities. Writing reduced to its barest essentials. Devoid of any awkward metre or hint of circumlocution, it sat flat on the page like a frozen dinner, able to be consumed in the most controlled and precise fashion where everything looked, smelled and tasted as expected, and the reader was never forced to suffer the indignity of not feeling in complete control. Surrendering to the imagination of an author was not part of the agreement made with this new style of writing. Instead it was believed that readers wanted *real* events set in *real* places to support a *real* story about *real* people. And if they were not real, then they had better be *based* on real people. No one wanted to feel lied to or manipulated, so everything needed to be coated in a thick syrup of familiarity. To ensure readers would recognise themselves in the work. For without such a thing there was a risk they might experience a different way of thinking. Or living. And who wanted to read a book like that!? Lucian did, that's who. And it was why he refused to give a damn about reality in his work. Making a reader feel secure in their values and ideas was not the purpose of his writing. In fact, he was committed to achieving the exact opposite. To destabilising his readers' reality in the hope that once they looked away from his pages they might see the world anew. Unfortunately book reviewers failed to understand why any writer would attempt such a thing. How could Lucian Clarke expect to ever become famous enough to teach creative writing to the most privileged students at the most prestigious universities if he refused to tell his readers what they already knew? That everything was okay. There was nothing to learn. Here are the same stories you have always been told. The same places. The same people. Relax. Don't question your existence. Life will soon be over. Then you can sleep. The book reviewers insisted that living at the bottom of the world had pushed Lucian Clarke's thinking in a strange direction. Don't follow him. You wouldn't like it. Keep your receipt.

Michael now understood why Lucian had not bothered to read the reviews, and returned them to the envelope without having learned anything he could add to his daily report. He hoped Lucian's newly found civility would endure past dinner time, otherwise he feared he was likely to receive an earful about value for money and renegotiating their agreement. Michael quickly threaded a sheet of paper into the typewriter, but his fingers hesitated above the keys. All he could think about was Lucian bringing him a cup of tea. It was as if he had wanted the incident about the sausages swept under the carpet and forgotten. But why? Lucian loved a fight. Even when he knew he was in the wrong. So why not this fight?

36.

I've had an idea for doing something different tonight.

Oh yes? What's that?

Instead of me giving you another page of notes, I thought perhaps you could recount some of the moments in your life that *you* think have been defining. That way I could write them down and keep them in mind as I work through your papers.

I see. That *is* an interesting idea.

It's exactly the same project, just a different approach. And it could help me to recognise things that I might not otherwise identify as significant.

Yes, yes. I see your logic.

As a safety measure against missing anything important.

Uh huh. Right.

Last night I suddenly realised how risky it was to have only my interpretation of what's relevant.

That's a good point.

After all, we're two different people.

Very different.

And if I knew a little more about your life then it could help me delve deeper between the lines.

Well I did say I wanted you to do that, didn't I?

It's a valid request, especially if you're intending to write the autobiography I know you're capable of.

You think it could be something good?

Of course it could. Without question.

Well that's very nice of you to say.

And I want to do everything I can to help you write it. So it occurred to me that a two-way exchange of information might improve our process. Instead of just one way, from me to you.

It all sounds very wise...except, I thought we had already established the guidelines for how this relationship was going to work.

Well I know we discussed a general process, but I didn't think it was set in stone. We can mix things up a bit can't we?

Mix things up? Sure, sure. However you do remember that I am the person who's paying you, right?

Of course, but...

As well as giving you proximity to me in case any of my talent rubs off. How's that working out for you by the way?

I don't really...

And I understand that being an academic you're used to appropriating other people's ideas to disguise the fact you have so few of your own. In fact I sympathise with it. It's part of the culture you've always worked in. And I can appreciate how difficult it must be to break a habit like that. I suspect that after a while you don't even recognise it as a habit.

I wouldn't exactly put it like that.

Of course you wouldn't. But I just want to clarify that I'm not some anonymous funding body handing out grants so you can sit around regurgitating my own ideas back to me. I'm paying you to do an actual job. To tell me about my life. And the last thing I need to hear is what I already know.

I wasn't intending...

To tell you the truth, your idea sounds like nothing more than an excuse for not having done your homework. What are you going to do next? Tell me that Sadie has eaten it?

No of course not, I...

Just what exactly have you been doing all day? You've been paid your wages. Yet so far all I've received in return are sausages that I didn't even ask you to buy.

But I thought you said...

Stop fucking interrupting me. The next time you try and pull shit like this you'll be out on your arse. I haven't given you a tough job. Even someone with your limited intellect should be able to manage it. So now I want two pages from you tomorrow, and they had better be impressive. In fact I want two pages every day from now on.

I was reading reviews of *Dismantling Ivan's Circus*. That's what I was doing today.

Well what the hell for? You think I can't remember everything I need to know about a book I only finished writing four years ago? I don't need to know anything about *Ivan*. What I want is information from the time of *Foxtrot* and *The Bombardier* and *Lady Cadaver*. That's what I need help remembering.

Right. Okay. I'll get onto it first thing tomorrow.

You can get onto it now. You think you're going to sit there and eat my food and smoke my weed and provide nothing in return? I want a page by the end of the day or the deal is off.

But I thought you said you wanted two pages tomorrow.

Two pages tomorrow, *and* one tonight. You've pissed me off kid. Now get to work.

37.

You're finishing late tonight, said Maureen as she turned off the lights over the fruit and vegetable stand.

Michael rubbed his hands together as he hurried towards the pot-bellied stove at the centre of the store. Busy day. Lots to do.

Don't let Lucian work you too hard. He's an old softie deep down.

Michael raised an eyebrow.

Well maybe not an old softie, but remember he probably needs you as much as you need him.

Michael admired the efficiency with which Maureen moved about the store – checking the fridge doors were properly closed and all the mousetraps had been set. It's okay, I'm not being exploited. I just got distracted reading something and had to stay late to finish off the day's work.

What was it?

Pardon?

What were you reading that was so distracting?

Just some old reviews of Lucian's books.

Oh yes? Which ones?

Dismantling Ivan's Circus mainly.

Anyone gush?

Hardly. In fact I don't think many of them even understood it. I can't understand why though. That book has always struck me as being pretty straightforward. Especially compared with his others.

Same here. I gobbled it up.

You've read it?

Maureen chose to ignore Michael's surprise. I've read all of Lucian's books. It's probably why I only see his polite side.

Which one is your favourite?

I read *Foxtrot* first, so I suppose it's always going to feel special to me.

Lady Cadaver was my first.

Yeah, lots of men like that one best.

Michael's cheeks glowed warm as he remembered how aroused he had become while reading Lucian's fabulist tale of a bordello whose girls had the ability to transform into exact reproductions of wives who had died. From the sound of their voice and the perfume they favoured, to their tiny mannerisms during the moment of climax, the women were able to offer a perfect imitation of a wife at any stage of life that a widower requested. The book was a brilliant examination of matrimonial sex that included the mundane routines alongside the perversions; the aggressive overtones as well as the loving connections, while at the same time contemplating ideas of death and grief and the changing nature of relationships across the course of a marriage. Michael shrugged. I said it was my first, not my favourite. I usually recommend *The Bombardier* to people.

So do I. Just so they can read him in the proper order.

You think there's an order to Lucian's books?

Maureen turned off another light. Order is probably the wrong word. His books are so different that it would be impossible to link their stories together. I think it's more about being able to enjoy the development of his style and themes from the beginning.

Loss of identity. Reincarnation. Struggle for a legacy.

But don't you think all those ideas have something to do with sacrifice? Haven't you noticed how Lucian's characters all have to lose something precious to gain something precious? I think that's the idea sitting at the centre of all of his books. Appreciating the price that needs to be paid just to make it through a single lifetime.

The sudden despair Michael felt at the failure of his thesis to address such an interpretation quickly gave way to delight at gaining a new insight into Lucian's work. I might have to go back and read them all over again.

Maureen offered a coquettish smile while she locked the cash register and turned off the store's CD player.

I suppose I should call a cab so you can close up.

Would you like a cup of tea first? I usually make one after I lock the front door.

I don't want to keep you up.

It's not *that* late. And I don't often get the opportunity to talk about books. Come on through to the kitchen. It's warmer in there, and if Tim hasn't scoffed them all you might get a homemade biscuit.

Maureen filled the kettle and cleared the plates from the dish rack as she answered Michael's questions about her previous life in Melbourne, and the circumstances behind her move with Tim to Tasmania. Eventually the tea was ready and she grabbed one of the biscuits that Michael had so far ignored. I suppose you'd prefer a cigarette?

What? No. I mean, I'm trying to quit. Eight days so far.

Good for you. I'm glad. I was only being polite. I hate the smell.

Yeah, it's not something you notice until you stop smoking. But now I can smell it all over my clothes and through my room.

Where are you staying?

At a B&B in Battery Point.

Fancy.

So people say.

Maureen took another biscuit and pushed the plate towards Michael. So what work are you doing for Lucian?

Just organising his papers and making notes about his past. I think he's planning on writing an autobiography.

I thought he was working on a new novel?

He probably is. I think he's waiting until I've gathered all the information together before he decides on whether he wants to do it or not.

Doesn't he hate autobiographies by writers?

That's certainly what I'd always thought, but he seems to have changed his mind. Michael dunked a biscuit into his tea.

It reminded Maureen of her grandmother who had the same habit, and fitted perfectly with Michael's other old fashioned traits. And not just his clothes, but the manner in which he crossed his legs, held a tea cup, and used a handkerchief instead of a tissue. So what did you find?

Pardon?

What did you find out about Lucian today?

I don't know if I can talk about it without Lucian's permission. He's quite a private person. And the last thing I need is for him not to trust me.

Who am I going to tell up here?

I'd better not.

Okay then, how about we play a game. I tell you something about Lucian that you didn't know, and you tell me something. Fair?

Michael had never considered Maureen as a source of information, but after seven years in Wood Green it made sense that she and Lucian would have got to know each other. All right, but you go first.

Gladly. Did you know he still has a piece of shrapnel in his leg?

From Vietnam?

That's right. Says it starts to hurt whenever it's about to snow. Your turn.

Okay. Let me see. Did you know that in seventy-seven he almost died from a knife fight?

Who doesn't know it? He's so proud of that scar he shows it to strangers. Come on, you've got to give me something better than that.

All right, um, how about this? Did you know that he wrote a book before *The Bombardier*?

Maureen leaned forward. No. Have you read it?

Michael shook his head. I don't think it exists anymore. But I've run across a few of the rejection letters it received. He must have been only fifteen or sixteen when he wrote it.

Not bad. Not bad at all. Did you know that Lucian cheats at cards? And that the first time he played Patricia he took forty pounds off her in a game of poker.

And it wasn't enough of a warning not to marry him?

Lucian says it was *why* they got together. Apparently Patricia was going through a rebellious stage and wanted to be treated like a real person, not just some debutante waiting for a man to protect her. That wore off pretty quickly though.

Have you heard how in Turkey he smoked a plant that sent him blind for three days?

Maureen rolled her eyes. Did you know that when Lucian was living in Paris he stalked Jean Genet. And when Genet walked across the road to confront him he ran away like a scared child.

You're joking?

It's true. Ask him.

Not on your life. I suppose you know about the affair he had with Patricia's best friend?

No, but it's hardly surprising. Has he told you how he knocked back an Order of Australia?

No. Do you know why?

He wrote to them and said that after allowing Patrick White's house to be sold they could take their award and shove it.

Good on him. Too right.

You still owe me one, said Maureen as she drained her tea.

Michael leaned back and searched his memory. Okay, here's a good one. Did you know that Lucian has a photograph of you?

Maureen appeared genuinely surprised, and a little cautious. Doing what exactly?

It looked as if you were out the back collecting eggs from the chickens. I don't think you knew it was being taken. At least it didn't appear that way. I saw it sticking out from a book on his coffee table.

What was the book?

Michael had not anticipated the question and closed his eyes to picture the cover. I think it was called *The Good Soldier*. Why?

38.

This way. Come right through. Tim held open the door to the hall so Carl and Fiona could walk upstairs and inspect the residence. Fiona smiled, winked and gave a secret thumbs up as she waddled past. The real estate agent wore silver-plated earrings, a cheap business suit stretched over her belly fat, and insisted on saying 'interiority', 'superiorfied' and 'caricature' when describing the renovations that had been made to the premises. A thick veil of perfume hung in her wake, though its scent was warped by the body odour lingering underneath. Tim could not accompany them upstairs. He had to tend the shop as Maureen had gone out for the afternoon. The inspection had been planned for more than three weeks, and the two of them had spent the past six nights making sure that everything was ready – cleaning, organising, camouflaging tiny faults. Then at breakfast Maureen had announced she needed the car to run an errand. It was infuriating and completely typical. But she knew it would not take the two of them to sell the business. A copy of their financial records had been emailed to Fiona a fortnight ago, so the only thing left to discuss were the quirks of the local community and the potential for Wood Green to grow in the future. Both of which Tim could handle on his own. Unfortunately it was an abysmal day for an inspection. So wet and cold that most locals would be staying inside if they could manage it. Tim had already received six home-delivery orders, and would not normally have bothered to pack them until Maureen returned with the car, but he wanted to give the impression of a business that was thriving even in inclement weather.

The ache of sentimentality Tim had felt after Fiona rang to inform him she had found a potential buyer was all but gone. He now acknowledged only the hard work necessary to keep the business afloat, and their daily struggle to appease the needs of customers so they did not take their money down to the supermarkets in Hobart. And what was the use of being sentimental when Maureen wasn't? She had always possessed an impeccable business sense, and if his wife was willing to let the shop go after all the effort they had put in, then he would be as well. Tim fed another piece of wood into the heater. He did not want the place to feel cold. Carl had spoken with a thick South African accent, and not unzipped his jacket when he walked inside, so he might be unaccustomed to such low temperatures and wet weather.

Fiona pushed opened the door and offered her best professional face. We're just going to have a look at the kitchen and backyard, okay?

Go ahead, said Tim. There's a couple of umbrellas beside the back door if you want to have a walk around outside.

The bell above the shop door announced Michael's arrival to purchase a litre of milk and a six-pack of tonic. As he stood at the cash register waiting to pay, Tim crouched below the counter pretending to look for something. He wanted to foster the appearance of a bustling store, and hoped to delay Michael until Fiona and Carl had walked back inside. But the moment they did Tim realised his mistake. Just when the time had arrived to conduct a private and frank discussion about a price for the business, Lucian's assistant had suddenly developed a deep interest in the dried pasta section.

Would you like a cup of tea or coffee to warm yourselves up? offered Tim.

No thank you, said Fiona. Carl, is there anything else you'd like to ask?

Carl looked up from his phone, wondering why he could not get reception, and glanced around the store. No, no. I have everything I need. Thank you for letting me look around your home.

Tim accepted Carl's excessively strong hand and was shocked at how cold his fingers felt. You're welcome. Good to meet you.

I'll be in touch, said Fiona before she and Carl dashed through the rain to the BMW parked outside.

Tim's heart sank. If Carl had been serious about purchasing the business he would have asked more questions. Or waited for Michael to leave so he could make an offer. Maybe it was just a reconnaissance trip. To gauge the competition before Carl opened up a general store of his own. And like an idiot Tim had shown him everything they did. He was too trusting. Taking advantage of people was not in his nature, so in turn he never suspected it in anyone else. He might have noticed something was wrong if Michael had not been in the way. Just when they were supposed to have a serious conversation, Lucian's nursemaid had decided to hang around and eavesdrop. Damn it all to hell, he thought as he watched the car begin to pull away. But then the BMW's brake lights flashed, the passenger door opened, and Carl ran with his jacket over his head towards Paul's pub.

You little beauty, said Tim.

What? asked Michael.

Nothing. Nothing at all.

39.

Maureen did not expect Lucian to answer his front door, but thought it only polite to knock before letting herself in with the spare key from under the wood box. And when he failed to open his bedroom door to confirm who had violated his 1pm rule, she assumed a sentence or idea had made him deaf to all distractions. So she decided to wait in the sunroom until Lucian felt the need to make himself a cup of tea.

His socks were what she saw first. Through the large windows at the rear of the house their dark-blue pattern caught her attention even before she had noticed the kettle boiling vigorously on the stove, or the back door hanging open. Maureen ran outside and knelt next to Lucian lying face down in the dirt with an arm bent awkwardly beneath his body. Heart attack or stroke were her immediate fears as she gently rolled him onto his back. No, not dead. Still breathing. Yes, he had a pulse. Lucian's skin was cold and wet but that was to be expected after lying outside in only a shirt and trousers. Maureen brushed away the dirt and leaves stuck to his forehead. Extracted a tiny twig entangled in his short beard. Lucian seemed to be stirring. His groans were growing louder, more regular, until finally his eyelids flickered open to reveal two blue irises surrounded by a dense web of red. Between the fingers of the hand that Lucian had fallen onto was a ridiculously fat joint, crushed.

Are you all right?

A vision...

Do you need me to get an ambulance? Have you had a heart attack?

...of beauty.

Yeah right. I bet I have two heads at the moment. Come on, can you stand up?

Lucian perched on the edge of the bath feeling weak, a little nauseous, but delighting in the way Maureen dabbed at the small graze on the end of his nose. There was music playing in the other room – *E Pluribus Unum*. Lucian could not recall selecting it, and thought how wonderful it was to be cared for by a woman who understood the restorative properties of Sandy Bull's music. He smiled as Maureen changed his wet socks for dry, and savoured the tender way she passed a warm washcloth over his face and hands.

Do you want to lie down?

Lucian shook his head. I think I'd prefer to sit in front of a fire. Do you have the time?

Maureen ignored the suggestion she might have somewhere else to be and escorted Lucian to one of the deep armchairs in the sitting room before preparing a pot of tea. Lucian sipped and listened to the music as Maureen built a fire. She had found some chocolate in the fridge and told Lucian to eat it all, but he refused to take a bite until she accepted a piece as well. Together they watched the flames take hold and engulf the wood.

It must have been the shock of the cold air, Lucian finally offered as an excuse. Probably made my blood pressure drop. And I didn't eat very much for breakfast this morning.

Smoking a joint big enough to fell an elephant might have had something to do with it as well, don't you think?

My spliff! I forgot all about it.

Don't worry. I put it next to the ashtray on the coffee table. But maybe you should think about taking a few days off.

Lucian held up his cup. Only one type of tea for me from now on.

I'm not here to tell you what to do. Are you hungry? Do you want some lunch?

Not at the moment. What time do you have to be back at the shop?

Maureen shrugged. Whenever I'm ready to go back.

You and Tim have a fight?

No. We've given up on fighting. There's someone inspecting the shop at the moment. That's what I came up here to tell you. I think we might have found a buyer.

Lucian sipped his tea and stared at the fire. When do you think you'll be leaving?

If it sells? In a month or two I suppose.

Any plans yet?

None that I can think of.

What about Tim?

Once we've sold up he can go wherever he likes.

So you'll be getting a divorce?

That's the plan. Though Tim never does anything in a hurry.

Lucian and Maureen finished their tea in silence.

I could stay around here if you'd like? Maureen knew she had said the wrong thing as soon as the words left her lips. Lucian had already decided the fate of their relationship, and what she wanted was never going to change his mind no matter how unfair it seemed.

Lucian pulled on his glasses and opened a nearby book – *Memoirs of Hadrian* by Marguerite Yourcenar.

Maureen picked up the empty cups. I'll start some lunch, okay?

All right.

Shall I make some for Michael as well? He should be here soon shouldn't he?

Lucian looked away from the page. Why don't we give him the day off? That way it can just be the two of us.

40.

Tempted you at last I see.

Sorry?

For lunch, explained Paul as he stood beside Michael's table.

Oh, yeah. I'm been meaning to stop by for ages. Michael was lying. As soon as he had seen the message 'Day Off' tacked to Lucian's front door he had intended to call a cab and return to Hobart. But Tim explained that at this time of day, when the drivers were changing shifts, he would have to wait at least forty-five minutes for a car to drive up to Wood Green.

We have three dishes on the menu today, but what you want is the salt and pepper squid.

I do?

Ask him if you don't believe me. Paul nodded towards a man sitting at a nearby table. How's the squid?

Fantastic, Carl replied with a mouthful of food.

Sold, Michael said. And a glass of whatever white you think would suit it best.

As Paul passed Carl's table he noticed a sheet of paper with a picture of the general store printed on it. Unmistakably a real-estate ad, it left Paul shocked. He had no idea that Tim and Maureen were thinking of selling. If they abandoned Wood Green and the general store went back to how it had been before it would make his task of turning the pub into a success even more difficult. He stole another look at Carl. Though the South African accent grated on his ears, he could not deny its owner was attractive. Tall, muscular, with a wide expressive face sporting just the right amount of stubble, and no wedding ring either. His leather jacket was a little too Tom Cruise, but it revealed a tidy physique underneath, and he certainly knew how to buy shoes. Paul handed Michael's order to Penny, a local single mum who worked in the kitchen during school hours and cooked better than half the chefs in Hobart. Then walked out the back of the pub for an armload of wood. The fire was low and the day was bitter, and who knew how sensitive a South African might be to such temperatures.

Carl pulled out his mobile phone to check again if his crime had finally made it into the newspapers back home, but for the second time that day he failed to find a signal.

You need to go upstairs and stand on the back balcony if you want reception, said Paul as he added split logs to the flames. We're in a bit of black spot here.

Really? Carl held up his phone and moved it around to confirm Paul was telling the truth. Nobody has tried to fix that?

I don't think anyone has complained about it. Tends to make life a little less complicated I suppose. Are you up here visiting friends or just sightseeing?

Carl slipped the ad back inside his manila folder. Sightseeing. Are you the proprietor of this pub?

Paul glanced at the walls, floor and ceiling. Yep, all mine. His eyes then fell on Brad's fat arse half hanging out his trousers as he leaned sideways to ask Phil to buy him a beer. All mine, Paul repeated to himself as he quickly returned to the bar to prevent the two old timers from erupting into a shouting match about who owed whom a drink.

Carl observed how all the bar stools were occupied, and took it as an encouraging sign that so many people were out in such foul weather. He had not expected Wood Green to be this cold, or this beautiful. The abundance of moisture and lush foliage was almost impossible to believe. And everything seemed so well maintained. On the drive up the mountainside he had seen council workers trimming trees away from power lines, and surveyors staking out huge plots of land for new residential constructions. His heart beat for the wild daisies growing along the edge of the road, and he had noticed how there were no potholes for Fiona to contend with as she steered the hairpin corners and talked about the opportunities in Wood Green for someone willing to take a chance. But what Carl liked the most was the fact that no one would ever think to look for him here. It was such a perfect place to hide and start a new life. He had already managed to set up a bank account with his new name, so now all he needed was something to do and somewhere to live. And Wood Green was unlike anywhere else he had seen before. He thought the shop might be too much work for just one person, but how much more difficult could it be than running a pub? And Carl felt confident he could hire someone local to help make deliveries or do the late shift. With the glow of a delicious lunch and a good fire, he felt warm and comfortable and wondered if the owners of the general store might be willing to accept a little less than their asking price. *Bon appetit*, he said to the man at the nearby table when his lunch arrived.

Michael raised his glass. He remembered the face from earlier in the general store, but had no intention of inviting the man to join him. He had started to jot down ideas for his book and was determined to capture every detail before they slipped away. If he made it home in an hour he would still have most of the afternoon and all night to himself. Of course there would be emails to answer. The leave of absence he had taken from his university job did not seem to have registered with some of his former students or colleagues. And he still owed Rachel a phone call. Guilt over ignoring her messages niggled at Michael's conscience on a daily basis, but every time he resolved to call and let her know how he was getting on, it suddenly felt like an imposition. As if he were relinquishing a reward he had earned or was entitled to. Michael looked at his hand and realised he had stopped writing. This was exactly what he meant. Just thinking of his former life had the power to distract him from his work. Imagine what effect speaking to Rachel might have? He did not care if he was being selfish. Lucian had given him the day off, and he was determined not to waste it answering emails or talking on the phone. All he wanted to do was work. At the moment he felt as if he could write an entire chapter in just one sitting.

41.

Wood Green? No problem. Been shopping for music I see. New CD? Which one? Vibra what? Hold on a minute there's a red light coming up. Give me a look at that. Vibracathedral Orchestra – *Wisdom Thunderbolt*. Never heard of it. Australian? Gee, you don't hear about many bands coming from Leeds. Bet you had to order that one in. What type of music is it? Doesn't sound like it's going to be one for the car. And if you're asking me that's a big factor for music in Australia. We spend half our bloody lives driving around, so if something doesn't play well in the car then it's not going to sell. Hell, it's scarcely going to get heard. It's why Australian rock is still so meat and potatoes. Cars demand syncopation. Simple beats and steady rhythms. Anything abstract or delicate just gets lost in the noise of the engine. But maybe I'll look that one up when I get home. Here, write it down for me on one of my cards or I'll forget it otherwise. And take a card for yourself in case you need a cab again. Believe it or not, it's not always safe to walk home at night in Hobart. Especially after the pubs close. Been to see any of the local bands yet? There's not much to choose from I'll admit, but you'd be surprised what can turn up. Occasionally we produce something interesting. You know Peter Sculthorpe was Tasmanian, don't you? Okay, well have you heard about Eileen Joyce? Not surprised. Few people have these days. Classical pianist from the nineteen-thirties. It's her playing Rachmaninoff's *Piano Concerto No.2* in the soundtrack to *Brief Encounter*. That's right. Born in a little town up the west coast called Zeehan. Hardly anyone living there these days. Less than a thousand people I hear. We've also got that bloke who records under the name Striborg. Does a lo-fi black metal that's quite popular in the Netherlands. It's as dark as Satan's bottom but it works well on an ambient level. I usually put it on when a storm is blowing and scare myself shitless. You ever hear that live album John Fahey recorded down here? I know he isn't Tasmanian, but I swear it's one of the best gigs I've ever been to. Can't listen to the record much anymore though. Played it too often, and it makes me sad to think he's never coming back. You know the best thing about seeing music in Tasmania? The crowds are mixed. There's so few people down here that anyone who's into music goes and sees everything. Mums and dads standing right next to the young kids. Makes a show feel more like a community experience. And keeps the mood relaxed. It's hard to start acting like a prick when there's old codgers like me in the crowd. Maybe Vibra-thingy will tour here one day. I could use a little psychedelic drone in my life.

42.

Good Morning. How may I help you?

I'm here to see Michael Pollard.

And you are?

Could you tell him that it's Rachel Atler please.

I see. Was Mr Pollard expecting you Ms Atler?

No. I wanted to surprise him.

Yes, yes, well that certainly explains why he failed to mention you this morning while we were having breakfast together. You're welcome to leave a note for him if you'd like, and I'll make sure he gets it.

You mean he isn't in?

I don't think it would be professional of me to disclose something like that. I'm sure you can appreciate my position.

Well could you call up to his room for me please?

I'm sorry but we don't have internal phones. This is a B&B not a hotel.

Then can you tell me his room number so I can knock on his door myself? I guarantee he'll be happy to see me.

Andrew leaned forward and whispered. I'm sure he would, but just between you and me, Mr Pollard has already left for the day. He said something about needing to do a little shopping before going to work.

Oh. I don't suppose you know when he'll be back do you?

As you're such a good friend of Mr Pollard's I'm sure you would not want me giving out his personal information to just anyone who walked in off the street. And in truth, I can't be expected to keep track of my guests' whereabouts.

I just thought you might know what type of hours he keeps.

Yes, yes, well look, all I am prepared to say is that he *usually* comes home quite late. Like I said, you are more than welcome to leave a message with your name and phone number on it and I'll be happy to pass it along to Mr Pollard whenever I see him next. Which will probably be at breakfast tomorrow morning I'd say.

I don't suppose I could leave my suitcase with you? asked Rachel as she wrote her note.

Unfortunately I couldn't possibly take responsibility for something like that.

You can't just put it inside Michael's room for me?

Not without Mr Pollard's permission. I'm awfully sorry.

Andrew watched the young woman dial on her mobile phone as she exited his B&B. She did not seem like the type of person that Michael would be friends with. Her heels were too high, and her hair was cut into one of those annoying fringes that made it look, to Andrew at least, like she was wearing a helmet. He found her voice too raspy, and the fact she wore so little makeup left him in no doubt as to her status as a feminist. Oh some might say she was attractive, though not him. Too tall for his taste, and the swing of her hips too provocative. He doubted she was Michael's type either. Not that they had discussed such matters. Their breakfast conversations usually consisted of weather predictions and amusing stories about the people who had stayed in the B&B over the years. Andrew did not encourage Michael to talk about the work he did when he left each day, and certainly never suggested they swap anecdotes about their sexual escapades. There were other guests having breakfast in the same room, and Andrew preferred not to offend their sensibilities as they listened in on his conversations with Michael. Instead he wanted them to appreciate how close the bond between them had grown. No longer businessman and customer, or even casual acquaintances, they were now genuine friends who could and would talk about anything. Andrew was proud of forming such a relationship at his age. The older he grew the harder it was to make new friends. Most people he knew in Hobart he had grown up with. And it was so difficult to meet the type of people he *wanted* to be friends with. People who knew how to talk. To listen. Oh yes, someone like Michael was to be cherished, and Andrew deliberated whether it might be best if he just dropped the message from...what was her name again?... Rachel, that's it...maybe it would be best if he just threw her note into the garbage. That way Michael would not become distracted from his work by someone who was clearly unsuitable for him. It was a harsh decision, but real friends looked out for one another. Andrew dropped the piece of paper into the wastepaper basket, then felt a sudden pang of unprofessionalism. Fulfilling his duties as a friend was one thing, but betraying his role as a concierge was quite another. There was the reputation of his B&B to consider. Friendships don't pay the bills. And what if Michael found out? What would he say? That woman was sure to blab about leaving him a message. Oh no, he would not fall for that old trick. He was far too clever. Andrew fished out the note and walked upstairs to slip it under Michael's door. There. His friendship was safe, and so was his B&B. No need to worry. Everything was fine. Michael had already paid in advance for the next month, and there was a strict rule about not have guests to stay overnight. Andrew did not want his breakfast time with Michael intruded upon. Surprises like that were what he had worked all his life to avoid.

43.

After six weeks spent tracking down Michael's whereabouts, Rachel had envisioned the culmination of her efforts as something far more satisfying than being stonewalled by a man like that. Her skin crawled at the memory of his smarmy smile and faux professionalism. What on earth was Michael doing having breakfast with such a person? He still wasn't answering his phone, and as Rachel rolled her overnight bag along the blustery streets of Battery Point in search of another B&B, she began to question the instincts that had told her to ignore all caution and just fly down to Hobart. So far the place had not endeared itself. Crazy cab drivers, freezing weather, and a B&B proprietor with a broomstick so deeply wedged it would take a team of surgeons to pull it out. There were countless other destinations she would have preferred to visit for a long weekend. But the flight had been a last-minute special, and after so many weeks of uncertainty Rachel felt compelled to confirm with her own eyes that Michael was indeed safe.

At least she could now stop worrying about whether Lucian Clarke had been telling the truth. His reply letter had been so free with information about where Michael was staying and what time of day he was likely to be home that Rachel had feared the author was making it all up. Had he shown Michael her letter? If so, and Michael had still not made contact, then there was little hope of reconciling their relationship. But if he hadn't seen her letter? Well then the note she had left at the B&B was going to come as something of a surprise. Rachel knew that Michael hated surprises, but after what he had put her through he deserved a little inconvenience. In the few minutes since she had stopped fearing for his safety, Rachel a re-examined her feelings, and found an unexpected ambiguity. Had her emotions somehow deceived her? Like a well-fed cat killing a bird for sport, was her quarry devoid of all attraction now the hunt was over? Did the decision to separate from Michael make good sense again? Rachel admitted there was a chance she had made a mistake, and that her search for Michael may have been motivated by wounded pride. Had she resented the idea of him moving on so fast? And taking the trip to Tasmania he had talked about so often, yet been too afraid to book while they were still together?

Rachel checked into a nearby B&B and fell on top of her bed with a sigh of relief. The effort of travelling to Hobart had left her exhausted, and the prospect of seeing Michael had inexplicably become a chore. How would she act? What would she say? The note she had left for him explained her intention to drop by early tomorrow morning, but she had no idea of what she was going to do until then. Rain had started to fall, and her clothes had already proven themselves inadequate for Tasmania's climate. Why on earth would anyone want to come to such a place? she thought, as her head nestled into a pillow. She inhaled the scent of lavender and groaned with frustration at how everything in Hobart seemed so old fashioned.

44.

1987 – Patricia visits her parents in England. She does not enjoy living in Berlin and all efforts to find an apartment in Paris have failed. Returning to Surrey does not appear to be an option for you. (Please fill in gaps if possible. Suspect sexual impropriety by the tone of the letters received from Patricia at the time.) Berlin is wet, cold and awash with heroin. You smoke it a few times but desist when a neighbour overdoses and nearly dies. A cough develops into pneumonia and you spend eight weeks recovering. During this time you consider abandoning *Foxtrot* altogether. (Please confirm????)

1988 – Istanbul is hot and welcoming. Patricia finds work in a local school teaching English. It is the first job she has ever had and appears to enjoy it. The first draft of *Foxtrot* is complete. Rewriting begins immediately. Your agent finds you work reading screenplays. Patricia is attacked on her way home from school. Only money is stolen but she is shaken and flies back to England alone.

1989 – Patricia is living with her parents while you rent a room in London and work as a cinema projectionist. An affair with an usher loses you your job and ends your marriage for good. You return to Tasmania, pick up whatever work you can, and complete the third draft of *Foxtrot*.

1990 – You turn forty. Cards arrive from friends in England. *The Australian* reports you as deceased. You refuse to correct the mistake and send the final draft of *Foxtrot* to your London agent.

1991 – *Foxtrot* is published, accompanied by the announcement you are no longer dead. Reviews of the book are glowing, though sales are sluggish. You turn down offers to teach at universities in England and Australia.

1992 – (No information for this year. Please let me know why and provide any leads.)

1993 – You fly to the United States and take up a six-month post at the University of New Mexico. You decline an invitation to extend your contract and begin travelling across North America.

1994 – While in Florida, building wooden decks for sailing boats, news arrives that Ursula has died of a brain aneurism. (No more information for another six months. Please assist.)

1995 – Work begins on *Lady Cadaver* in Mexico.

45.

Oh, I've got something for you.

Lucian read to the end of Michael's notes then looked up to accept a small plastic bag containing a CD. What's this?

I was reading about Pärson Sound and saw this band mentioned in relation to them. I checked your collection. I don't think you have it already.

No, no, I've never heard of them before. That's very kind of you. Why don't you put it on and I'll roll us some dessert.

With their plates from dinner (roast pork stuffed with thyme and prunes) still on the coffee table, Lucian and Michael proceeded to lose their minds to a concoction of rhythms that blossomed, unwound and cohered again in a gloriously unconventional eruption of sound. Michael watched Lucian for any signs of boredom or irritation, but saw only deep concentration and a gentle nodding to the riotous clatter of Vibracathedral Orchestra.

When the album ended a vacuum of silence engulfed the room and Michael shivered as if a blanket had just been yanked off his body. He needed to move, and picked up the dinner plates to carry them to the kitchen.

Sorry, announced Lucian, but I have to listen to that again.

Michael was still hopelessly stoned and felt the music align with his labour, so much so that he could not stop cleaning the kitchen until the CD had once again finished. When he returned to the sunroom Lucian was lying along his couch with an arm across his eyes. He looked smaller and more frail than Michael remembered. But maybe it had been a tiring day, or he was no longer able to stay up so late. Michael decided to let him sleep and was about to creep down the hall when Lucian suddenly spoke. Jesus, who needs mushrooms when you've got music like that.

I'm glad you enjoyed it. Hopefully it'll prove good to write to as well.

Simply by the way Lucian removed his arm and turned his head, Michael knew he had said the wrong thing. But the raised voice he braced himself for did not materialise.

You want to know what writing is? asked Lucian as he slowly sat up and scratched his beard. You want to know what *real* writing is?

Michael presumed that Lucian did not expect an answer.

I'm going to let you in on a secret that ninety-five per cent of the hacks out there are yet to grasp, and probably never will. Real writing *is* music. So long as there's a rhythm strong enough to lift the reader and carry them along, you can do whatever you like in a book. Anything with the story. Anything with the punctuation. Anything with the structure. Look at Malcolm Lowry. William Gaddis. Virginia Woolf. Joseph Conrad. D.H. Lawrence. George Eliot. You know how they all achieved so much on the page? Because their writing contained rhythm. Give it whatever name you want. Melody. Metre. For writers like that it's as strong as a bull and authoritative as a heart attack. That's what sets them apart. And it's the difference between real writing and just putting ink on a page. I see it all the time. The bookshops are full of authors who approach sentences as if they were mathematical equations. This word plus this word equals this expression. And the result is a flat, lifeless writing without an ounce of musicality to it. I tell you the only rule of writing you ever need to worry about is that your work sings. And the only way to achieve that is to listen to its rhythm. But how the hell can you do that if you've got music playing in the same room? As soon as an author starts listing their favourite albums to work to I immediately lose interest because it just proves they don't understand the first thing about writing. It's voice and tone. The rhythm of the story. The beat of the chapters. All working together like different sections of an orchestra. Or like the record we've just listened to. On the surface it might sound like noise, but underneath there's a whole encyclopaedia of ideas at work. And to hear it you have to listen closely. In silence. You can't even *listen* to two records at the same time, so imagine trying to compose music while something is playing in the background. Well that's what writing is. Composing. Why do you think I live on this mountain? Because it's quiet enough for me to hear my work. To make sure it sings. You look through all the records I own and you'll find they're predominantly concerned with rhythm. Well the same goes for the books I write. Underneath their stories are melodies of words. If you haven't discovered that then you've missed half their point.

46.

Michael stood in the middle of his room holding Rachel's note and weighing up if he needed to go back out and buy cigarettes. After rebuffing so many of her emails and phone messages the prospect of facing his former girlfriend reignited old anxieties, and their incumbent remedies. He re-read the note and wondered when she had delivered it. Where she was staying? How long she was staying? How the hell had Rachel found out where *he* was staying? Michael caught himself gnawing his index finger and remembered when Maureen's face had wrinkled in disgust at his hands. He had never considered how they might appear to other people, and since then had tried to banish the habit along with his addiction to nicotine. An image of Maureen's broad smile and avian eyes intruded upon Rachel's small and elegant features, as if Michael were trying to meld the best of both women into a third of his own design. It made his head swim, and he opened a window to cut the viscosity of the internal heating. As the chill of midnight air penetrated his room Michael wondered what time Rachel intended to arrive, and felt irritated at the prospect of his morning routine being intruded upon. After putting up with Andrew during breakfast his reward was meant to be the freedom to work on his book uninterrupted. It was evolving so well that Michael had become defensive of any time he had to himself, and resentful of anyone attempting to impinge upon it. Maybe he could sneak off to a different B&B before Rachel arrived. There were plenty in Battery Point, though it was hard to believe he would find a room to compare with the one he had. Or a proprietor as easily manipulated as Andrew had become. Which meant that Michael was stuck where he was. And should he simply refuse to answer his door then Rachel would just sit outside and wait. Hadn't she tracked him all the way to Hobart? Michael knew exactly how persistent Rachel could be. It was one of her most impressive qualities, as well as one of her most annoying. Maybe he could say he had needed a clean break. Explain that because his love was so strong it had been necessary to wrench himself away and go cold turkey. And her arriving now, so soon into his rehabilitation, was like an addict revisiting old haunts populated with old friends who wanted to share old habits. But perhaps that was how Rachel had also interpreted his silence. Did she think there was still more for them to share? Surely, like Michael, she knew it wasn't true. He was not only trying to keep Rachel away. He was trying to keep his entire old life away. Of which Rachel was just one part. He was trying to reinvent himself. Become the person he had always wanted to be. Here in Tasmania, through proximity to Lucian Clarke, he was hoping to unlock new dimensions of himself. Already there had been different experiences. And not just the drugs, but books and music he might never have otherwise been exposed to. Not to mention the progress he had made with his novel. So why the hell would he want people around to remind him of his former life and his former self? He closed the window, undressed and climbed into bed. He didn't need a cigarette. That was the old Michael. The new one just needed to go to sleep so he could write well the following day. When Rachel arrived he would greet her as if everything was fine and nothing extraordinary had taken place. They would kiss. Eat lunch. Even see some sights. Then he would pack Rachel back off to Sydney without the slightest doubt that their relationship was over. There was no room for her here. Michael turned off his bedside lamp and watched the Derwent River glisten with a reflection of the Milky Way. Hobart contained so few streetlights that a thick, inky darkness descended upon the city every night, and as he waited for sleep Michael marvelled at how the silhouetted hills of the Eastern Shore appeared to fuse with the sky above.

47.

You look older, said Rachel, struggling to appear nonchalant as she leaned against Michael's window. Though her strategy had been to act as if there was nothing unusual about her sudden arrival in Hobart, the shock of Michael's appearance – tired, pale, red-eyed and heavily whiskered – had undermined her resolve. Quickly she searched for her cigarettes.

You can't smoke in here. Sorry. House rules.

That must be fun for you.

I quit. Three weeks tomorrow. Michael had not expected Rachel to knock so early and began to shuffle together the papers scattered about the ornamental writer's desk that stood against the wall.

Nice view you've got here.

Yeah. It can be distracting sometimes though.

What's that over there?

Michael pushed the pages of his novel beneath Lucian's copy of B. Traven's *The Death Ship*. No idea.

Well you're not much of a tour guide, are you?

Haven't had a chance to do any sightseeing yet.

Too busy working.

You might say that.

I assume you haven't had breakfast. Do you want to go out and get something together?

Sure. Just let me take a shower.

Rachel glanced through the handwritten pages Michael had so unsuccessfully attempted to conceal and was surprised to discover they were fiction. Her assumption had been that he had disappeared to Tasmania to write another book on Lucian Clarke. Of course she knew about his ambitions to one day publish a novel, but it had always seemed as likely as her own dream to someday grow an inch taller. Immediately she identified Lucian's influence and wondered if Michael was aware of how derivative he was being. Rachel put the papers back and glanced around the room. Besides a few of Michael's possessions, there was nothing in it she recognised, and the idea that he had established a different life in her absence began to offend her self-esteem. Quickly she discarded her clothes. The bathroom was small and cramped, and more than likely they made too much noise, but the hard clean surfaces seemed to encourage a sense of play reminiscent of what they had enjoyed at the beginning of their relationship.

As she dressed, Rachel made sure that Michael was watching. He had always been fascinated by the process; enthralled by the mysterious reconstruction of a feminine mystique that minutes before had been utterly unveiled. They then walked downstairs side by side, and Rachel waited on the footpath while Michael informed Andrew that he would be going out for breakfast today.

How did he take it? she asked as they began to look for a café.

Like an evil stepmother.

Were there tears?

Almost.

You've certainly got yourself a dedicated new friend. Couldn't you have adopted a pit bull instead?

It's a small price to pay for the deal I'm getting on the room.

Well it *is* pleasant, I'll give you that.

And Andrew is okay once you know how to manage him.

You mean with a feather boa and whip?

Hardly. He just wants to talk.

But you hate talking in the morning.

Well luckily Andrew only needs me to listen. So it all becomes white noise after a while.

And the rest of the day you get to enjoy your room.

Exactly. You see, a small price to pay.

Until you have to go to work.

That's not until the afternoon.

Sounds cushy.

Most of the time it is. Hey, you still haven't told me how you tracked me down.

Buy me breakfast and I'll consider revealing my sources.

I bet it was Brian. I swear that man could never keep a secret.

Who's Brian?

My old neighbour in the apartment across the hall. I'm sure I introduced you to him.

Rachel opened the café door and felt the warm air relax the skin of her face. The room was busy, and the table where they sat down needed to be cleared of plates and cups.

Wait a minute, Michael asked as he watched the waitress work. What do you mean I look older?

48.

Rachel focussed on her dinner as she tried to avoid Michael's eyes. The realisation that they had exhausted their conversation left her embarrassed, and confused as to why had she come so far for someone she had so little in common with. And why on earth had she exerted so much energy worrying about him? Rachel was sure that in Sydney the flow of their talk had never stalled. But since moving to Hobart Michael seemed to be different somehow. Quieter. More at ease in his own skin. Less willing to participate in their little games of sarcasm and contempt. But perhaps she was just tired. Visiting the local museum, browsing book stores, eating a lunch of battered seafood, and catching a movie in an attempt to stay warm was hardly the busiest day she had ever experienced. Yet Hobart was such a baffling place that Rachel found it taxing just walking around. To her, the streets seemed altogether too wide and too clean. And where was all the traffic? Was that why there were so many vacant parking places? And who paid so little for parking in the middle of a city? The shops also seemed to have too much stock. Rachel had found a pair of stockings that had been sold out in Sydney for weeks, and a new cardigan that fit her perfectly. But the experience was so lacking in the anxiety and disappointment and frustration she normally associated with shopping that it completely undermined the pleasure of her success. The cakes in the cafés were enormous, but the people serving them needed to back off. What did they want? Why were they being so nice? What was their problem? The coffee was shit, but Rachel could never find a decent cup outside of Sydney. Even in Paris or New York. Hobart reminded her of a country town more than a city. No matter where you looked there were mountains or trees or the water. And everyone was so white. So hetero. Rachel was sure they would not be able to get a table at the restaurant she had read about online, but they had walked in off the street and been seated immediately. And the food was delicious. Generously portioned. Fairly priced. The whole place unnerved her.

Michael unnerved her. All day he had acted as if everything in Hobart was perfectly normal. And there was nothing unusual about him buying a fruit cake from the Country Women's Association shop. Or describing a place that sold work boots as the most wonderful shoe store he had ever visited. Who was this guy? And where had he hidden the real Michael Pollard? The man seated opposite her at dinner seemed so changed from the one she remembered. And not just because he had ordered eel for his entrée and roasted goat for his main, or suggested they indulge in a second bottle of wine. It wasn't even the whiskers, or giving up cigarettes, or his decision to write fiction. It was the little things that disturbed her. Like Michael's sudden awareness of the music playing in every place they visited; the way his walking pace had slowed down, and the attention he seemed to give to every dog they passed on the street. And in the shower that morning there had been moves that Michael had never made before. Predilections that caught Rachel by surprise. The memory made her a little ashamed, and worried it might have been a mistake. What would her friends say if they knew? After all the trouble Michael had caused her, after all the worry. Rachel had just wanted things back to how they had once been. For Michael's attention to again be turned in her direction. But after a day spent in his company she was no longer certain if she even wanted him to come back to Sydney.

49.

The vibrations of Michael slamming the front door reverberated along the walls of the house as Lucian stood in the kitchen struggling to calm down. For the past fifteen minutes the two men had stood shouting at one another, with Lucian insisting he had absolutely no recollection of receiving any letter enquiring about Michael's whereabouts, or replying to it with details of the B&B where he was staying. Internally, Lucian admitted that it sounded exactly like something he might do. Just to stir things up and check if Michael's commitment could resist the pull of his former life. But it did not mean that Michael was entitled to give himself the day off to show his girlfriend around Hobart. Why the hell would he consent to something like that? He was paying Michael to work seven days a week, and he expected to get seven days in return. Lucian knew there was no time to lose. Winter was almost upon them. For a moment he feared he had chosen unwisely. Perhaps Michael was the wrong person for the job. Was he nothing more than an opportunist? Ready to steal whatever he could lay his hands on, even if it was only a day that had been paid for in advance? Lucian felt his trouser pocket for the shape of his billfold. Looked to his CDs for any unusual gaps in his collection. Hurried down the hall and locked the front door. Pulled back the hall rug and pried up a loose floorboard. His secret stash of cash and marijuana did not appear to have been tampered with, so next he checked his bedroom and Michael's office. But who would want to steal newspaper clippings and old clothes? Books, however, were an entirely different matter and Lucian was shocked to discover the number of gaps in the shelves of his library. It was not ordered alphabetically. More a system of French here and American there. German and Italian together. Icelandic and Irish. South American, Eastern European and Japanese all had shelves of their own, while English and Australian were over there. And everything else wherever it might fit. But where the hell was Céline? Lucian checked the small piles of books that had been left around the room, but *Journey to the End of the Night* was nowhere to be found. He put *Owen Glendower*, Clarice Lispector, Sadegh Hedayat, Elizabeth Smart, *Felix Krull* and Halldór Laxness back in their proper places, though Lucian could see there was still something missing from the Germanic section. Finally it dawned on him. No Thomas Bernhard. Lucian wondered if Maureen had borrowed them. But she was usually so good about returning books. Being a reader Maureen understood they were more than just objects or possessions. Books were friends. Companions for life. And what type of person steals someone else's friends? The gaps in the shelves appeared to Lucian like holes in a brain, and moments later his vision blurred with tears. His memory was getting worse. He was running out of time. What did it matter if Michael stole his books? What did it matter if Michael stole everything in the house? Soon enough none of it would mean anything to him. He could not take his possessions where he was going. Everything he had enjoyed in life was about to end. Only the novels he had written would remain behind. Lucian pulled a copy of *Dismantling Ivan's Circus* from the shelves. Had his most recent novel successfully conveyed everything he wanted to say about the weakness of the male mind? The ability of men to delude themselves at the expense of the people around them? Lucian flicked through the pages, intending to refamiliarise himself with what he had written. But after one or two sentences he hurriedly returned the book to its place. If something was wrong or lacking from the story it was too late to fix it now. Better not to know. Much better not to know.

50.

So is it true?

Tim looked up from his newspaper and saw Paul on the other side of the counter holding a tube of toothpaste and a bottle of bath salts. What's that?

You and Maureen are selling the business?

For a moment Tim considered lying. He had wanted to keep the sale private for at least another week, if not two, but Paul seemed already in possession of the facts and to be seeking only a nod of confirmation.

When did this happen?

It's been on the market for a couple of years now.

But I thought you two loved it up here.

Let's just say our priorities have changed. Tim was unwilling to publically discuss the reasons for his marriage breakdown. It's hard running a business together.

You should try running one on your own.

Good point. You see, you never know what it's like for the other person. Look, if you wouldn't mind, I was hoping to keep this quiet for as long as possible. Otherwise I'll be fielding the same questions for the next month and a half. Everyone will learn about it soon enough when they see us start to pack up.

You mean you've found a buyer? I thought it was just on the market.

Tim squirmed. He had always had an unfortunately big mouth. Someone made us an offer and we've decided to take it.

The South African?

His name is Carl.

Paul detected a ripple of excitement at learning the handsome stranger's name. So how much longer do we have you for?

If everything goes smoothly with the exchange of contracts, we should be out of here in just over five weeks.

I can't believe it. Wood Green won't be the same without you and Maureen. Do you know where you're going to go, or what you're going to do? Are you going to buy another business together?

I doubt it, said Tim as he closed his newspaper and started to ring up Paul's groceries. We haven't really made any plans yet. But look, don't let it worry you. Carl seems like he's really keen to make a life for himself up here. And the shop is pretty successful, so I don't imagine he'll try to change it too much. That'll be $9.50.

Paul unfolded his wallet. I bet he can't make coffee and croissants as good as Maureen. Where is she? Out the back? Can I go through and say hello?

No, she's in town at the moment.

Well tell her I want to see her for a drink as soon as possible.

Will do. And like I said, it would be great if we could keep this quiet for a couple more weeks. You know what people around here are like. As soon as they learn we're leaving they'll all start acting as if we've betrayed them.

51.

Maureen lowered the venetian blinds and angled their dusty slats so the hotel room was striped with sunlight. The blue bedspread she threw inside the cupboard, followed by the two cheap prints hanging on the walls, and the kettle provided for complimentary tea and coffee. The room had only one chair, and Maureen faced it towards the door. Her dark green coat reached to her knees, but when she sat down and crossed her legs it became clear that she was wearing nothing underneath. Maybe sitting wasn't the right position. Maureen wanted her unveiling to be a surprise. Perhaps she should wait in the bathroom. Or just ditch the drama and slip between the sheets. Maureen was aware that the scene she had constructed was a cliché, but so long as it worked she didn't give a damn. Her time in Wood Green was running out, and she was determined to spend as much of it as she could in Lucian's company. Hopefully he would turn up. There was always a chance the note she had pushed under his front door earlier that day had not been found in time. Or he had decided he was not in the mood for an afternoon rendezvous in North Hobart. Maureen regretted the 'please' she had written as part of her message. It made her sound too needy. Too easy. She rolled her eyes. How much easier could she get? Maureen admired the skin of her thigh and thought of Lucian's fingers moving across it. Around it. Underneath it. She stood up to cool her desires. There was no need to rush the afternoon. Tim could take care of the shop. She could stay out all night if she wanted to. After dabbing water behind her ears Maureen inspected herself in the bathroom mirror. Thick eyeliner and red lipstick were not her usual style, and neither was allowing her hair to fall loose about her face. But she thought it softened the lines at the side of her mouth, the same way a turned up collar seemed to shade the wrinkled skin at the front of her neck. Maureen opened her coat and leaned her pelvis against the cold porcelain of the sink. But rather than temper her lust it seemed to heighten it. Where the hell was Lucian? she thought. Seconds later the hotel door swung open. Lucian's woollen beanie and brown cords made Maureen feel ridiculous, but it was too late to stop the show now. She offered no greeting, just dragged the chair across the room and wedged it forcefully beneath the door handle. The buckle of her coat easily unfastened, and in a single swift movement the garment dropped to the floor. Maureen waited for Lucian to scan her figure, then pulled off his beanie and loosened his trousers. She could feel him growing hard in her hand. It's working she thought. She crawled slowly across the bed, arranged the pillows into a pile, and lay on top of them. Only then did she look back at Lucian undressing. His jacket, shirt, socks. Lucian raised his singlet above his head, but when his face reappeared it was covered with red.

You're bleeding, cried Maureen as she ran to the bathroom for toilet paper.

Lucian watched large droplets of blood splatter onto the bathroom tiles. I didn't even feel it.

52.

Thanks for coming to see me off. I know how much planes make you nervous.

Michael slid his hand across the back seat of the taxi and linked his smallest finger with Rachel's. It's the least I can do after you came all this way.

It won't make you late for work?

No. I'm taking another day off.

I thought that was against the rules. I don't want to get you into trouble again.

Since when?

Rachel lifted her hand from Michael's so she could raise her sunglasses and admire the midday sky. It had given a idyllic hue to the fields around the airport, and helped diminish the sense of frustration she had felt for much of her time in Hobart. It's so pretty down here. I can understand how the place grows on you. A few more weeks and I might stay myself.

Michael doubted it was true, but left Rachel's moment of self-deception unchallenged as he tried to comprehend why his hands were dry and his heart was not racing. Yes, he understood he was not boarding a plane, but there had been too many moments of terror at too many airports for him not to have developed a Pavlovian response to even the sight of a terminal. Michael's chest, however, did not feel tight at all.

Rachel's overnight bag was small enough to be carried on board, and her phone held the details of her boarding pass, so the two of them joined the queue for the security checkpoint. Rachel watched her bag disappear inside the X-ray machine and walked through the electronic doorway to the departure lounge. Michael followed but was stopped by a security guard. After emptying his pockets of change, and removing his shoes and belt, he walked through the metal detector for a second time. But the alarm went off again.

Any metal pins for broken bones? the security guard enquired as her hand-held device continued to beep.

No.

Nothing sewn into the lining of your trousers?

Of course not.

Could you step inside this room for a moment please sir.

Rachel waited impatiently for Michael to reappear, frustrated by his insistence to stay at her side until she had boarded her plane. What was the use of dragging things out? They had both agreed to have a break until Michael finished his book. Then when he returned to Sydney he would give her a call to see how things stood between them. But Rachel already doubted the likelihood of a successful reunion. Just a few weeks apart had revealed features of Michael's personality that she had never noticed while they were a couple. So four more months of separation was likely to expose even more. And anyway, she was not the type of woman to wait around for someone.

Their equipment must be faulty, said Michael as they walked towards the newsagency. I was down to my underwear and that thing was still lighting up.

Too much iron in your diet.

Told you I was the man of steel.

Aluminium more likely. Rachel was surprised at the bitterness in her voice and sought to correct it. You should have told them you were just seeing me off.

I think it was too late by that stage. They wanted to know exactly where I was hiding my nail clippers.

As Rachel paid for a magazine Michael noticed a stand dedicated solely to books about Tasmania, and a solitary copy of *Dismantling Ivan's Circus* standing on a shelf below rows of travel guides, glossy photographic journals and literary non-fiction. Michael had followed Lucian's advice and not given the novel much attention lately, but as soon as he began to read he realised what a mistake he had made. The voice in *Dismantling Ivan's Circus* was almost identical to the way Lucian spoke in real life. And it occurred to Michael that perhaps its narrative about a demoralised circus proprietor making one final attempt to hold onto his business might reveal more about Lucian than any of his other books. It was a novel filled with the lies that men told themselves, and the price such behaviour exacted from the people around them. Which was why there were so many strong women in it. Some critics had lazily interpreted this as Lucian's attempt to address the accusations of misogyny levelled at him after the publication of *Lady Cadaver*. But Michael knew the female characters who populated the book were there to offer a damning contrast to the circus proprietor's farcical behaviour. Though the story began in rural England in the nineteen-fifties, it was quickly transported to the north coast of Tasmania, where the failures Ivan had hoped to escape fell upon him without mercy. Lucian had always used the fantastical nature of catastrophes to undermine his readers' perceptions of reality, and in this book he perfected the technique. There was a freedom to the writing that Michael had never appreciated before, and Lucian was right, in every sentence was a rich melody to carry the reader along as they surrendered to the authority of the author's imagination.

Rachel folded her magazine into her handbag. I haven't read that one yet. Any good?

It is. In fact I think I should read it again.

He's lucky to have you, you know.

I'm not sure Lucian sees it that way.

Then he's an old fool. How many people out there could organise his papers with the knowledge you have?

Michael returned the novel to the shelf. It's a means to an end, that's all. I get time to write a novel, and he gets the information he needs to write an autobiography.

I'd be very surprised if that's what he's really up to.

Of course he is. Why would you say that?

Just think about it. The short temper. The forgetfulness. From what you've told me it sounds as though he's losing his memory. And I'll bet the real reasons he's brought you down here is to help him hold onto his past for as long as he can.

53.

Hello? Hello? Lucian stood in the hall as he waited for a response from either the other side of Michael's office door, or the kitchen. When the house remained silent he hurried to the sunroom and checked the backyard. It was late, but there was still enough light to see that Michael was not outside taking a break. As Lucian lay on his couch he saw the note he had left on the coffee table explaining how he would be spending the afternoon in Hobart. It had not been touched, and Lucian felt a spark of fear in his chest. What if Michael had decided to quit? Was his assistant the type to hold a grudge? Had that girlfriend of his convinced him to give up working for such a cranky old bastard and fly back to Sydney? Lucian now remembered the letter she had written, and fathomed the mistake he had made by replying to it. He had never expected her to board a plane and come after Michael. What was wrong with a phone call? Didn't everyone just text these days? Stupid. Stupid. To put his entire plan into jeopardy all for the sake of a test. If Michael wasn't committed then why would he have come all the way to Wood Green? Stupid. Stupid. The last of the daylight left the top of the forest and the sunroom fell into darkness. Lucian's breathing grew strained. He needed to stand up and take a taxi to the airport. Maybe Michael's flight had not departed yet and there was still time to explain the truth. Well some of the truth. Just enough to change Michael's mind. He would promise to be better behaved. Provide more advice about writing. Look over Michael's novel. Whatever it took. But what if Michael's plane had already taken off? How was he going to find him? The address Michael had used during their correspondence was no longer valid. He had given up his apartment to move down to Tasmania. Then maybe he was still at the B&B. Michael would have had to pay in advance, so perhaps he was using the remainder of the time to work on his book. It was what Lucian would have done. It was what any writer would do. If Michael did not turn up for work tomorrow then Lucian would pay a visit to Battery Point. The idea helped him rationalise his fears. He was tired. That was why he was panicking. Though he had spent the afternoon lying in bed with Maureen, the effort of speaking about everything other than her imminent departure from Wood Green had been exhausting. And he was probably still recovering from the loss of blood. The nosebleed had taken more than an hour to stop. And by Maureen's expression, Lucian presumed it had left him looking pale. Food. He needed food. Except it was Michael's turn to cook. God damn it, Lucian shouted as his panic reasserted itself. Had their argument really been too serious to forgive?

54.

With the first sip of his fifth beer Michael's body chemistry abruptly revealed just how drunk he had become. For much of the afternoon he had been trying to drown the realisation that Lucian had deceived him; tricked him; fooled him into thinking he had been hired as a researcher for an autobiography. But it appeared no amount of alcohol would allow him to forget that he was in Hobart to do nothing more than nurse Lucian Clarke through his failing memory. Rachel was right. As soon as she had pointed to the evidence he knew she was completely right. He had almost made it. Almost got her back to Sydney without his world being destabilised. But in the few minutes remaining before Rachel boarded her plane she had managed to undermine everything he thought he knew. Maybe it was payback for not replying to her messages. Or forcing her to fly to Tasmania. Whatever the reason, Michael now needed a drink. As his taxi re-entered Hobart he had asked to be dropped at the nearest pub to Battery Point where he could be left in peace. The driver, however, had scoffed at the idea that such a place existed and continued further down the road towards Sandy Bay.

Two TVs, on mute, each screening different sporting events, shone at either end of a room that was isolated from the outside world by heavily tinted windows; decorated with posters advertising gambling websites, and serviced by a cash machine standing ready at the door to the gaming room. Though the front bar had been empty when Michael entered, it now contained a pair of builders getting a head start on their night out, a newly minted grandmother pushing a pram back and forth, two students slumming it until their parents transferred more money, and a bald man of imposing size sitting four stools away and smiling at his latest text message. The barman had finished restocking the fridges for the night shift, and stood at the far end of the bar in case Michael attempted to initiate a conversation about his predicament again.

There was no chance of that. Even to Michael's ears his complaints had sounded petty. So instead he tried to rationalise his situation. Look for a positive side to the idea of Lucian having dementia. Could he somehow turn it to his advantage? Michael knew there was cash hidden somewhere in the house. Maybe Lucian would forget how much there was. Or how much Michael was supposed to be paid each week. He might even forget about the book he was writing. Was he now facing the opportunity to steal Lucian Clarke's latest manuscript? Who would there be to dispute it? Certainly not Lucian. Michael was sure that one success was all he needed to establish a literary reputation. After that his name would become a brand under which he could publish whatever he wanted. Being drunk and feeling lazy, the idea was particularly appealing to him. But even in the midst of such a tenuous grasp on reality he knew that being recognised for someone else's work was not what he wanted. Michael needed to know if *he* was a writer. If the story he was creating was as good as he suspected it might be. So perhaps the only thing to do was to leave Hobart and use what time he had left to finish his book. But go where? Back to Sydney? Back to Rachel? He had no intention of doing that. The relief of seeing her plane leave the tarmac confirmed their relationship was over. Then why not stay in Hobart to write? As long as he maintained their breakfast relationship, Michael was sure that Andrew would allow him to rent his room for as long as he liked. So why not keep on with Lucian as well? Stay and see what happened? Who cared if Lucian had lied? Their arrangement seemed to be working fine. He was writing wasn't he? What more did he want? He would have to confront Lucian at some point though, if only to stop the arguments and...

Hey mate?

Michael looked over his shoulder in the direction of the grandmother sipping a Raspberry Breezer.

Shut up will ya? You're gonna wake the baby.

Then turned back to the bar and his thoughts.

You're gibbering, said the bald man with his eyes still on his phone. Why don't you shut up for a while and give us some peace.

When the barman also nodded Michael realised he had been speaking his thoughts out loud. What had he said? How long had it been going on for? He was more drunk than he realised. He should go home and sleep it off.

Then go, insisted one of the students.

Both of them sported thick beards that reminded Michael of his post-grads, and the risk he now faced of returning to his old life.

Go on, piss off, one of the builders shouted. You're boring us stupid.

Michael unstuck himself from his stool, found his balance, lost it, then found it again before shouting, Why don't you all fuck off and leave me alone.

I bloody well knew it, the grandmother said as her grandson wailed in protest at the sudden noise. She stood up and started to push his pram around the room. You're a fucking wanker, you know that.

No place for a baby anyhow, said Michael with a haughty tone.

Time for you to go mate, said the bald man as he switched off his phone.

I'm having another drink first.

Pub's closed, said the barman.

Then why are all these people here?

Because they can shut up, said the grandmother.

The bald man stood up. Are you going to leave?

A flicker of common sense flashed across Michael's addled brain. Okay. Okay. He walked towards the door, glanced outside and felt the sting of daylight. He then turned back to the room and shouted, Fuck you all, while brandishing both middle fingers. He then turned and hit his face so hard against the doorframe that blood gushed from his nose.

55.

Morning.

Good morning Michael. Tea or coffee?

I'll have whatever you're having.

Oh I'm sorry but I couldn't possibly have breakfast with you this morning. I'm far too busy. Tea or coffee?

Coffee. Strong please.

Bacon and eggs? Or pancakes?

Could I have bacon with pancakes?

No. I'm sorry. It's either one or the other.

Pancakes then. You're sure you can't spare a moment to sit and chat?

Andrew wrote down Michael's order.

Just a cup of coffee?

Pardon? Oh no, no, not this morning. I've much too much to do. It's a lot of work running a B&B you know. I've been up for hours. No afternoon shift for me. And I probably won't get to bed until late.

Of course. I understand.

Will you be having cereal as well?

Yes, I thought I might have a small bowl this morning.

Well that will be an extra $4.50. I'll just add it to your bill, shall I?

Michael nodded and watched Andrew disappear through the doorway to the kitchen.

56.

Penny was broad hipped and buxom, with dark hair, darker eyes, a longstanding commitment to retro fashion, and a dwindling interest in tattoos since they had entered the mainstream. She was thirty-two, self sufficient, always willing to lend a hand, and barely reacted when Paul revealed that Tim and Maureen were selling up. The two of them scored squid, mixed salad dressings and changed the oil in the deep fryer with such a sense of solidarity that Paul felt bad withholding the news. If his livelihood was going to be affected by the sale of the general store then so was Penny's, and she deserved his loyalty more than Tim and Maureen. They did not care about the community of Wood Green. In a few weeks it would be nothing more than a memory; just a place where they had once lived and worked. Penny had been cooking in the pub for five years. Ever since her son Matthew was old enough to begin kindergarten. On school holidays he would help in the kitchen by shelling peas, sweeping up, or manning the dishwasher, and Paul would use any tips to cover his wages. The money lasted Matthew all term, and took the pressure off Penny when it came to buying toys and DVDs. Paul thought Matthew was about the best kid he had ever met, and for the first few days after the new school term started he would sit in the kitchen lamenting how quiet it was.

What do you mean you already knew?

Everyone saw the real estate agent's car. You don't get too many BMWs up here during the week. Or South Africans for that matter.

His name is Carl.

Already on a first name basis are we? Sounds promising.

Tim told me. I get the impression that he and Maureen are separating once they sell the place.

Penny disappeared inside the cool room then emerged carrying a tureen of three-root soup. That'll happen when you screw around.

Tim cheated? With who?

Penny transferred the soup to a pot and lit the gas burner underneath. Not Tim. Maureen. She and Lucian have been at it for years.

No!

Penny rolled her eyes. Exactly how long have you been living up here?

I don't know what you lot get up to.

Pretty much the same as what you boys get up to.

Does Tim know? Is that why they're selling?

Penny shrugged then stepped out the back to pick a handful of parsley.

Isn't Lucian a little old for her? Paul asked on her return.

Don't they say that intelligence is the ultimate aphrodisiac?

He'd have to be damn smart to make me go there.

It's probably a dirty old man thing. And Tim's no catch. But Maureen is.

You think? I've always found her a little vacant.

Maybe that's what the problem is between her and Tim.

I'd say it's more likely to be working and living together in the same place all day. Not many people can pull that one off.

I wouldn't mind the chance to try.

It'll happen. You wait. One day he'll just be there and you won't even remember the life you had before.

Paul admired the way Penny refused to be cynical about love even though Matthew's father had run off with someone else. And once again acknowledged that she was probably the most emotionally stable person he knew. The only times that Paul could recall Penny arriving at the pub in a bad mood was when Matthew had broken his arm, or her ex had tried to make contact. Otherwise she was the same person every day of the week. At one stage Paul had considered offering Penny a partnership in the pub, but suspected that if she had any capital to invest she would used it to buy a home for Matthew instead of renting Mrs Harding's dilapidated cottage.

You think it's going to affect the business?

Maybe, said Penny as she washed her hands and dried them on her apron. Hard to say until we see what the new owner is like.

But Carl could make the general store even better. He might improve it.

Penny smiled. Caaaarl might indeed. We don't know what Caaaarl is capable of yet, do we?

57.

Michael spooned steaming *ribollita* into his mouth until he felt his gnawing hunger begin to abate. There had been no snacks that day. Since 1pm all he had done was stay in his office catching up on work and trying to avoid a confrontation with Lucian about taking the previous day off. But now his stomach had ceased to rumble, and he felt less light-headed, the speech Michael had been internally composing for the past thirty-six hours would no longer be contained.

I think we need to talk about our situation, he said. And see if we can come to a more amicable understanding.

Last night Lucian had vowed that if Michael turned up for work he would try his best to get along, and this was his first opportunity to put his pledge into practise. He had selected *Um Violão Em Primeiro Plano* to accompany their dinner. The album by Brazilian guitarist Rosinha De Valença was a gentle, spacey affair filled with summertime dreaminess and slow bossa grooves that immediately diffused any hint of tension in the air.

Okay.

First, I need to ask you a question. And it would be great if you could answer me honestly, and in a civil manner

Of course. Of course.

Michael felt wrong-footed by Lucian's affability, but was determined to maintain his resolve. He wiped his mouth with a cloth napkin. Usually Lucian provided only a sheet of paper towel, and Michael felt a twinge of guilt that the serviette would now have to be washed.

I need to know if you're having problems with your memory.

Lucian paused and stared across the coffee table. His instinct was to deny everything and counter attack, and it was taking a surprising amount of will-power to resist both.

I don't think the reason you've hired me is so you can write an autobiography. I think the reason I'm here is to help you keep track of your past so you can either finish the book you're currently writing, or just prevent people from learning there's a problem for as long as possible. Because there *is* a problem, isn't there? I can tell. The short temper. The forgetfulness. If we're going to continue working together then I need to know what's happening, otherwise we're going to keep having these misunderstandings that become full-blown arguments, which are both boring and exhausting. I can appreciate why you'd want to hide something like this. It must be incredibly upsetting. And I won't pretend I understand what you're going through. But I think now is the time to do me the courtesy of telling the truth. Because if you don't I fear you're going to lose an assistant, and I'm going to lose the privilege of working for you.

Lucian sat back with a sad, defeated smile. Here I was thinking I was doing such a good job at disguising it... but it appears not. You're right of course. Something is wrong. I'm not sure what it is exactly, but I assume it's Alzheimer's. I can't really be bothered to go to a doctor to have it diagnosed. I don't need a name for whatever it is. And I doubt there's anything that can be done to slow it down. I'm old enough. I've had a good time. And I don't want their drugs getting in the way of my thoughts while I'm trying to finish a book. You're right, I'm not writing an autobiography. But writers are always incorporating people and places from their lives. It's unavoidable no matter how hard we try to resist. That's why I chose you specifically. Because you already know so much about me and my work. I need you to help me remember the things I might have forgotten. That I probably have forgotten. I need you to be the part of my brain that's dying. And after I'm gone you get to write the definitive biography of Lucian Clarke. But only *after* I'm gone. Until then you work for me, and finish that novel you've started writing. A book will teach you more about what it means to be an author than all the stuff in that office. And I only need three more months. After that, if I'm still compos mentis, we can reassess the situation. Of course if I start losing it before then you're free to call the doctors and have me taken away. I've instructed my lawyers to give you power of attorney. And I've filled out a 'Do not resuscitate' order. But all that's a long way off. Things aren't too bad yet, and won't be for quite a while. I can still cook and write and listen to music, and smoke as much pot as the next man. For the moment it's just a bad case of forgetfulness. So at present all I need you to do is not tell anyone and keep working. But maybe at a faster pace. Days off are a luxury I can't afford anymore.

58.

1998 – While working on the final draft of *Lady Cadaver* you agree to take care of a friend's apartment in Pisa for nine months. At night you walk along the River Arno, attend open-air cinemas screening Hollywood blockbusters overdubbed with Italian, and visit the nearby monuments that appear to be made of phosphorescent bones. A nunnery adjacent to your apartment has pigeon chicks hiding in its eaves. Down the street an opera singer practises every evening at 6pm. The owners of a nearby café learn what time you take your coffee and try to teach you Italian. The only words you master are numbers and the names of the vegetables you buy at the daily market in the town square. The butcher yells 'kangaroo' in greeting whenever you enter his store to buy a chop. And every other week the local baker attempts to give you back the wrong change. It is perhaps the happiest place you have ever lived. The tourists bus in, look at the leaning tower, the Baptistery, the Duomo, then leave. In the rest of the city their presence is barely felt. On particularly hot days you catch the train to Livorno to swim in the ocean. The journey takes thirty minutes and all the windows are left open for the cool wind to blow through the carriage. You see Grace Fergusson struggling to tame her straight red hair as the wind whips it about her head and gives her the appearance of a Fury. She tries to control it but eventually relents and allows her mane to blow wildly while she reads *Wide Sargasso Sea*. Her skin is heavily freckled and pink from the sun. She has broad shoulders, and a sharp nose with nostrils that flare provocatively. Her Italian is even more limited than your own, and when the train conductor disputes her *biglietti* you intervene on his behalf to explain how she needs to validate her ticket in a machine on the platform before boarding a train. Grace has come to Pisa to assist with the opening of an Irish-themed pub. She works nights and you work days. At 2pm you meet for lunch then sleep together until five.

1999 – Grace is the first person to read *Lady Cadaver*. She is shocked. Mistakes the characters for versions of you. Their desires for your own. The relationship is momentarily destabilised. Your London agent writes back suggesting changes, and questions the wisdom of such a darkly explicit book at the turn of the new millennium. She passes on the rejection letters the manuscript receives from your former editors. Grace reads your two previous novels and begins to understand the type of writer you are. *Lady Cadaver* finds a publisher.

2000 – Conservative outcry at the content of *Lady Cadaver* ensures good sales and plenty of reviews. Trips to London allow you and Grace to test your relationship outside the insulation of Pisa. She is fifteen years younger and her parents express concerns about you being too old. They are lifetime residents of Galway, and insist you and Grace marry in their local church. The reception is subdued, and along with half the guests you are struck down with food poisoning.

2001 – Promotion of *Lady Cadaver* takes you and Grace across North America and Australia. You visit Tasmania for only a few days.

2002 – For six months you live in Melbourne where Grace tries to fall pregnant and fails. Translated editions of *Lady Cadaver* are released and necessitate a return to Europe for a publicity tour.

2003 – The Irish pub Grace opened in Pisa is struggling and she is offered the role of manager. You return to Pisa but the city feels different. Your first attempt at a new book fails painfully. The marriage begins to fragment.

2004 – Grace has an affair with a co-worker and falls pregnant.

2005 – The marriage dissolves and you return to Tasmania alone.

59.

Frigid wind pierced all three layers of Michael's clothing as he stood on the highest edge of Bronwyn's Chin – a giant bolder that jutted out from the forest on the south face of Mount Wellington. His shoulders hunched, nose began to run, teeth hurt, and it took no effort whatsoever to imagine that beyond the sharp line of the horizon stood Antarctica. However, as soon as he had established a reliable footing Michael was able to concede that the two-hour hike had been worth it. Below him he could see the course of the Derwent River all the way to the ocean, and the pattern of beaches and bays it had carved through the southeast corner of Tasmania. Surrounded by such ancient trees, and standing on an enormous slab of metallic grey stone, Michael felt an urge to connect with the landscape. To interact with it more profoundly than just moving across its surface. He wanted to feel nature beneath his skin – in his blood – an interaction that would remove all sense of disconnection between himself and his environment. He was struck by such a wave of yearning it almost sent him off balance.

Lucian grabbed his arm. You all right?

Thanks. This wind is a little intense.

We should get back. Those clouds look as if they're heading our way.

Michael shuffled to the lowest edge of Bronwyn's Chin, jumped to the ground and grabbed a tree trunk to steady his landing. Lucian felt less confident in his abilities, and sat down to slide back inelegantly to the forest floor, where he landed unevenly, fell to his knees and swore with abandon.

You okay?

Of course not. Here, give me a hand up. As Lucian lowered weight onto his left foot a barbarous pain shot through his ankle. Jesus.

Michael kept hold of Lucian's elbow. Is it broken?

How do I know? Feels like it might be.

It was already past 3pm. In a couple of hours the sun would be gone for another day. They did not have enough clothes and food to spend the night in the open, especially if the weather was about to turn. And if Michael went ahead alone it would take four or five hours for help to get back, presuming of course he could retrace his steps in the dark. Once again the possibility of stealing Lucian's latest novel occurred to him. But he knew the manuscript was not yet complete, and the circumstances of a bush-walking accident were far too dubious.

Think you can lean on me?

Let's give it a try.

Lucian reached across Michael's back, grabbed his far shoulder, and took a few clumsy steps. On such a steep incline it was difficult for the two bodies to stay knitted together, so Michael unfastened his belt, linked it with

Lucian's, then rethreaded it back around his trousers. He then took off his jacket, removed his shirt, twisted it into a rope and tied their knees together. Lucian's calf was about four centimetres shorter than Michael's, so his injured foot remained off the ground as they three-legged it in the direction of Wood Green.

After an X-ray at The Royal Hobart Hospital a doctor pronounced Lucian's ankle to be severely sprained and, with a generous dose of painkillers, instructed him to stay off it for at least two weeks. Michael accompanied the injured author back up the mountain, and slept on a couch in the sunroom in case Lucian needed anything in the middle of the night.

60.

Tim leaned through the kitchen doorway. That was Carl on the phone. He's coming in next week to do some training.

Maureen looked up from *The Gallery* by John Horne Burns. What day?

Thursday.

Okay.

Tim waited for his wife to expand on her confirmation but her attention immediately returned to her book. Does that mean you'll be here to help?

Maureen held her eyes on the page. It's only Friday, so who can say? But if I'm here I'm sure I'll lend a hand.

Well that's big of you. Thanks. Me and the rest of the stock will all be waiting to see if you'll grace us with your presence.

Are you implying I don't do enough around here?

I didn't say anything of the sort. Those words never even left my mouth. Once again you're accusing me of things you've imagined I've done.

Don't try to play that bullshit game. Who the hell closed up shop for the past four nights because you had a little sniffle? And then you insinuate I'm not pulling my weight. What a jerk.

And you're a crazy bitch.

Fuck off.

Watch me. The moment this place is off our hands you won't see my dust.

Go now if you want. I'll send you a cheque.

I don't think so. Your idea of fifty per cent is not always the same as mine.

Now you're accusing me of being a thief? Anything else you'd like to add? Murderer? Adulterer?

The possibility of Maureen being unfaithful had never occurred to Tim before, and with it came the realisation that once they separated she would be free to have sex with whomever she wanted. Tim had dedicated countless hours to imagining himself with women other than his wife, but so far had failed to picture Maureen undressing for anyone beside himself. It sparked jealousy in his veins. And like the moment when all the features of the office had abruptly emerged, Tim was now suddenly awake to qualities of Maureen's beauty that years of marriage had allowed him to take for granted. The soft lines beside her eyes; the elegance of her stockings and shoes; her perfect stillness as she read a book; the tips of her painted fingernails holding open a page. Tim stood staring. Thinking. One more time. After all the years they had spent together...just one more time. The anger that sought to continue the argument was suddenly usurped by another internal drive.

You're right, he said in a conciliatory tone. I'm sorry. I shouldn't have said those things. I didn't mean to be so rude. I know how hard you work. And I appreciate it. I really do. I can take care of Carl's training. How difficult could it be, right?

Maureen refused to concede the moral high ground and pulled herself away from her book. I'm sorry too. Let's not do that again. Remember we promised. No more arguments.

Agreed, said Tim, who looked for a moment longer, then returned to the shop.

61.

Andrew held his head down pretending to read a very important document while waiting for Michael to walk past the reception desk. Found yourself a local girl have you?

Pardon?

She'll be expecting a ring if you keep spending the night at her place.

Um, I don't have a...

Don't worry. I won't give your secret away. A man like you *should* have a girl in every city. Why not? Life is for the living, right? If that one from Sydney calls I'll just tell her you're working late.

No. Please. Don't do that.

So I should tell her you haven't slept in your room for three nights? That seems a little harsh don't you think? And it's not really my responsibility to let her know you've found someone new.

I don't need you to tell her anything. And I doubt if she'll even call. I'm not seeing anyone else. I'm just helping a friend who has injured his leg and can't move around very well at the moment.

Oh, yes, yes, I see.

It's the truth.

I believe you. Why would you lie?

So you won't say anything if Rachel calls?

Is that her name? No, I'll just take a message.

Thank you.

What are friends for. Will you be staying out again tonight? I find it helpful to know in advance so I don't bother preparing your breakfast. I can't stand to see good food going to waste. Every penny counts you know.

Yes, unfortunately, I think I will be. The doctor has told him to stay off it for at least another week. I've just come home for a change of clothes.

Another week! My, you *are* a good friend. Well this is a B&B so I suppose you're entitled to treat it like a hotel.

Is there something you need to talk to me about? asked Michael.

Me? No, no, nothing. All good here. You just carry on. I can see you're busy.

Andrew returned to pretending to read and waited for the sound of Michael's footsteps on the second landing. He then looked up and sighed. As if he was going to believe such a blatant invention. A friend with an injured leg. How ridiculous. He knew Michael had no other friends in Hobart. How could he? Look at how disrespectfully he treated the one he did have. Lying. Deceiving. Really, it was as if Michael believed that Andrew had no brain in his head. But he knew people. They were the bread and butter of his business. Hundreds. Thousands of guests had passed through his B&B over the years, and Andrew had come to appreciate that they were all essentially alike. Michael was no exception to the rule. He had revealed himself to be the same as everybody else. Greedy. Self-centred. Inconsiderate of other people's feelings. Nothing special. Nothing exceptional. Andrew checked his ledger to see how long it was before Michael was due to pay next month's rent. Eight more nights. Eight more breakfasts. He drew a line beneath the date to mark the occasion when Michael would witness the real Andrew Tiller. Not the servant who always kowtowed to the petty needs and demands of his guests. But the man, the specimen, the human being of rare and outstanding qualities.

62.

Surprise, said Maureen. Hello, said Lucian. Me too, said Penny. Who's for champagne? said Paul. I brought you the papers, said Tim. What a lovely surprise, said Lucian. We heard you were injured, said Maureen. Oh, what are those? asked Lucian. Peppers stuffed with anchovies and capers, said Maureen. And these are lamb and eggplant balls, said Penny. How's the leg? asked Tim. It's nothing serious, said Lucian. Is everyone having champagne? asked Michael. Of course everyone is having champagne, this is a party, said Paul. A get-well party, said Maureen. You don't mind do you? They kept asking if they could pay you a visit, said Michael. Mind? With meatballs like these? said Lucian. See, I told you he'd love them, said Paul. I just thought it might be too early in the day, said Penny. Let's have some music, said Maureen. To mountain climbers everywhere, said Paul. Cheers, said Michael. Cheers, said Maureen. Cheers, said Tim. Cheers, said Penny. Cheers, said Lucian. I'm just going to get in some more wood for the fire, said Michael. Well that goes down nicely, said Tim. I forgot the music, said Maureen. The CD in the player should be perfect, said Lucian. Is this your library? asked Tim. It's cold today, isn't it? said Penny. Logs coming through, said Michael. They're predicting snow, said Paul. You've read all those books? asked Tim. Have a meatball, said Penny. I need to wash my hands first, said Michael. You should have told us about your ankle, said Maureen. Down Sadie, said Michael. We could have made you something to eat, said Penny. I can cook, said Michael. I heard about it from Paul, said Tim. I thought you told me, said Paul. You're not drinking? asked Maureen. I haven't heard music like this in years, said Paul. It's a little early for me, said Penny. Who is it again? asked Paul. Dorothy Ashby, said Lucian. *Afro-Harping*, added Michael. We should play something like this in the pub, said Paul. I can finish my own sentences, said Lucian. My, these chairs are deep, said Penny. I know you can, said Michael. Did you hear that snow was predicted this week? asked Tim. Paul said, said Michael. Better get ready for the shut in, said Tim. What's that? asked Michael. The road sometimes gets closed when there's a heavy snowfall, said Maureen. What a beautiful painting, said Penny. Yes, I forget where I got it from though, said Lucian. Barcelona, said Michael. Could you pass me another of those peppers? asked Paul. Fill her up please, said Tim. I'm fasting twice a week and it's really helping me to lose weight, said Penny. When I was a boy it seemed to rain all the time in Tasmania, said Paul. See how many shops are closing down along Elizabeth Street? asked Maureen. You can't tell me things were better when Gunns was around, said Penny. House prices won't climb much higher, said Tim. Sorry, I'll clean it up, said Michael. Stop fussing, said Lucian. Matthew is with his grandmother today, said Penny. My leg has been aching all week, said Michael. Pretty good for local bubbly, said Tim. Doctor says I'm not to sit at my desk at the moment, said Lucian. What are you two whispering about? asked Tim. Nothing, said Maureen. I was just saying that you get the government you deserve, said Michael. You've been hanging around Lucian too much, you're starting to sound like him, said Paul. Where's the bathroom? asked Penny. Any discussion of Australian literature that doesn't include Alexis Wright's *Carpentaria* is irrelevant, said Lucian. We need a new CD, said Michael. Carl is coming in this week to learn the ropes, said Tim. Have you started packing yet? asked Paul. I love this Nathan Davis album, said Maureen. Your kitchen is so clean, said Penny. That's Michael's doing, said Lucian. I should be going. We open up in half an hour, said Paul. That's my cue too, said Penny. We'd better go too, said Tim. Really? asked Lucian. Sadie stay, said Michael. Reminds me of the parties I used to attend in London, said Lucian. When was that? asked Tim. Thanks for coming, said Michael. Oh a long time ago now, another lifetime, said Lucian. We had a lovely time, said Penny. Thanks, said Tim. See you soon, said Paul. He seemed to enjoy himself, said Michael. If there's anything you need, just ask, said Maureen. Come on flirty, he's doing fine, said Tim. That goes for me too, said Paul. I will, thanks, said Michael.

63.

Michael cracked a window to clear the room of stale air, kicked off his boots and started to pull clothes from his back, all the while trying to ignore the sheets of paper piled on top of his desk. Under the shower the sound of Lucian's offer echoed between his ears. To repay for all the cooking and shopping Michael had done over the past seven days he would be happy to have a look at his manuscript...if that was what he wanted. Except Michael no longer knew if it was. Towelling himself dry, he thought it might be unwise to have his work critiqued before it was finished. Michael could feel how fragile the process was. Vulnerable to insecurity; second-guessing. And a dose of Lucian's sarcasm might bring his current progress to an abrupt halt. Michael reread the scene he had most recently completed and realised that a similar situation would suit his novel. The aspiring writer showing his latest work to the established author. The worry and anxiety that went along with it. The advice that ensued. Its possible misinterpretation by both characters and readers. The tensions that might emerge between the aspiring author and his new wife. An accusation that she no longer had his best interests at heart. Or a creeping suspicion that she was falling in love with the established author. Could that be another idea developed throughout the book? Another misdirection to put before the reader? Thirty minutes later Michael realised he still had no clothes on and had written an additional two pages. It was like that now. The writing would just happen. Michael would see himself holding a pen, but it felt like someone else was moving it across the paper. The same as when he read a book so good he was unaware of turning the pages. He hoped it was an indication of doing real work. That by escaping the restrictions of the physical world during the act of composition – fleeing gravity; travelling through time; guided by a voice different from his everyday consciousness – he was writing something true enough to also displace his readers. Michael trembled with a sudden recognition of the effort necessary to create something new. And now understood why certain novels of obscure experimental fiction had endured despite never topping a bestseller list. They were vessels. To convey readers into a unique world of no compromise. A singular state of mind that vanished the moment the final sentence of the book was complete. It must have been tortuous for their authors to realise it was gone forever. And Michael theorised that what divided writers was the decision either to spend a career trying to recapture it, or to move on with the understanding that the value of the achievement lived not in the moment, but in searching for its existence. How could anything new be discovered without looking somewhere different? Michael acknowledged that this was what Lucian had done throughout his career, and how it would be folly to decline an offer of assistance. Who knew for how long Lucian would be able to bestow such a gift. Michael dressed quickly and stuffed the opening chapters of his book inside his satchel. He glanced around the room and scarcely recognised it. His laptop and mobile phone had acquired a layer of dust and appeared to belong to someone else. His waste-paper basket was empty, his bed was made with fresh sheets, and someone had turned the pictures on the wall to face the right way. The bathroom awoke memories of Rachel's visit, and with it recollections of his former life in Sydney. Michael felt little for either the people he had left behind, or the places he had frequented. All he wanted was to get onto the streets of Battery Point. Find a shop. Buy some groceries. Hail a taxi. And return to Wood Green with its trees and quiet and friends like Maureen and Paul. It was where he felt most at home. More so, he realised with surprise, than any other place he had ever lived.

64.

Maureen was not surprised to feel Tim's hand upon her hip. He had been awake when she came to bed, and all day there had been casual touches of her arm, her shoulder. One time she had caught him spying at her from behind his newspaper, and of course, it had snowed. The first fall of winter had kept them inside for most of the day. The only time Tim had stepped out was to shovel clear the path that led to the shop's front door. He re-entered the kitchen sweating; red faced, with veins bulging at the side of his neck, and it reminded Maureen of how he had looked when they were first married. When their sex had been good, sometimes even great. Maureen caught herself revisiting one or two incidences of particular eroticism. There was nothing else to do. The snow had made everything so quiet. She closed the shop early and was not nearly as tired as usual. Tim waited for her to settle into bed. The room to grow still. Then turned on his side and reached across. If only he didn't speak, Maureen thought. Just removed her pyjamas and nibbled at the back of her neck the way she liked. Didn't kiss her too much, or say anything to imply he was trying to save their marriage. If only he caressed the small of her back: attended to her breasts; licked his fingers first; made her feel his desires were urgent, passionate; so long as he didn't tickle her; try to talk dirty or make that sound at the back of his throat. He needed to understand that this was the last time, so he should make the most of it and respond to her body, touch her inner thighs, give her hair a gentle tug. Not resort to tired positions, come too fast, take too long, sniff in her ear, or ask for anal. If only he gave Maureen no reasons to change her mind then she might find the right position and tap into a fantasy, banish all thought and finally lose herself in the moment.

65.

Dear Michael,

Thanks for this. I'm sure that showing your work to someone before it's finished must be a terrifying experience, but you needn't have worried, the writing is fine. In fact it's better than fine, it's good. You appear to have found a story of interest to yourself and, I'm pleased to say, readers as well. You also seem to have reached that point where you can begin to relax and enjoy the experience of writing. I usually have to wrestle my way inside a book, but once I'm there and I'm sure it's alive I start to breathe easy and allow it to grow under its own momentum. Be careful though. Such a pleasure is fleeting. So enjoy it while it lasts because soon enough you'll need to wrestle your way out again. But while all of that is still ahead of you I thought I might offer a little advice. Not hard and fast rules, as I'm sure you know that no such things exist. Just an understanding, which after years of writing I hold to be true. A writer can only use the voice he or she was born with. And if it makes them a success or not is simply luck.

In fact, to be honest, whether you get published or not is down to luck as well. Your voice is your voice and it's the one you're stuck with. Unfortunately, choice is not a factor. Popular fiction writers can't understand why they never win literary prizes. Literary writers are frustrated that they can't achieve the big sales. Yet it's all because neither of them can escape their voice. And those that try tend to fail miserably. Also, don't worry so much about being neat and correct. Awkwardness is fine. Rough edges are good. Think of the millions of novels that have been published. It's rarely the smooth and palatable ones that endure. It's the books that get stuck in my throat that I tend to remember. Be yourself. Let your personality seep into the work. Be true to what's inside your head. How else will you uncover the things you never knew existed? Write the book *you* would want to read. That way whether it sells or not becomes irrelevant. Publishers will always insist that this is a business. And for them it is. But for you it can never be. Writing has to be an artistic pursuit otherwise you're just wasting trees and distracting yourself until death. And believe me, you are going to die. We all are. So why not make your own mark. State what *you* think is real. More than likely it will be real for others as well. And in the process you'll furnish yourself with a purpose in life that billionaires will envy.

Lucian leaned away from the typewriter to scan his letter. His back was sore, his ankle throbbed, and he was actually more interested in what might be for lunch than composing platitudes. Did Michael really need to hear this? Did he not already know it all instinctively? So what was the point of blathering on like this? Encouragement? What real writer needed that? You either had to write or you didn't. And if you did then good or bad was beside the point. Lucian had no recollection of a time when he had sought someone else's validation of his work. He just wrote and hoped for the best. Consequences be damned. What other choice was there? And wasn't that the measure of a real artist? It had certainly always seemed that way to Lucian.

He reached forward and yanked the paper out the typewriter. The machine rattled in protest at being treated so roughly, but Lucian assumed he would not need it for much longer, so what did it matter if it broke. He screwed up the letter and threw it to the floor for Sadie to chew on. The dog raised her head, sniffed the paper ball once, then grabbed it between her slobbering jaws. Michael, however, would be expecting some kind of response to his writing. On a fresh sheet of paper Lucian wrote in an untidy hand, 'Good work. Keep going.' And placed it on top of the manuscript. Really, what else did he need to hear?

66.

Michael slipped and fell in the snow. He had managed to remain upright all the way down the road to Tim and Maureen's store, but on his return to Lucian's house had tripped over hidden stones and lost his balance so many times that his trousers were now completely wet through, with the sleeves of his jacket only marginally drier. Appreciation for the blanket of white that had descended upon the mountainside, its incongruousness with the dominant eucalypts, the sight of wallabies venturing into front gardens, and the general otherworldliness of walking through falling snow, had all begun to fade as Michael struggled back along Brenan Street. Maybe it was because he was walking up hill. Or perhaps his feet had grown too numb to work properly. Fear of frostbite tried to take hold in Michael's imagination, but he told himself to stop being childish and step in the footprints he had made on his way down.

By the time he reached Lucian's verandah he was shivering. He suspected the leather of his boots was frozen, and slipped them off inside the front door as he announced to Lucian that the roads were closed and he was taking a bath. No response came from the other side of the bedroom door, and Michael was thankful for the chance to shed his wet clothes without the delay of having to explain himself.

Lucian's bathroom was a remarkable time capsule of nineteen-seventies fittings and tiling. Respectable to the point of functionality, it was nevertheless developing an impression of antiquation, bordering on neglect. As Michael waited for the long deep tub to fill slowly, he inspected his reflection in the medicine cabinet mirror and wondered whether marijuana was turning his hair grey. He knew he could not smoke it every night without consequences, and saw how the creases across his forehead had grown deeper. The discolouration of his teeth also appeared to be worse, even though he had avoided tobacco for nearly two months. Maybe he wasn't getting enough sunlight. Being cooped up with Lucian all day looked like it was making his skin grow pale. And a layer of flab was developing around his neck that Michael was convinced had not been present when he first arrived in Tasmania.

He examined the contents of the medicine cabinet. Not in search for illicit pharmaceuticals, of which there were plenty elsewhere in the house, but for clues about what medication Lucian might be taking to help him manage his condition. After almost a fortnight of caring for the author and his sprained ankle, Michael had identified definite signs of Lucian's decline. Most obvious was his incessant opening and closing of cupboards and drawers to persuade himself he knew for certain the location of the peanut butter or the tea bags. The sound of double-checking created an atmosphere of anxiety that permeated the entire house, but in accordance with their tacit agreement the two men refused to acknowledge the unease, its source, or anything else to do with Lucian's memory loss. For the moment such a pact was only mildly inconvenient, though Michael could foresee a time quickly approaching when he would have no choice but to speak the name of Lucian's misfortune, if only so they could begin to face its ramifications head on.

As Michael lay in the bath, his body tingling beneath the hot water, he again acknowledged the quiet that had descended upon Mount Wellington with the snow. It seemed to amplify every sound, from the ripples of the bathwater to the creaking of the house constricting against the icy air. Michael was surprised not to hear the clack of Lucian's typewriter, and wondered if he was reading instead. He sank lower into the bathwater. Maybe Lucian was reading the opening chapters of his manuscript. Michael had not anticipated being in Wood Green while this occurred, and decided to hurry to his office as soon as he exited the bathroom. That way it might be hours before they encountered one another. Plenty of time for Lucian to become distracted...and maybe forget all about the limitations of Michael's abilities.

67.

I'd like a room please.

Really?

You don't think your own pub is a good place to stay?

It's not that. It's just that people usually go back down to Hobart if they need a hotel.

Yeah, but if it snows again I won't be able to get back up the mountain. They closed the road on Thursday, and it was pretty slow this morning as well. You should have seen the meter in my taxi.

How did you get on with Tim today? He show you the ropes?

I'd say that running a general store is deceptively difficult. Much like running a pub I presume.

Deceptively difficult sounds about right. Don't worry, you'll soon get the hang of it. How many nights do you think you'll need? Or do you want to wait and see how you feel at the end of each day?

I'll need two nights at least. Maureen is showing me the morning shift tomorrow, and depending on how it goes I might do it again the next day. Sunday I assume is pretty slow, and it would probably be worth my while hanging around until Monday so I can meet all the delivery guys. But yeah, let's play it by ear. Do you want me to pay upfront? I've only got cash I'm sorry.

No, no, I know where you live. Or where you will live. Just settle up at the end of your stay. So what would you prefer, quiet or warmth?

Both if you've got it.

Well room three shares the chimney so it's warm all the time, but the sound of the pub will come up through the floorboards until closing. Or you can have room five, which is at the back of the pub over the kitchen, away from everything. There's a small heater in there, but if it snows overnight it could get a little chilly.

I'll take room three please. Noise doesn't bother me.

Good choice. The bathroom is next door, and there's no one else staying here at the moment so you'll have it all to yourself.

No ghosts?

None that I've noticed. If you hear someone walking around in the attic it's just me stumbling into bed, so don't worry. Breakfast is included. Nothing fancy. Orange juice. Coffee. Scrambled eggs and bacon, if that's all right? Here's your key. Up the stairs and the second door on your left. Have you had any dinner? Of course you haven't. Where could you? The kitchen is only open for lunch, so most nights I tend to make myself something. You're welcome to join me if you'd like.

I don't want to put you to any trouble. I can wait until breakfast.

Nonsense. But I don't usually eat until late, when people are drinking a little slower.

No problem. I like to eat late as well. Thank you, that's very kind of you. I might take a shower then come back down for a drink.

I have some South African wines in stock if you're interested.

No thanks. That's all behind me now. A Tasmanian wine is what I'd prefer. No use moving to a new place and wishing I was back home. Up the stairs and to the left?

That's right. Anything you need just ask.

68.

Maureen cursed inwardly as she rolled and bent pastry into the shape of a croissant. The forlorn expression on Carl's face as he stood in the kitchen and sipped coffee was ridiculous. To the point of being odious. No one had forced him to stay up late drinking with Paul. Maureen certainly hadn't. Self pity during a hangover was a bugbear she could never shake, and it undermined the kindness behind her decision to help train Carl with his takeover. She felt her time was being wasted. Carl wasn't listening. He was barely awake. Maureen vowed that if he started to doze she would kick him out. Tim and Lucian were enough. Teaching a third man the meaning of gratitude was too much. Running a general store would soon reveal to Carl the consequences of neglecting personal responsibilities in favour of instant gratification. And if, like Tim, he failed to discipline his decision-making, then this mountain and its community would quickly cut him adrift. The timer on top of the stove announced the first batch of croissants were ready. Carl winced at the volume of the alarm, so Maureen left it ringing until the second tray had been placed inside the oven.

It was a cruel trick to play, but it was too early in the morning to put up with people being inconsiderate of her effort.

Would you like one? she asked.

Maybe later. I think I need to wait a while before I try to eat anything.

Come on then. I usually start to get the store ready while the second batch is cooking. First I light the fire. That way the store is nice and warm by the time you open up. If you're smart you'll get the wood and kindling ready the day before. Gives it more time to dry, and means you don't have to go out into the cold. Then I wipe down the fridge doors. It only takes a minute or two and they look so much nicer without a build-up of condensation. Next I sweep the floor and empty the mousetraps. You don't catch one every night but at this time of year they tend to come inside to escape the cold. Maureen saw Carl's revulsion as she dropped three dead mice into a plastic bag. Glamorous, isn't it?

Carl nodded, fidgeted, and turned to the knock at the front door.

Get that will you. It'll be Bill.

Carl said good morning and tried to smile, but the edifice of hospitality crumbled under a wave of nausea.

Bill walked inside carrying a cup, returned Carl's greeting with a hint of surprise, then softly called out, Maureen?

She reappeared with two warm croissants wrapped in paper napkins and placed them on the counter. Coffee?

Yes please.

This is Carl. He's taking over the shop. Carl, this is Bill. District Court Judge and local poet.

Now, now, said Bill.

Carl extended his hand, determined not to show any sign of nerves in the presence of the law. Nice to meet you.

And you, replied Bill. Hope you're paying attention. Big shoes to fill here. These are the best croissants in all of Tasmania. Bill was a tall man with wavy silver hair and a bulbous nose that indicated an enthusiasm for wine. It suited his friendly face, and the quiet voice with which he spoke slow, well-considered words.

I'll do my best. Carl tried to project an air of respectability, but knew it was a first impression he would have to mend at a later date.

Of course you will.

Here's your coffee, said Maureen.

Bill accepted the cup and hastily made his farewells.

He's up in Launceston this week, explained Maureen. So he has to leave early.

He doesn't pay?

Of course he does. Didn't Tim show you the ledger? Maureen pulled a blue notebook out from beneath the till and entered a date and amount on the page headed with Bill's name. He settles up at the end of each month. Judges can't just take things for free.

No. Of course not.

There are about fifteen people we extend a line of credit to. Their names are all in here. You'll get to know them quickly enough. And we've never had a problem with people paying what they owe. Maureen switched on the store's amplifier and inserted a CD by Grouper – *Dragging A Dead Deer Up A Hill*.

You seem to do an awful lot to make people feel welcome. I don't see how I'll be able to keep it up on my own.

Just do what you can. You'll figure it out. We've found that if you care about the people as much as their money they'll respond with loyalty. Most people would prefer to shop locally. I can't remember the last time I walked into a supermarket.

Well I suppose it's not too far ahead of you now.

Maureen unlocked the till and checked the float. What's that?

Shopping in a supermarket. Unless you're intending to open up another store?

Not in this lifetime. But look, if you want my advice, you'll need to decide pretty early on if this is going to be an investment or a way of life.

Can't it be both?

Of course it can. Maureen looked around the shop with an expression of regret. But it's a tricky balance to achieve. And even if you do, it's a hard one to hold on to.

69.

Lucian knocked, then opened Michael's office door. If I'm making lunch, you're making dinner, okay?

Michael swivelled in the captain's chair. Pardon? He had been typing on Lucian's spare machine and had not heard a word.

What are you wearing those old things for?

Michael glanced down at the ornately printed shirt and blue pinstriped trousers he had borrowed from the cupboard in his office. My clothes were wet from the snow, and I didn't want to disturb you by asking for something to wear.

Why didn't you just get a cab home?

The roads are closed. Remember? I told you when I came back in.

Lucian repressed the urge to dispute such a claim and offered a perfunctory, Oh yeah, right, before changing the subject. I remember buying that shirt in Rome. I've no idea where I got the trousers from though.

Michael stood up and held out his arms. I expected them to be too small, but they seem to fit perfectly.

I was probably bigger then. You tend to shrink a little when you get older.

I'll put them back as soon as my clothes are dry.

No rush. It's not as if I'll be wearing them any time soon. Lunch'll be ready in about ten minutes.

Michael placed his two pages of notes about Lucian's life on the coffee table, then began to eat from the platter of hummus, olives, flatbread, cold toast, grilled haloumi, fried zucchini, slices of salami, pickled eggplant and anchovies in olive oil. Lucian poured them each a glass of wine, and carefully draped three of the largest anchovies across a slice of luxuriously buttered toast. Tactlessly Michael winced at the sight, making Lucian grin mischievously while he chewed. The enchantment of the platter subsided only when a detritus of pips, bread scraps and smears of dip were all that remained. They had drunk their wine and sat docile on the couches, listening to The Khan Jamal Creative Arts Ensemble – *Drumdance to the Motherland*.

Michael looked down and noticed a small stain of olive oil on his trousers. He wiped at it with a napkin, all the while reassuring Lucian that he would get them dry cleaned as soon as he returned to Hobart.

Lucian sighed and shook his head. You know how long I've owned those clothes for? If they didn't mean anything to me; if they didn't possess some intrinsic value, even if it's just sentimental, then why would I keep them? Lucian enjoyed watching Michael's face cloud over with humiliation and fear. It's about respecting other people's possessions. Just because *you* don't hold them in high regard doesn't mean that other people are the same. If you can't put yourself in someone else's shoes when it comes to something as simple as that, then how do you expect to do it for a novel? Same goes for putting CDs back in their cases, and the butter back in the right compartment of the fridge. I've got a memory problem at the moment, unless you hadn't noticed, and not finding things where I know they ought to be kind of fucks with my head.

You're right. I'm sorry. It won't happen again.

Lucian sighed. Well I suppose this is as good a time as any to come to a decision about our circumstances. After two weeks of having you help me with my leg I think we can both agree that this little arrangement isn't working out. I won't deny that in many regards you've been a big help, but I don't believe things can go on as they did before.

They're just a pair of trousers, I can get them...

Lucian held up his hand. This whole situation has become too incompatible with what I originally planned. I see that now, and I apologise for prolonging my decision. I just wanted to be absolutely sure before I said anything.

Has something happened? Do you feel as though you're getting worse?

No, no, nothing like that. In respect to this issue my thoughts are refreshingly coherent. I appreciate you being so sensitive to my condition, however I have made my decision. You spending half of every day at my house has become too inconvenient. And I'm sure your expenditure on taxis must be financially crippling. Which is why I think you should move in permanently. Who knows how much more snow is going to fall this season, and if you can't catch a taxi up here then no work gets done, and the whole plan falls apart.

Michael's woebegone expression instantly vanished.

There is, however, one very important condition to this offer.

All right.

We go back to our established routines. Writing until 1pm, then you do your research for the rest of the day. Deal?

Deal.

70.

In retrospect, Andrew regretted the sense of amusement with which he had accepted Michael's invitation to join him for breakfast. His plan to listen to Michael's stories about finding true love in the arms of a local girl, before explaining how the rent for his room could no longer be discounted, had gone awry almost immediately. Instead he had heard Michael reveal that he would be vacating his room that very day so he could move into his 'employer's house' up in Wood Green. The underlined date in the register confirmed that Michael's second month was up, and Andrew had presumed that his presence at breakfast for the first time in two weeks was little more than a cynical ploy to re-establish their friendship before renegotiations began for the next four weeks. But Andrew quickly learned that Michael had come home only to pack; that he was ready to leave straight after breakfast, and did not intend to make any gesture to indicate their friendship would endure beyond the boundaries of the B&B. There was to be no offer to exchange phone numbers or email addresses; not even a half-hearted agreement to meet for coffee some time in the future. How cold, thought Andrew. How calculating. While calmly performing the conventional smiles and nods his profession had taught him to execute, the B&B proprietor wondered how much more friendship he needed to bestow before he received some in return. Exactly what defects did he possess that seemed to invalidate every effort he made to form a meaningful relationship? This was not some game he was playing. His motives were genuine. Sincere. Surely Michael could distinguish how authentic he was compared with everyone else in Hobart. And yet once again he had failed to forge a connection. Well Andrew refused to believe it was his fault. To think of oneself as always in the wrong was macabre. And it was out of proportion with the evidence. Michael had never been sympathetic to his needs. Instead he was always talking about himself. Obstinately, habitually reverting to the idea that he was the centre of the universe. It was so unsophisticated. Nothing more than a persistent self-infatuation that lacked all introspection, and proved to Andrew that, like so many of his guests, Michael was emotionally retarded. A lost soul isolated from the rest of humanity; skirting the periphery of society without ever managing to actually participate in it; viewing every interaction as simply a transaction to be conducted with as few scruples as possible. Andrew understood how humiliating it would be for Michael to realise how transparent he was being. And it was not his job to pull the wool from his customers' eyes. If Michael could not perceive his own limitations then whatever Andrew did or said was unlikely to help. No, there was nothing amusing about this situation. It was sad and tiring, and Andrew could ill-afford to expend any more energy upon such a person. He drained his coffee cup and explained how he needed to get back to work. Just leave your key at the front desk if I'm not there, he said as a goodbye. Then set about collecting the plates and bowls that had been abandoned on the other tables. A faint regret that he would no longer see Michael in the halls or in the breakfast room twinged somewhere inside Andrew's chest, but he pitilessly quashed such a useless sentiment and disappeared into the kitchen.

71.

Airport? Oh, okay. Sorry. Just saw your bags and thought you were flying out. Wood Green it is then. Buckle up. Nice day for once. It's meant to get a lot colder later on though. Hope you brought your woollies with you. They're predicting we're in for some more snow tonight. You know, in ratio with the rest of the country, Tasmania gets more snow than...

I don't mean to be rude, said Michael. But I can feel a bit of a headache coming on, and I'd really appreciate just a quiet drive.

Sure, sure. No problem. I understand. I've been to Sydney too.

72.

Tim armed himself with another empty box and set about extracting the business books and Bryce Courtenay hardbacks that Maureen had relegated to the bottom shelf behind the reading chairs. She had explained that such heavy volumes needed to be placed low to stabilise the shelf, but Tim knew that his wife hated the sight of his books and was terrified a visitor might mistake them for part of her collection.

As he stood in the lounge room looking for what else needed to be packed, Tim caught himself making small farewells to objects Maureen owned and that he had grown fond of during their marriage. The aromatic candles were not part of this process, however Tim was surprised to find the Toby cup on the mantelpiece was. Along with the orange glass vase. Goodbye to the hatstand, he thought. Goodbye to the magazine rack. Goodbye to the tiny metal horse that stood on the windowsill. Goodbye to the reading chairs that Maureen had bargained for when he had claimed the desk in the office. Goodbye to the cushions she had sewn using the old curtains that had come with the shop. He checked their bedroom. Goodbye to the triptych of strange paintings, full of ferocious, gnashing figures that Maureen had bought in Budapest on her first trip overseas and hung in every bedroom she had lived in since. Goodbye to Alexander Trocchi's *Thongs*. Being free of Maureen's books was something Tim was eagerly anticipating, but there were a few volumes he knew he would have to buy his own copy of, and *Thongs* was one of them. Maureen kept it in the bookshelf beside the bed, and even though it had been years since she had read it aloud, Tim often revisited the most explicit pages whenever he found he had the room to himself and was confident of not being interrupted. Goodbye to the mechanical fish his father-in-law had played with as a boy. Goodbye to the perfume that lingered in the bathroom. Goodbye to Maureen's hairbrush that made such an excellent back scratcher. Goodbye to her footsteps on the stairs. The delicious biscuits she baked. Goodbye to her calm, problem-solving mind. And good riddance to the arrogance that came along with it.

Tim found himself standing at the bottom of the staircase. He could hear Maureen serving a customer in the shop, and smelled soup simmering in the kitchen. Such trances of nostalgia were occurring more frequently as the day of their departure drew closer. And each time he woke from one Tim felt the real world to be more pronounced; more raw. Fuelling the fear, somewhere at the back of his mind, that his readiness to leave Maureen was not yet fully established. And reigniting questions about whether he had chosen an incorrect path for himself; if the decay of his marriage was as irreversible as he had presumed.

Was he guilty of exaggerating their problems? Even if he was, such self-questioning was too frustrating. Years of uncertainty in regards to whether they had done the right thing by moving to Hobart had left him desperate to make a decision and just live with it. Right or wrong, in less than a week, he and Maureen would no longer be together. And clothing that fact in uncertainty was not going to change the course he had set for himself. Nor would regret for the loss of Maureen's possessions. Tim was tired, and he knew it always made him susceptible to fear. What did it matter if he was leaving things behind. It was the prospect of what he might find in the future that had given him the courage to accept Carl's offer for the shop. Tim ladled himself a bowl of soup. Nothing ventured, he thought as he sipped, nothing gained.

73.

I bought you a housewarming gift.

But aren't you the one who's moving in?

Well then I bought it for both of us.

Another CD. Two!

I couldn't decide so I ordered both. I've been reading about them online and I thought they might be of interest. You don't have them do you?

No. Never heard of either of them. Shall we put one on?

You go ahead. I'm going to finish unpacking, then I'll start lunch.

Lucian tore off the plastic wrapping and put the CD in the player. From the cover he could not identify if it was a band or solo musician, and whether they called themselves ovalprocess or that was the title of the album.

As soon as the music started Lucian knew it was going to be unlike anything he had heard before. Electronic. Unharmonic. Full of unruly clicks and ticks and beeps. All bubbling up with no discernable melody or structure. For a moment he thought the CD was skipping, but then the suspect glitch became incorporated into the composition and Lucian realised a strange, untutored creativity was at play. One with a significant ingenuity at its core that could recontextualise microscopic fluctuations and digital hissing into a ritualistic noise as oddly tender as it was astonishingly futuristic. At first the effect was disorientating. Like an electrical storm erupting inside the house. Setting off waves of overdriven static and whistling fireworks in all directions. But as the album progressed, and Lucian's ears acclimatised to the astringent alien electronics, he began to notice a sculptural technique at work, and a maverick chamber music. One where regular metre was obliterated, and margins were redrawn using murky melodic threads and pulsating dissonance. It was a psychedelic experiment by an unforgiving machine. A sensory overload of combustible details and digital scrapings welded together with an abstract logic to deliver a radiant drone. A delineation of sound. A volatile spasm. Harmonically complex and elaborately constructed, the album seemed formless and unfiltered until the polyrhythmic atmosphere congealed into a sonic realm of oscillating vibrancy: unpredictable salvos; nettled tones; software eruptions and snaking voltage. Not a single noise betrayed traceable ancestry with traditional instrumentation. The rattling compositions sounded entirely computer generated, yet were nonetheless capable of conveying genuine moments of ache and bliss. Lucian realised it was as much about unlocking the rhythms hidden within the torrent of sound as it was about absorbing the mercurial forms and tonal fanfares. He observed the interminable repetition of squawking, snarling and squealing gradually shift in nature to unveil the secret orchestration of the inner machine. And comprehended how the sweeping imagination inherent in the cyclical patterns and interlocking algorithms heralded the arrival of a stunning mutant beauty.

It was not the possessions Lucian would leave behind that made death so difficult to accept. It was things like this. The music he had not yet heard. The books he had not yet read. Had not yet been written. All the things he would miss out on because he would be no longer conscious. It seemed so unfair that he should stop living while the rest of the world continued to grow. He was not tired. Lucian felt he had the energy of a twenty year old. So why couldn't he stay awake forever and see what was going to happen?

What's the new CD like? asked Michael as he returned to the sunroom.

Lucian looked up and blinked away his tears. It's...

74.

I made a mistake, okay?

Penny put down her knife and stepped sideways, closer to Paul, so her son would not overhear. It was the first day of school holidays and Matthew was loading plates into the dishwasher. Losing your wallet is a mistake. Or forgetting to set your alarm clock. That, however, was not a mistake. That was an assault. And it was not your fault.

Paul touched his bruised eye socket and assumed it was going to be even darker by the end of the day. He already had a reputation for clumsiness, so the elaborate story he concocted about hitting his head on a low beam in the cellar was not questioned by any of the regulars who sat along the bar. But Penny knew from experience what domestic violence looked like and refused to be complicit by pretending to believe such a ludicrous tale. It irritated Paul that she would not mind her own business. And at the same time he found it comforting to know that someone cared for his welfare.

Carl didn't mean it, Paul explained. It was just a misunderstanding.

All he needed to do was tell you he was straight. He didn't have to hit you.

We were both drunk, and I suppose things had gone a little too far.

What do you mean? How far did it go?

Paul looked over his shoulder at Matthew. Can we perhaps discuss this at another time?

No. Penny grabbed Paul's hand. We're going outside to pick some parsley, she told Matthew. Go stand at the door and keep an eye on the bar. Come and get us if anyone starts serving themselves, okay?

Matthew pulled off his rubber gloves. He recognised the expression on his mother's face from the times he had got into trouble at school, or forgotten to do his homework. Can I have some chips? he asked.

Of course you can, said Paul.

No you can't, corrected his mother. It's not even lunchtime yet. Now go and do what I asked.

Paul stood under the back awning watching rain fall in heavy sheets of grey. The air was freezing, and he could see that the back of the pub needed a fresh coat of paint. More money, he thought. How was he supposed to pay for something like that?

Look, I appreciate your concern, but I can take care of myself.

Penny lowered her voice so no one in the men's toilet could eavesdrop. I know you can. I didn't say you couldn't. But I thought we all took care of each other. You, me and Matthew. And I don't intend to let anyone hurt you, no matter whether you think you deserve it or not. This guy might have all the money in the world, but it doesn't give him the right to give you a black eye.

Carl's not that rich.

Well he certainly acts as if he is.

It was just a mistake. I think you're overreacting.

So how far did it go?

I'm not giving you any details.

Did you kiss him? asked Penny. Did he kiss you back?

We'd been drinking all night. That's all I'm telling you.

So you had your tongue in his mouth and he suddenly remembered he was straight?

It wasn't like that.

Well then tell me what it was like, because it sure as hell isn't obvious to me.

Paul leaned forward so he could whisper. All right, look, I was giving him head when I touched something he didn't like.

His cock was in your mouth and he didn't want to be touched? Exactly where didn't he want you to touch him?

Where do you think? Paul could see the confusion on Penny's face. His bum.

So his dick is ok, but his arse is out of bounds?

I know, I know. I just thought he was being playful so I started to play along too. But then things got out of hand.

Too right they did. That eye is going to take weeks to heal.

It won't happen again. I promise.

No, I promise *you* it won't happen again. Because if it does I'll make sure that no one in Wood Green buys a thing from his store, and we'll send that bastard bankrupt faster than you can say South African prick.

Paul smiled at Penny's protectiveness, but knew she understood little of the nocturnal subtleties that went on between men. And certainly would not have been able to accept that he and Carl had already reconciled.

The kitchen door opened and Matthew leaned outside. Wobbly Bob fell off his stool and no one is helping him to get back up.

Let's give him a hand, said Paul. Come on, then we'll bring in some wood for the fire. It's colder than the North Pole today.

Matthew checked his mum's expression and saw it had grown more benign.

Then can I have some chips?

75.

Michael opened the front door to Maureen holding a cardboard box full of books. Hello.

Hi. These are Lucian's.

Oh, okay. Here, let me take them for you.

I can manage. All right if I go through to the library?

Of course. Michael stepped aside as Maureen kicked off her boots and crossed the threshold. I can do that for you if you'd like, he said as she began returning the books to the shelves.

I don't mind. I know where they go, and it'll probably be the last time I get the opportunity.

When are you and Tim due to leave?

In a couple of days.

How's the packing going?

Well I've finished the books. Is Lucian working late today? I waited until the afternoon so I wouldn't disturb him.

No, he's asleep. He got up feeling unwell and went back to bed pretty much straight after breakfast.

That's not like him. Is he all right?

He doesn't seem to have a temperature.

Have you checked him?

I did a couple of hours ago. I think it's just the flu.

Mind if I put my head around the door to see if he's okay?

As Maureen stood inside the bedroom watching Lucian's chest gently rise and fall, she felt a tinge of jealousy that Michael had been allowed to share the author's house when she had not. But a moment's reflection of her current circumstances – selling the store; separating from Tim; no particular plans for the future – clarified the reason why Lucian had chosen Michael. Business arrangements were always so much easier to negotiate than emotional ones.

I'd better get back to my packing.

Michael pointed to the kettle on the stove. I was just about to make us a pot of tea.

Maureen lowered herself into Lucian's regular position on the leather couches and watched Michael move about the kitchen. He seemed so at home – aware of where everything lived – as if he had made the tea a million times before. The coffee table was littered with the usual offenders, and Maureen wondered if being stoned might make packing boxes a little more bearable. Mind if I put some music on?

Go ahead.

Maureen selected Terry Reid's *River*, just because it had a swing like no other record, and placed the album cover on her lap to admire the artwork. Do you think Lucian would mind? she asked holding up the half-smoked spliff that had been left on the ashtray.

Michael delivered a tray of tea and biscuits. I doubt he'd even notice. Maureen had placed her black stockinged feet on the edge of the coffee table and Michael caught himself admiring their shape. Sadie leapt onto the couch and rested her snout on top of his thigh.

Looks like you've made yourself a friend.

Yeah, we're getting there. I feed her most days so she's started to accept my presence.

Did you bake those yourself?

They're not very neat but I think they taste all right. Lucian has been going to bed early, and there's not much else to do up here besides read and listen to music and bake.

They're delicious.

Michael beamed. Thanks. That means a lot coming from you.

I'm not *that* good a cook.

The moment you're gone I'm sure everyone on this mountainside is going to realise exactly how good you are.

If I get stoned I might grow greedy with those, so stop me at three if I forget myself.

No problem. So long as you do the same for me.

Maureen pressed her hands to her cheeks. Her jaw was aching from laughing so much. They had eaten all the biscuits, and after Michael closed the sliding door to the sitting room he had turned up the music and rolled another joint. Maureen acknowledged there was a frisson in the room. More than once she had caught Michael admiring her legs or holding her gaze a little too long. But perhaps the pot was making her imagine it that way. They had graduated to Gal Costa's debut album, and were so involved in a conversation about José Saramago's *Blindness* that both of them squeaked in surprise when Lucian slid back the door.

In his dressing gown he appeared sleepy, and perhaps a little cross.

Having a party without me?

Sorry, we didn't mean to wake you.

How are you feeling? asked Maureen.

Better, thank you. You didn't wake me. I think I've had enough sleep for one day.

Would you like a cup of tea? asked Michael.

Yes please, that would be lovely.

Maureen shifted across the couch so Lucian could occupy his regular position.

He felt the warmth of her body in the leather and admired her black stockinged feet curled up beside him. What brings you here?

I was just returning a box of your books...but I seem to have become a little distracted.

Lucian scanned the evidence on the coffee table. So it seems.

Having Lucian and Michael in the same room confused Maureen's antennae. She felt she had to be a different person for each of them, and could not decide which Maureen she preferred to be.

Are you going to have another cup as well? asked Michael.

You know I don't think I will. I really should get back to the shop. It's not going to pack itself, and I'm only half done.

Lucian stood at the front door while Maureen pulled on her boots.

This is for you, she said as she slipped an envelope into the pocket of his dressing gown. Their kiss goodbye felt indifferent and perfunctory, though Maureen assumed the pot was again clouding her perception of reality. Well of course it was. That was what it was supposed to do. The cold air struck her face like a bucket of water. Anarchic. Intense. And in the end, amusing. As Maureen walked down Brenan Street she felt her head begin to clear. And noticed the mountainside – quiet and damp – was even more exquisite than usual.

76.

Tim knew he needed to time it exactly as he had before. Allow Maureen a few moments to get settled, then gently reach over when she turned on her side. Why not one more time? This was going to be their last night together. Ever. So it was not unreasonable for him to make an approach. On the contrary, after the last time she might be waiting for him. Expectant. Eager for a repeat performance. A frenzied last hurrah. Impersonal. Depraved. Surely all modesty was redundant at this stage in their relationship. There, she was in position. Tim knew it was not the moment to hesitate. It was already well past midnight and in a few hours the removalists would be knocking at their front door. Seductively he touched Maureen's hip.

No fucking way, she shouted, and violently pushed Tim's hand aside.

77.

Lucian glanced up from the biographical notes that Michael had written during the afternoon. Pardon?

Why are there no photographs of you around the house?

What would I want to look at myself for?

Okay, sure, but I haven't found anything in the boxes either. The only picture of you I've come across is the same publicity shot that all the newspapers use, which must have been taken when *The Bombardier* was published.

Lucian shrugged and went back to his reading. Don't worry too much about photographs. They tend to be a pretty unreliable source of information.

But you must have a photo album somewhere. And it might help me to place you in different locations.

Lucian pretended not to hear and continued to read.

What about those pictures on your bedroom wall? Michael knew there was a risk that Lucian might complain about his privacy being violated, but as a carer there could be no corner of the house he was prohibited from visiting.

What about them?

You're not in any of them?

Had a close look did you?

Michael stood at the kitchen bench waiting for Lucian to stop being childish.

I'm not in any of them because I'm the person who took them. Seems obvious to me.

But shouldn't we go through them and identify who's who so I could add them to my notes.

Sorry. Can't help you. I don't remember half the faces in those photos. They're strangers to me as much as they are to you.

Michael reproached himself for his lack of sensitivity. Sorry.

No problem. I sometimes forget why you're here as well.

But what about the people you do remember? You don't think it's worth writing down who they are?

Lucian set Michael's notes on the coffee table and stood up with grunt of effort. Come on, come with me. I've told you this before but it seems I have to explain it to you again. He walked into the library and indicated to the shelves lining the room. This is my photo album. An entire lifetime of reading. Every one of these books contains a memory of a place or an event or a person that's more vivid in my mind than any photograph.

All right then, said Michael as he sat in the chair next to Sadie's basket – she rolled onto her back and offered her stomach for him to rub – let's put it to use.

Right now?

Michael reached for the pen and paper that was always on the small round table at the centre of the room. You want to wait until you forget this as well?

Lucian could see that Michael was determined to have his way, and conceded there might be merit in the idea. He turned to his bookshelves looking left and right, up and down. The main difficulty was that there were so many books to choose from. And Lucian was surprised at how many stories he could actually remember.

All right, here we go. *Death Comes for the Archbishop* by Willa Cather. You see for me that book is Ladbroke Grove in London. Grey streets. Grey sky. A basement flat with traffic just outside my front door. Crap job, which after rent and food left me with barely enough money to go to the cinema. Terrible homesickness. And a constant yearning to see the sky. Thankfully the pages of this book are filled with sunlight. Well for me they are at least.

Here's another London one. *Gormenghast* by Mervyn Peake. By the time I was reading this I was on my feet a bit more. Had a better-paid job, knew my way around Soho, and was sharing a house in Kensal Rise with some people who worked in the bookstores along Charing Cross Road. It also reminds of the National Portrait Gallery in St Martin's Place. You ever get the chance to visit it, go and see Mervyn Peake's self-portrait. Captures his sensibility perfectly.

Lucian selected a worn paperback of *The Third Policeman*. Read this in Venice. On the top floor of an apartment in the Jewish Quarter. Like most people the first time I went to Venice I got hopelessly lost. But the second time – the time I read this book – I used public transport and seemed to find my way around just fine. Ate like a king. And I'll never forget the Peggy Guggenheim Collection. More Jackson Pollocks than I'd ever seen before. And you could stand so close to them.

Okay. Here we go. *The Book of Ebenezer Le Page* by G.B. Edwards. To me this book is Greece. A small island with one shop, two restaurants, lots of donkeys, and the sound of turkeys gobbling just before sunset. Stayed there for six weeks doing nothing but reading and writing. Lived in a converted boatshed right on the harbour. Fantastic swimming. And the most exquisite little chapel I've ever seen. The book is set on an island as well so it must have been why I decided to take it with me.

Lucian shuddered as he pulled out Gilbert Sorrentino's *Aberration of Starlight*. I dropped some heavy acid in Canberra once that completely messed with my head, and I remember reading this book three times while I stayed in bed trying to recover. Sorrentino can be a steely mother, but you need that when the bedspread is pulsating.

Whereas this one reminds me of Wood Green, said Lucian as he handed Michael a paperback of *The Man on a Donkey* by H.F.M. Prescott. A friend in London sent it to me after I left Pisa. He thought it might help take my mind off Grace. And I suppose it worked for a while. But now it just reminds me of how bad I felt at the time. Which is a shame really. It's a wonderful book. Should be better known.

The Cardboard Crown by Martin Boyd. Patricia's mother gave me this. Kind woman. Excellent mother-in-law. Tried to make me feel welcome in the family by reading an Australian author. I think it was her first. Reminds me of the deerhound they had as a pet. I'd be reading this on the lawn and he'd walk over and drop down right beside me. Almost on top of me. Lovely animal. I think his name was Fin.

Found this in New Mexico, Lucian said half to himself as he pulled out *The Hearing Trumpet* by Leonora Carrington. Incredibly imaginative book. Unlike anything else I'd read at the time. I must have recommended it to my students because what it reminds me of most is staring at their blank expressions after I asked them what they'd thought of it. I suspect that was the moment my teaching career officially ended.

Lucian gently passed a hand over the cover of *Kristin Lavransdatter* by Sigrid Undset. Softly fanned its pages and inhaled their scent. Smiled. Still smells of Portugal, he said. Angela Carter sent this to me after she read *The Bombardier*. She was working at the University of Adelaide and wrote to her London publisher to buy me a copy on her behalf. But by the time it reached me, and by the time I got around to reading it, she had passed away. Stupid, childish mistake. Imagine not thanking the person who introduces you to such an incredible book. One of my biggest regrets.

78.

Jesus, it's cold.

Paul reached behind and pulled Carl even closer. Warm breath tickled the back of his neck, and toes burrowed into the bottom of his feet. He should have been up half an hour ago, but fear that this might be the last morning Carl spent in his bed made him reluctant to move. For the past week Paul had been counting the days until Carl became a permanent resident of Wood Green. Yet now the date of Tim and Maureen's departure had arrived he wished he could delay it a little longer. He knew that as soon as Carl had a warm house of his own it would be impossible to convince him to spend the night in his poorly heated attic bedroom. Cancelling out the one and only contribution he currently made to their relationship. Carl was already the wealthier of the two. The better educated. Wider travelled. And unquestionably more attractive. His body was refined. Firm. Preposterously strong, with stomach muscles that fascinated Paul's fingertips. Together they had capsized the pub owner's common sense. Propelling him into a reality where he was absent-minded, guileless in conversation and susceptible to crippling bouts of self doubt that exaggerated every tiny fault. How would the two of them ever develop a lasting relationship when they were so uneven? The thought left Paul agitated. Feeling corpulent. Angry that his beauty was insufficient. And determined to better himself. He stopped snacking during the day. Drinking full-fat milk. And refused to use the stool behind the bar in the hope that if he sat down less often he might lose more weight. The effect of which was that his feet and legs ached, he was hungry all the time, uncharacteristically irritable, and oversensitive to the way Penny bristled whenever he mentioned Carl's name. Yes, he could sometimes be pompous and a little too distracted by his mobile phone, but on the other hand Paul liked Carl's audacity, and perseverance to get exactly what he wanted, when he wanted it. Paul knew he needed to develop something similar in himself, and if that meant suppressing other parts of his personality then it was a small price to pay. For the consolation was no longer being alone. Maybe that was what Penny was so upset about. Did she detect his happiness and feel threatened by it? Was she scared that he and Carl were falling in love and it was going to leave her alone with Matthew? Was Carl simply too inconvenient for Penny? Paul's thoughts digressed further and further until the carnal movements of Carl's hands returned him to the present. All the happiness he had felt upon waking suddenly rematerialised and dispelled his anxiety about thick ankles and getting up late. He was just thankful for everything he had, and reached behind to pull Carl even closer.

79.

This going as well luv?

Maureen turned to the perspiring man pointing at the Formica table. Heavy feet were still moving in the room above her head, though it appeared the removalists were about to start work on the kitchen. She nodded, then returned to staring at the backyard and feeling betrayed. The note Maureen had placed inside Lucian's pocket had invited him to pay a final late-night visit, and it was 2am by the time she realised his silhouette was not going to appear behind the frosted glass in the back door. The secret hole in the wall beside the rosemary shrub where they had previously left all correspondence was also empty, leaving Maureen to conclude that in spite of all the effort she had invested in their relationship, Lucian's icy reserve remained intact. It clearly existed somewhere deep beneath his skin. So his hands and prick were warm enough to enjoy her tits and arse, while his vital organs remained insulated from her touch. Maureen stepped into the drizzle to farewell the chickens. Carl had reluctantly agreed to take over their care, and she assumed it would be a matter of only weeks before one of them ended up in the oven. Hope that Lucian would appear from the scrub behind the coop was quickly usurped by a fear that perhaps something had gone wrong. Had Lucian fallen down in the dark? Was he lying in the bush somewhere waiting for help to arrive? Wondering why Maureen had not organised a search party to comb the forest? His leg had better be broken, she thought, otherwise he was being particularly spineless and cruel.

This going as well?

Maureen returned to the kitchen and found the biggest, hairiest removalist about to wheel out the refrigerator. No, sorry, that's staying. Look, let me show you what needs to go.

As she passed through the house noting how small it looked without any furniture, Maureen lamented the way every detail would eventually fade from her memory, just like all the other houses she had lived in. The thought perturbed her, and she looked about the shop – the only room left undisturbed – to try to memorise its features. The counter. The till. The fridge doors and coffee machine. The bell above the front door whose tinkle infiltrated her dreams. She knew she would also miss the pot-bellied stove – its smell of hot iron and ash, and the late-night warmth that had made her feel more content and happy than at any other time in her life.

Through the shop window Maureen saw a small crowd gathered in front of Paul's pub. Half the people she would never think of again, while saying goodbye to the other half was sure to make her cry. If only Lucian has been braver, Maureen thought. She wanted to put this period of her life behind her, yet knew it would be impossible to untangle herself from Wood Green until Lucian had bestowed a parting kiss. Did he know this as well? By not turning up was Lucian somehow saying he wanted her to stay? But that, Maureen acknowledged, was probably the most sentimental thought she had had all morning.

This too luv?

She turned. Yes thanks. That too.

80.

The dozen people standing beneath the rusted awning at the front of Paul's pub shuffled slowly back and forth to keep warm and avoid the drizzle being blown sideways by the wind. They had congregated to give Tim and Maureen a community farewell, but their patience was waning as the removalists continued to load out what seemed to be an endless supply of boxes and furniture. Some had already returned to their stools saying they had never liked that prick Tim anyway, and were boasting about how they still owed the shop twenty-five dollars. Fuck's chance of getting it now, they said with a laugh at how clever they had been.

Matthew stood inside his mother's coat with her arms folded across his chest, and looked up as Michael made small talk about the lunch menu.

I'd recommend the curry today, Penny said. It'll keep you warm all afternoon.

You live with Lucian, don't you? asked Matthew.

That's right. Are you helping your mum in the kitchen today?

Matthew nodded. I made the hamburgers.

Well maybe I'll have one of those instead.

You get chips with it.

Sounds too good to resist.

Matthew scrunched up his nose. But the curry is better.

Penny beamed and kissed her son's crown. This is Matthew.

Good to meet you Matthew. How old are you?

Nine, but I'll be ten in January. Do you like Lego? I've got six Lego figures from the Batman series. But I'm going to buy two more at the end of the school holidays.

You know I do like Lego. But I don't get much of an opportunity to play with it these days.

You could come to our house. I've got heaps.

Thanks. I might take you up on that. Maybe not today though, I've got to get back to work. But another day for sure, okay?

Okay. Any time you want.

There he goes, said Paul as Carl crossed the street.

Shouldn't be long now, said Michael.

Finally the truck roared to life and the removalists began to negotiate the winding road down the side of Mount Wellington. With the large vehicle gone everyone could see inside the shop as Tim handed over the keys to Carl.

Is Lucian coming down? asked Penny.

No, he's in bed with a cold.

Where are Tim and Maureen going? asked Matthew.

We don't know yet, his mother answered. They're staying in Hobart for a few nights, then I think Tim is flying to Melbourne.

But who's going to help Carl?

We all are, said Paul.

I'm not giving that prick my money, murmured a voice from within the crowd.

Paul tried to pretend he had not heard it, and felt the birth of a suspicion that Penny had already begun her campaign for a boycott of Carl's business.

The front door opened and Tim walked into the middle of the road to look back at the general store. Those waiting at the front of the pub could see he was enjoying a moment of reflection, but it was too cold to indulge him for long.

Hey Tim you bastard, you still owe me a beer.

Tim held up his wallet and announced he was buying everyone a drink.

The crowd gave up a cheer as Paul said, Bloody hell, and dashed inside to man the taps.

Maureen did not look back as she crossed the road. A Mars bar and two rolls of Life Savers appeared from her pocket as she winked at Matthew and handed him the booty. Stole 'em.

Matthew checked with his mum, whose smile confirmed that Maureen was only joking and it was fine for him to accept the gift.

Lucian is still sick, Michael blurted out before she could ask.

Well tell him I hope he feels better, and give him this from me. Maureen kissed Michael on the side of his mouth.

Best of luck, he said.

You too.

Michael then walked inside the pub to say goodbye to Tim and order a take-away lunch for two.

Meanwhile Penny and Maureen made promises to keep in touch and visit one another, which both of them suspected they were never going to keep.

81.

How are you feeling?

I think I might have the same thing you had. All I want to do is sleep. And I ache all over. Like my whole body is being squeezed in a vice.

Well just rest and you'll probably feel better tomorrow. Lucian leaned into the room and placed a cup of herbal tea at the head of the daybed where Michael lay prone. Have you taken any aspirin?

Yes, thanks. Sorry about this. I'm the one who's supposed to be looking after you.

Nonsense. I can still take care of myself.

I'll get up and do some work in a couple of hours. All I need is a little more sleep.

Forget the work. Just get better and we'll catch up over the next few days.

Michael nodded, pulled the blankets to his chin and shut his eyes.

Lucian closed the office door and returned to the sitting room where Sadie dozed in front of a cheerful fire, and everything needed for an extravagant spliff had been arranged on the table between the two armchairs. Lucian knew he should probably eat lunch first, but all he wanted was to wallow in his thoughts while watching the flames grow animated. No music. No reading. Snow lay thick on the ground outside and more was forecast for later that evening. The roads would be closed for at least forty-eight hours. No cars or newspapers. No need to step outside except for a breath of fresh air. As he assembled his joint Lucian noticed the skin of his fingers was dry and thin; growing translucent so he could watch his life force slowly draining away. Though his sprained ankle had healed enough for him to walk, it still hurt most days, and Lucian could tell that his balance would never be the same again. So he willed it to become even worse as he inhaled deeply on his spliff. The task for the afternoon was to discover just how high he could become. An idea so enticing that Lucian considered rolling a second joint even as his respiration grew constricted and his blood pressure stepped off a cliff. Fortunately he was already sitting down so there was nowhere to collapse except further into his chair. It reminded Lucian of the day Maureen had found him face down in the backyard. Despite his veneer of indifference, her departure from Wood Green had left an ache inside his chest that he could neither dismiss nor ignore. The decision to end their affair had been necessary to protect Maureen from the calamity of what he was about to go through, but sometimes the misfortune of not meeting her earlier in his life felt too cruel to bear. If only he had had a few more years then Lucian was certain he would have proposed. But to burden such a bewitching beauty with an old man whose memory was disintegrating felt immoral. The fortifications of Lucian's reality began to crumble and his thoughts wandered to Grace and the question of whether she still lived in Pisa. Or had she returned to Galway to look after her ageing parents? More than likely they were dead by now, along with Patricia's mother and father. A fraternity Lucian would be joining in the not too distant future. It was not so bad, he thought. As long as he managed to finish his latest book he did not really want for much more. And even if he did, he would not allow childish longing to undermine the pleasure of his remaining days. He had recently arrived at the reassuring revelation that the world did not depend on him to exist. In his absence, all the things he loved in life would continue to flourish. And it made his approaching departure feel more tranquil. It had been a strange life. And at no point could he remember ever feeling in control of it. It had never been boring. There had been plenty of laughter, ample love, and though writing had exacted a terrible price, Lucian could think of no occupation he might otherwise have dedicated himself to. Unwittingly, he realised that he was content, and his traditional bag of worries were not worthy of further consideration. After all of life's struggles and sacrifices he was able to sit on top of a mountain, or on the side of it at least, and have a happy death. The idea caught him so unawares that he wondered if he was merely being frivolous. Would he have felt an equivalent epiphany without a skull full of THC? He reminded himself that he still had a book to finish. That it was necessary to maintain the fire in his belly right until the end. But he could not deny the interior transformation that had taken place. At last he felt ready to take the next step without regret or despondence. What was there to fear? The others had done it this way, and now it was his turn. And anyway, how could he avoid it? Why on earth would anyone wish to do so? At this stage, dying was what he was meant to do. And it felt closer to living life to the full than some strange wish for immortality in a world that was done with you. Twenty years was twenty years, and this was just part of the bargain. A necessary process for things to move forward. The most logical progression.

82.

Michael could feel himself laughing with Ursula as he looked down at her sock covered with mud. Without explanation he knew her gumboot had become stuck in the field and she had stepped out of it by accident. There were two teeth missing from the front of her mouth, and her hair was tied back in a ponytail that reminded him of their mother. Plovers standing like sentinels of the vacant lot flew up into the air as Ursula lost her balance and toppled over. When he reached forward to help her up, her face changed into a Vietnamese girl whose terrified expression vanished as a bullet tore though the side of her head. He saw John Driscoll lower his rifle without emotion and insist they had no time to take prisoners. The small hand fell from his grasp as his father stood at the back door and called for them to come inside and get clean. He recognised the house he had grown up in, and the cellar door he had hid behind to set alight pieces of paper rolled into pretend cigarettes. He could hear his aunt running around above his head yelling, Fire, Fire, while two policemen entered through the side gate to club a large water rat curled into the corner of their back fence. When the show was over they returned to a Sunday lunch noticeably lacking in meat. So he took Ursula fishing at Blackmans Bay. The wind kept blowing his line into the shore but a man sitting outside the shops offered to buy them fish and chips if Ursula would come for a drive in his car. She said it wasn't fair that he got to go away to Vietnam while she had to stay in Tasmania. Their father stood at the back of the crowd and touched the brim of his hat as tugboats steered the ship away from the pier. He tasted the salt of the ocean and saw before him a table strewn with lemon wedges and an empty bottle of tequila. Outside the sun was raging and he knew it was time to leave for work. His stomach hurt and he walked to the kitchen for a glass of milk. Except there was too much sand piled in front of the refrigerator door. He pulled so hard the handle broke off and he fell into the mud next to his sister, laughing at the mess they had made of themselves.

83.

Michael woke in pain. The aspirin he had swallowed before going to bed had run its course and now his body lay entirely unprotected from the symptoms of the virus. He tried to go back to sleep, but the disturbing images still sloshing about his brain, and the menace of the ache humming along his skeleton would not be ignored. He had been working too hard. Why else would he be dreaming about Lucian's life? Michael tried to banish all memory of the dead Vietnamese girl, and Ursula's smile as she sat in the car eating fish and chips. How did he even know what Ursula looked like at that age? He didn't of course. It was just a dream. A stupid dream. No matter how convincing it had all seemed, none of it was real. Michael told himself to open his eyes. He was feverish. Surprised to find himself damp with sweat. Unsure if he was able even to move. In the hours since lying down gravity appeared to have become heavier and more hateful. Michael started to pant with fear. This did not feel like any flu he had suffered before. He forced himself to sit up. Ignore the tenderness in his legs. And stand, no matter how dangerously he swayed, or close he came to colliding with boxes. The house was dark but he could find the bathroom without turning on a light. The glowing embers in the sitting room fireplace revealed Lucian slumped in an armchair. The familiar reek explained the situation perfectly, but Michael felt too frail to assist the aged stoner into bed. The cold tiles of the bathroom floor soothed his bare feet as his fingers located nail scissors, tweezers and dental floss. However the aspirin proved elusive and forced him to pull the cord for the small light above the medicine cabinet. Its brightness stung his eyes and he hurriedly located the large rectangular box of pills. An excessive dose measured out, Michael bent to the tap to wash it down. He then shut the mirrored door and saw skin with no colour, teeth in urgent need of brushing, and eyeballs red and sore. Captivated by a face he scarcely recognised, Michael prodded his chin and nose to confirm they were indeed his own. Despairing, he turned off the light, took another sip of water and shuffled back through the house. He must have woken Sadie as he could hear her claws tapping the floorboards behind him. When he lay down she leapt onto the bed and settled on top of his feet. Michael appreciated the additional warmth and impatiently willed the aspirin to blunt his pain so he could drift back to sleep and have dreams that this time would hopefully reference people and places from his own life.

84.

Midday, thought Carl, and only three customers so far. He had been up since 5.30am, baking and burning croissants, and in that time had sold only one litre of milk, four tomatoes, and a pack of cigarettes. How was he supposed to cover costs with sales like that? He had not expected the residents of Wood Green to be quite so shy. But perhaps the snow was keeping them inside. Carl knew *he* certainly would not have got out of bed if it had been possible, but Tim and Maureen had insisted that days when it snowed could be some of their busiest. People running out of food, hiring DVDs, or just looking for a little conversation beyond their immediate family, especially before the pub opened its doors. Carl fed the pot-bellied stove another piece of wood.

Jesus it's cold, he exclaimed as the bell above the front door sounded.

Paul sent me over to ask if you wanted any lunch, said Matthew.

No thanks. Carl returned to the counter. Tell him I'm finishing off the leftovers from last night's dinner.

Matthew scanned the shelves where the novelty toys were stocked and picked up a plastic pink pig that released a sugared pellet from its rear end every time its tail was raised. Tim had sometimes given him toys like this for free, but it was not yet clear whether Carl was planning on being as generous.

We're having sausages and mash today. With gravy.

Sounds good, said Carl as he picked up his phone and began a fresh search of South Africa's news sites.

Or there's vegetarian lasagne for people who don't like meat.

Well I'm not one of those.

Me either. I like sausages. They might be my favourite food after spaghetti bolognese and lamb chops. Matthew continued to fondle the toy. It was the last day of the school holidays and he wondered how much money Paul was going to pay him for his work in the kitchen. Maybe it would be enough to buy his Lego figurines *and* the pink pig. He returned the toy to the shelf. Carl wasn't going to give it to him for free no matter how long he stood there admiring it.

Well I'd better get going.

By the time Carl looked up Matthew had crossed the street and disappeared back inside the pub. It was generous of Paul to offer him lunch, but Carl felt he was already growing fat from standing behind a counter all day. He was used to being more active, driving around in his car, drumming up business deals and taking meetings. When such work made him tired and frustrated the idea of serving inside a shop all day had seemed like heaven. But being so sedentary offered fewer pleasures than he had imagined. Already he was feeling trapped. Carl understood that a degree of disenchantment was to be expected at such an early stage in a new job, in a new place. And yet each afternoon he found himself spending more and more time on the internet, and questioning whether coming to Wood Green had been a good idea. What he needed was to hire someone to help. That way he could take a few hours off to relax and investigate what else Hobart had to offer. Someone like Matthew's mother would be perfect. Paul was always going on about how hard Penny worked in the kitchen. And if he offered cash in hand then it wouldn't cost that much. Otherwise he was going to have to start keeping shorter trading hours. Lack of sleep always affected his optimism, so staying up half the night with Paul probably wasn't helping either. He enjoyed their time together on a physical level, but their lack of common interests was becoming a trial. Once they had finished discussing whether Mrs Whatshername was going to move into a retirement village, and if the new house being built up the road was too large and too ugly, Carl wanted to talk about news and politics and where the local economy might be heading. But every time he tried to raise such topics Paul's face expressed utter bewilderment as to how such things could possibly be of interest.

85.

The sheets were clean. There was no blood on his fingers. His head did not feel sore or seem to have a bump on it. He looked under the covers. Two old feet at the end of pyjamas. Out the window the sun was shining but inside it felt cold. He pulled the blankets tight around his body. Who were the people in those photographs on the wall? He stood up. Scanned their faces. Nope. No. No. No. He didn't recognise any of them. Shivering. Maybe he should go back to bed. He turned to the desk. Saw a note stuck to the wall above it. 'Read the papers in the bottom drawer.' Bottom drawer of what? The filing cabinet of course, don't be stupid. He sat on the floor. Opened the drawer. There were fifty or sixty pages. All typed with dates and names. But who was the *You* they talked about? Maybe the *You* was one of the people in the photographs. He stood up. Left the papers on the floor. Did people still use old typewriters like that? He was cold. Tired. Then he heard someone walking in the hall. He hurried back to bed. Listened to the clatter of an old typewriter. Watched the one on the desk but saw the keys weren't moving. He pulled the blankets to his mouth. Someone else was in the house. Maybe a murderer. Come to kill him. Or a burglar. To steal his possessions. But what possessions did he own? He got up. Removed the photographs from the wall. Piled them on the end of his bed. The robber can have those. He didn't want them. Who were they of anyway? Maybe if he studied their faces...The typewriter stopped. Had there even been a sound? The keys of the machine on the desk certainly weren't moving. There were the footsteps again. He got back into bed. Some of the photographs fell to the floor. Who was out there? What did he want? Was it even a man? It might be a female burglar. Then what did *she* want? A knock at the door. He refused to answer. Pretended he wasn't there. Maybe then the burglar would just go away.

Lucian? Are you all right? It's time to get up.

Who was Lucian? What were all those photographs doing on the end of the bed? Who had taken them off the wall? The doorknob was turning. Someone was coming into the room. *His* room. At least he thought it was his room.

Lucian? Are you awake?

He saw a man. Just standing there. Was that the burglar? He needed to go to the toilet. He was going to the toilet. Tears on his cheeks. He was cold. But out the window the day looked sunny.

Lucian isn't here, he shouted. I don't know any Lucian. Lucian isn't here.

86.

No doctors.

But what if you...

No doctors or the deal is off.

As Michael sat on the floor of the sitting room he could smell the pot of tea brewing on the kitchen bench and feel the vibrations of the washing machine's spin cycle. You don't think what happened is cause for concern?

Lucian had become hypnotised by the ripples travelling back and forth across the surface of his bath.

Lucian, are you all right?

He groaned. Stop asking me that. Of course I am. And of course I think what happened is cause for concern. But I can't pretend it's unexpected. You thought it was going to be just cocktails and discussions about Hemingway? Well guess what? Papa caused more trouble than he was worth, and so might I. There's no guarantee that what happened today won't happen again. But that's what you signed up for. And it'd be pretty gutless to try and back out now things are getting a little unsavoury.

I haven't any intention of backing out. I just thought a doctor might be able to prescribe something to slow down the process, or help with the pain.

I'm not in any pain, and if I were I'd choose my own form of medication thank you very much. And why on earth would I want to slow down the process? You think I like being this way? Wetting the bed and being treated like an invalid? Fuck extending that. I'm ready to check out the moment my book is finished.

Michael took the opportunity to change the subject. So how's it going? How far are you through?

Why? You want to know how much longer you have to hang around for?

Stop being childish, of course not. I'm a fan of your work, remember? I can't wait to read what you're working on.

Lucian splashed at the ripples in frustration. Well it's coming along I suppose. A first draft might be all I get finished, but I reckon you can tidy it up for me.

You mean that?

I don't imagine you'd mess it up worse than anyone else. Just promise me not to touch the punctuation. Start unravelling that and you'll never get it back together. And try to remember that it's okay *not* to change things. If you don't understand something then the fault may not necessarily be with the book. Same goes for when you feel the urge to smooth out one of my sentences. Those rough edges and awkward rhythms are there for a reason. It's called character – my character. Don't worry if you don't feel in control. I probably don't want you to be. Personally, I read so I can have a break from being in control. Let someone else steer my consciousness for a while. That's why it's relaxing. That's why it's stimulating. I get to visit another person's mind and witness how it works. Learn what it knows. I'm not scared to have my way of thinking challenged. In fact I'm bloody grateful when it happens. Being shown the world in a different light is what makes a book great, isn't it?

Of course it is.

Well then keep that in mind when you're about to use your red pen.

I promise I'll be more than careful with it. I'm just so flattered you'd give me the responsibility. I really am. I'd be happy to have a look now if you're worried about it.

No thanks. I've always had a policy about not showing my work to anyone before it's finished.

Sure, I understand. Do you want your tea in there?

Yes please. I haven't had a bath in ages. I'd forgotten how pleasant it can be. Push play on the CD player while you're out there.

As Michael poured the tea the house filled with a squealing horn, steady snare, and deep, lugubrious voice. He delivered Lucian's cup to the corner of the tub then returned to his position outside the bathroom door. You wouldn't prefer to listen to something a little more peaceful?

I'm not dead yet, said Lucian. And there are few records more peaceful to my ears than Bailter Space's first album.

Is that one of the records you'd...

What?

Forget it. It was stupid idea.

I can't stand it when people don't finish their sentences. Tell me.

I'd really prefer not to.

Well now you bloody well have to.

Michael sighed. I was just wondering if this was one of the records you'd choose to have played at your funeral. Sorry. It was stupid. I spoke before I thought.

Jesus, you're a morbid person to have around. I have one little episode and already you're measuring me for a casket.

I tried not to say it but you insisted.

Who cares what they play at my funeral. I won't be able to hear it. Although I suppose it is the last opportunity I'll have to force my taste on other people. What about you? Have you got a song in mind?

Michael remained silent.

Not too pleasant to think about is it?

It's not that. I'm just trying to come up with something.

'The Black and Crazy Blues' by Roland Kirk.

That's what you'd like?

It's the opening song on *The Inflated Tear*. I'd play the whole album if I could. But if I only get one song, then that would be it. Sweetest, saddest tune you'll ever hear.

87.

Tim sipped his coffee and again judged it as inferior to the brew that Maureen used to make every morning. It was just another of the changes he had struggled to acclimatise to, along with waking up alone in bed and not being able to bite into a freshly baked croissant as soon as he walked downstairs. There were a few new faces in the B&B's dining room, and as he listened to their discussions about the day ahead it occurred to Tim that he too was free to go shopping or sightseeing if he liked. With no cartons of milk or boxes of chips to load in, no firewood to chop, customers to serve or small-talk to make with the drinkers in Paul's pub, he could spend his time whatever way he liked. His financial arrangements with Maureen had been finalised the day before, after which they had amicably shaken hands and walked in opposite directions. Now it was just a matter of waiting the necessary months before he could apply for a divorce, which he could do from anywhere.

Tim opened his newspaper as Andrew returned to the room carrying a tray of bacon and eggs. After three mornings of listening to the proprietor's stories about people who had stayed at the B&B – the majority of which had ended with a tone of grievance about some incident of selfishness or rude behaviour – Tim had made sure to enter the dining room with a newspaper under his arm. Andrew seemed to get the message and haughtily transferred his attentions to another guest who was sitting alone. The young woman tried to disguise her disappointment, but convinced only Andrew that she was not being inconvenienced by her sudden acquisition of a breakfast companion. From behind his newspaper Tim overheard the same stories he had been told a few days ago, and commiserated with the woman who was nodding her head and eating her breakfast as fast as she could. The sight of Andrew occupied encouraged Tim to take his time, enjoy his meal, scan the headlines, and admire the models advertising an underwear sale. A news story about food being wasted due to poor refrigeration procedures held his professional interest for two or three paragraphs, but a line about tomatoes came too close to reminding him of his own irregular practices. As Tim brought the sides of the newspaper together to turn the page he saw Andrew sitting at his table. Tim looked around the room and realised he was the last person to finish his breakfast.

Anything in the news this morning? enquired Andrew.

No, nothing important. Just the usual.

Yes, yes it seems the same every day, doesn't it? You know I've often wondered if they just repeat the same stories over and over. Sometimes I'm positive I've read them before.

I think they'd get in a quite a lot of trouble if they were caught doing something like that.

Yes, yes, I suppose you're right, although someone would have to notice it first, wouldn't they?

Tim folded his newspaper. Someone would notice. They always do.

Really? You think people are that observant?

About things like that? Definitely.

My experience is that people are only ever interested in what concerns them directly, and what they can get for themselves.

I can understand how you might feel like that sometimes. I used to work in the service industry myself. But I guess it just gets back to that old argument of whether your glass is half full or half empty.

You know I've always been a little confused by that one. If my glass is three-quarters empty, does that mean I'm pessimistic because I don't think a quarter of a glass is enough?

Tim pushed back his chair. It's an interesting point. Unfortunately, I've got to get going. Lots to do today.

Yes, yes, I'm busy as well. We should pick this up again tomorrow. I rather enjoy a philosophical discussion to start the day. Andrew followed Tim to the dining room door. What part of the service industry were you in?

Huh? Oh, I used to own a general store up on the mountain. In a place called Wood Green.

Oh yes, I know someone who lives up there.

Really. What was their name? Maybe I know them as well.

You know, isn't it always the way. As soon I mentioned him his name completely disappeared from my brain. Maybe it'll come back to me tomorrow. The same again for breakfast?

Yes please, said Tim as he started up the stairs.

Coffee? Tea?

Tea please.

But you had coffee today. And the day before that. In the mood for a bit of change are we? Well they do say it's good for us. See you tomorrow at breakfast.

88.

Cautiously Michael leaned backwards, ready to grip the edge of his desk should his chair suddenly tip sideways and try to spill him onto the floor. With the latest pages of his book in hand, he was checking for the spelling mistakes that inevitably appeared whenever he used a manual typewriter. Michael wrote his initial draft by pen, but recently had started revising using Lucian's spare machine. The ailing author said he found the sound soothing, and Michael was only too happy to provide comfort any way he could.

He needed to start thinking about dinner. It was his turn to cook tonight. It was his turn to cook most nights these days. Michael didn't mind. Lucian's more recent meals had begun to reveal the extent to which his memory was unravelling. Dubious combinations of ingredients and under-cooked meat; while other times it was clear that Lucian had lost track what dish he was supposed to be preparing. Michael just ate it. Pointing out mistakes only detonated Lucian's temper, and unleashed latent accusations about catastrophic injustices. Reiterations of disputes that had already been resolved, and a deluge of emphatic claims about blatant disloyalty. In the aftermath of such insensible rancour Lucian wallowed in grief; made heart-felt promises never to do it again, and scattered fresh memos around the house that repeated the same logical advice but failed to rectify any of the problems. The most unfortunate outcome, however, was a further decline in his health. He dozed more often. And increasingly gave a stupefied expression to the most simple questions. Other times Lucian was his old self. Sharper than Michael could ever hope to be. Shrewd. Dominant. Confident. Priceless. And during those moments Michael was able to believe that nothing was different. Though they never lasted for long.

He stood up and stretched. His back was sore and his eyes felt tired. He knew he probably needed glasses, but a visit to the optometrist would have to wait until he had more time. In the hall he listened for the plod of Lucian passing through the house like a sleepwalker. When he heard only silence, Michael peeked inside Lucian's bedroom and found him dozing in the chair beside the window. The blanket that usually lived on top of Lucian's bed was soaking in a bucket, so Michael searched around for the old dressing gown that Lucian was so fond of wearing. He found it hanging on the back of the bedroom door, in front of an old photograph that he had never noticed before. He draped the dressing gown over Lucian's lap then carried the picture to the hall. It was the first he had found in the house that featured a face he recognised, but it was not Lucian he saw in the middle of the five uniformed men standing arm in arm on the streets of Saigon. The face staring back with a cigarette dangling from the side of his mouth was his own. Michael rushed to the bathroom and looked at his reflection in the mirror. Then the photograph. The mirror. Then the photograph. It was uncanny. A thinner version to be sure, but it was unmistakably his face.

89.

Penny tapped the bell to announce that two lunches were ready to be picked up, and waited for Paul at the service counter. Why do you think I would do something like that?

Paul inspected the plates as if he needed to check Penny's work before he served it to his customers. It just seems strange to me, that's all.

You think I have that much influence in this town?

Paul rearranged a lettuce leaf then carried the plates into the pub.

Penny started to pack up the kitchen while she waited for Paul to return and finish the argument that had begun as soon as she arrived at work. Penny had not suspected anything was wrong. Matthew was back at school, over his small cold, her car had started on its second try, and Mrs Harding had finally agreed to call a plumber to fix the dripping taps in the bathroom. All was right with the world. Then bam! The moment Paul walked downstairs he had started levelling accusations at her about trying to ruin his life and destroy his happiness.

What are you talking about? asked Penny.

Don't pretend you don't know.

Actually, I really don't.

I told you he wouldn't hit me again and he hasn't.

So this is about Carl?

Of course it is. He's quickly going broke because of you.

What have I got to do with it?

Because you told everyone in Wood Green not to shop at the general store, didn't you.

No. Of course not.

Don't lie to me Penny, you're no good at it.

Paul, I never said a word to anyone. And why are you being so rude to me?

Because if you don't stop it he's going to leave and I'm going to be alone again on this bloody mountain.

I'm not doing or saying anything. What happens at the general store has nothing to do with me.

Then why is no one shopping there anymore? Tell me that.

I have no idea. I bought some butter from Carl just yesterday. And I see people going in there all the time.

Not as many as before though. You'll have to admit that.

How should I know? I'm not sitting around watching who goes in and out.

Carl says that some days he's not even close to covering his costs.

Well he's got to give it time. It's only been a few weeks.

Still, it doesn't make any sense. And if I find out you're telling people not to shop there I'll...

You'll what?

Jesus, said Paul as he turned and walked into the pub. You're supposed to be my best friend.

And you're supposed to be mine, she called after him.

The tension between the two of them persisted all day, and as a result Paul poured beer with either too much head or too little, while Penny cooked as if it were just a job. Only when the last plates from lunch were going through the dishwasher did Paul return to the kitchen.

I'm sorry for talking to you that way, he said. I don't want to fight anymore.

Penny stood with her arms folded, leaning against the sink, refusing to speak.

It's just that Carl said he thought it was strange how so few people were coming in, even for things like bread and milk. And I remembered what you said that time he hurt my eye, about sending him bankrupt, and I guess I just put two and two together and got five. I'm sorry. I won't do it again. I promise.

Penny could see how Paul was suffering. You're in love with him, aren't you?

Paul shrugged. I suppose. I feel like rubbish most of the time, I can't pour a beer to save my life, I'm yelling at my best friend, and I'm imagining things that aren't real. Yep, I'd say I'm in love. Either that or going crazy.

It's often a fine line.

I always thought it was supposed to make you happy.

That's just the marketing.

Paul nodded. He didn't know what else to say but still wanted to talk.

There's nothing you can do, said Penny. If Carl can't make the general store work then it's not your fault...or mine for that matter. He wouldn't be the first. You of all people know how many owners it's had. And Tim and

Maureen were the best. Carl can't expect it to be the same straight away. It took them years to get it right. Remember what it was like when they first arrived?

Paul shook his head.

Well I do. And they had each other to share the load. Carl is on his own. Of course he has you, but you've got your own business to run.

He's tried to find someone to work part time, but he says there's no one around here who wants a job.

Well that doesn't sound right, does it? This is Tasmania. There are always people who need work.

That's what I said.

What's he offering for wages? The people I know who need a job are not school kids looking for extra pocket money.

Yeah but he's just starting out. He can't afford to pay top money.

I don't think anyone around here would be expecting anything more than fair wages. It's what you've always paid me. We've not been put on earth for Carl's benefit.

I know, I know. But I can't help feeling that people are ganging up on him. They're such a closed-minded bunch in this town. They never like anyone new. Least of all some poof from South Africa.

Penny put away the last of the plates and threw her apron in the laundry bag. I don't know anything about that. But I do know they've never had a problem with their publican being gay.

90.

Try to eat a little more if you can.

Lucian shook his head. He was sitting on his couch in the sunroom watching the wind bend trees and scatter leaves across the backyard.

Michael finished his own bowl of pasta then carried the dishes to the sink. Are you warm enough?

Yes, thank you. Don't let me keep you from your work. I'm perfectly happy sitting here.

It's okay. I'm pretty much done for the day.

So early?

I've been doing extra work at night.

Yes, I suppose I'm not a very exciting companion to live with these days. Early to bed. No appetite. And sleepy as soon as I wake up.

Shall I put some music on?

Not at the moment. I'm enjoying listening to wind blow down the chimney.

Would you mind if we talked a little?

Not at all. What would you like to talk about?

I've found something, and I don't quite understand what it is.

May I see it?

Michael returned to the sunroom with the photograph he had discovered on the back of Lucian's bedroom door.

The author's thumbs caressed the frame as he stared and smiled and muttered that he could never bring himself to get rid of this one.

What do you mean?

Lucian held up a finger, briefly closed his eyes, then pointed to each of the five faces. Bill, Nick, Lucian, Frank and Jerry. How's that for a memory. More than forty years on and I still know their names.

Had Michael not been preoccupied with another matter he would have been impressed. You say that's you in the middle there?

Of course it is. Well an earlier version of me. Who else could it be?

You don't think there's a resemblance with anyone else?

Who do you have in mind?

Well, me, for instance?

Lucian glanced back and forth between Michael and the photograph. I can see that. But I'd be worried if there wasn't by this stage.

Sorry?

You're already at least twenty-eight, if not thirty.

I'm thirty-four actually. But what has that got to do with it?

Here, you should put this in the garbage.

Michael suspected that Lucian was slipping into another episode of confusion.

Maybe I'll keep it a little while longer.

You can't stop what's happening, so why try? he said as he handed back the photograph. That's what all of us have been told right from the very first one.

The first what?

Lucian of course.

I thought you were Lucian?

I am.

Maybe it's time you had a lie down.

There'll be plenty of time for that soon enough. You need to listen to what I'm trying to tell you.

Okay. But perhaps you should rest first.

Put that photo in the garbage. It'll only confuse matters. I can tell you everything you need to know. There's no need to go snooping and digging. Nothing has been hidden from you. What would be the point of that?

All right, don't get upset. This is nothing important.

Upset? Of course I'm upset. No one wants it to end. Especially after so much effort. In 1992 this moment seemed like a lifetime away. But twenty years feels pretty short when you're at the end of it. Do me a favour and don't waste your time like I did. Too much fooling around with women and drugs. Thought I had all the time in the world. But take the advice that was given to me when I was in your position. Buckle down. Do the work. It's what all of us have been striving towards, and now it's up to you to bring it home. I doubt there are going to be any more. And the rest of us have worked too hard for you to mess it up. You're the closing chapter. If it's going to work then you've got to come through for us. We need a strong finish, otherwise it'll all have been for nothing.

Bring what home? Who are these others you're talking about?

Lucian scrunched his face with impatience. Others. Others. Seventy-two, and the one you're holding in your hand.

Listen. You're not making any sense. All I need is for you to tell me how I came to be in this photograph.

But it's not you.

I thought you just said it was.

No I didn't. I said it was Lucian.

91.

1958 – On the morning of your first day at school you inform your teacher how unfair it is that Ursula is not allowed to attend with you. She has been crying, you say, as if no further evidence is necessary to prove the injustice of the situation. At lunchtime you walk the mile and a half home to tell Ursula that it will soon be over, and find her playing happily with your aunt. For a moment you feel betrayed, as if she has lied to you, or forgotten you, or simply replaced you. But then you feel relief that Ursula is going to be all right. You return to the playground and tell your teacher how your sister has stopped crying, and receive a smack with a ruler as punishment for leaving the school grounds. Ursula says she is never going to a school that gives out smacks, and your father insists the teacher did the right thing. Ursula declares that before she is sent to school she is going to run away and marry a king who will let her lock all the teachers in a dungeon and throw the key in the moat. Beneath the dinner table you hold Ursula's hand to prevent her from growing too angry as it always makes your father angry as well. After dinner you describe the games you played, and the new friends you made. How the smack was not so hard. Certainly not as hard as Father's. But Ursula insists she will never go to school, and if anyone tries to make her she will call the police and have them taken to jail. You lie down beside her and feel the anger pulsing through her limbs. You try to make her think of something else, tell her stories about your mother. The way she smelled of apricots, or the funny names she called you both. None of it is true. Your mother died when you were too young to remember anything about her. But the stories have become as real as any memories might be. Lying by her side is the only way to get Ursula to sleep when she is upset, and often you wake up next to her in the morning. Your father says it must stop. That soon it will be time for the pair of you to grow up. But until you depart for army training you remain the person Ursula says goodnight to last of all. And for weeks after you ship out she cannot sleep until she has rolled one of your shirts into a ball and placed it on the pillow beside her head.

92.

From the reading chair beside the bedroom window Michael watched Lucian's eyes gradually close. It had been the same every day for the past two weeks, ever since Lucian had insisted he wanted nothing more than to stay in bed and listen to Michael read aloud from the notes he had written. Lucian said he had forgotten almost everything about his life. The places he had been. The people he had known. He wanted to be told what he had done with his time. And asked questions about the books with his name printed on them. Who were the women he had married? Had he been a good husband? And why were there no pictures of his children and grandchildren for him to look at? To Michael it felt as if their roles had been reversed. Instead of interviewing Lucian about his life, Lucian was interviewing him. And Michael was surprised at how many questions he could answer with authority. He realised that this was the moment for which he had been hired. The task he had spent months preparing for. To recount to Lucian the story of his life. The remarkable things he had achieved. And every day, at almost the same hour, Michael watched Lucian fall asleep with an expression of satisfaction on his face.

93.

Lucian lay perfectly still and covertly scanned the details of Michael's face. Does he know? Does he even suspect? Has he noticed any irregularities? Surely he must have seen the hairs growing out of the pores at the end of his nose. The size of his ears increasing? I'd be surprised if he'd failed to notice something like that! Too busy writing perhaps. He's clearly been bitten by the bug. And once you start down that road you can never turn back. Lucian closed his eye and listened to Michael reading the details of his life. It was intoxicating. Even the events from before 1992 were vivid in his mind. As real to Lucian as if he had actually been there. Was this how it had felt for the one who had listened to the first forty years? Or had the second Lucian suffered from a sense of regret? Of being short-changed? In the end did he judge the sacrifice as too great for what he had received in return? Lucian doubted it. He too had given up much, but knew he would do it all over again if offered the chance. Michael would be the same. He won't try to fight it. He was born for a deal like this. Why else would he have agreed to come down here to take such a job? With no family or wife, what did he have to lose? A life of teaching books that other people had written? No, he wanted it. And who knows, being the last there was always a chance he might get more time than any of us. Imagine that? Living as Lucian for longer than twenty years. I thought for a minute it might be me. That somehow I had won the lottery. But no. There needs to be a fourth. There has always needed to be a fourth. Does he realise? Maybe I should tell him more. I can feel the time approaching. Faster than I expected. Perhaps it's because he's ready. I can hear it in his voice. Reading those details like he knows them by heart. As if they were already part of his bones. Maybe I should warn him? But if I don't will it even matter? Won't he just know? The same way I did? Or did I? Hard to remember that far back. Memory is flagging. Too many spliffs. Again Lucian partially opened an eye. I can see it's already happening. He's lost some weight. Too late to change anything now. I wonder if he suspects? But wouldn't he have asked? Hasn't mentioned that photograph again. Stupid mistake not to throw it away. Sentimental old fool. Nearly spoiled everything. Can't say I'm surprised he found it. I faintly recall doing something similar. All those clothes. Who could resist trying them on? Now I can't even remember who that person was. The name has been completely erased from my mind. Naive to expect it to still be there. Lurking some place for me to find. An old portrait hidden in the attic. Once you break with your past like that you can't go back. And why would you want to? Happy to be Lucian. Worth absolutely everything. Had a blast. Had a blast.

94.

Rachel closed the stall door and sat on the lid of the toilet as she scrolled through her phone messages and texts. They were having cake in the office to celebrate the intern's engagement, and she refused to pretend it was cause for a celebration. Not that Rachel had met the groom to-be, but after hearing stories about his gym business; fast new car; how he had less than two per cent body fat, and an uncle on the local council, she felt sure she already knew what the world could expect from him. He would have that intern impregnated before the end of their honeymoon, after which she would be pressured into giving up her job and any chance of the career she had spent the past four years and $30,000 trying to achieve. All for the thrill of staying at home to take care of a child and its father. The same man who would likely start screwing around three months before the baby was born, if he wasn't already. Then there would be a second baby almost straight away, if not twins, and at the same time his business hours would grow steadily longer, and his nights out with mates later and later. She would have suspicions, but only when he left his phone at home by accident would her fears be confirmed. And only then would she realise that the cake they had sliced and passed around the office had been full of ashes. The burnt remains of her wasted potential.

Rachel shivered at how malicious her thoughts had become. It was not like her to be so scornful of love. Although she was disappointed to see someone so young, with so much potential, acting so conservatively, it did not mean the girl's marriage would not work out. What the hell did she know about relationships? Maybe risking a career for love was the right thing to do. Maybe it was what she should have done herself instead of working ridiculous hours and following ex-boyfriends halfway across the country. Rachel decided to contribute fifty dollars to the wedding gift from the office. Maybe even a hundred.

As she scrolled her perfectly manicured thumb hovered over Michael's number. It had been four months and still he had not called, leaving Rachel to consider three possible conclusions: he had found a new girlfriend and stayed in Hobart; failed to finish his book and was too embarrassed to admit it to her face; or returned to Sydney and decided not to contact her. Strangely, it was the second scenario that bothered Rachel the most. On her return flight from Hobart she had had a strong hunch that unlike so many journalists and editors she knew, Michael was actually going to finish the book he had set out to write. She hoped it was true, and that his silence was simply a case of not wanting to rekindle their affair. Rachel had hardly been sitting by her phone waiting for him to call. She had more pride than that. There had been five dates since her return to Sydney. But all the men had talked about was how much money they made, while flashing their expensive wristwatches as if they were some symbol of virility. And even when Rachel found herself in bed with one, all he had wanted to do was re-enact scenes from his favourite porn films and share his dreams of driving across America on a Harley Davidson. She might have wanted a relationship with someone different from Michael, but she needed a little more imagination than that. And a hell of a lot more passion.

Rachel decided that a text would be best. Less of a shock and more time for him to think before he responded. She could hear people entering the bathroom to wash sticky cake off their fingers. High on an afternoon hit of sugar and chocolate, their voices were loud and full of laughter. Rachel's red thumbnail became a blur as she typed her message.

Hi Steve. Sorry about last time. You caught me by surprise. Still no word from Michael. You? Just wondering... still interested in chasing me around the couch?

95.

Where the hell were the aspirin? Michael searched the shelves of the medicine cabinet but failed to find the rectangular box of pills. He had again been woken by pain. Aching bones. Cramped muscles. Itching skin. Dry eyeballs. Watery nose. The cold he had just recovered from appeared to have returned for a second round, and he despaired at the prospect of being unwell again. The bathroom light hurt his eyes, and a tune was looping inside his head – Judee Sill's 'There's a Rugged Road' – which Michael realised must have been playing in his brain while he was asleep. He drank one, two glasses of water. Pressed a cold washcloth against his face. Was aspirin going to be enough?

He switched on a lamp in the sunroom and set about rolling a joint of serious intent. His fingers were so swollen that they fumbled with the papers. And his tongue was dry again. Perhaps he was dehydrated. Another glass of water before he began to inhale deeply. The marijuana dulled the pain to a point, but the idea of a few aspirin to help him get back to sleep was insistent. He gave the bathroom cabinet a repeat inspection then decided to check Lucian's bedroom.

Michael switched on the hall light and partially opened the door, allowing just enough glow inside the room to see the box on Lucian's bedside table. The spliff was still burning between his fingers, and rather than put it down or out Michael stood in the hall smoking with purpose.

As the roach fell into the sitting room fireplace he realised he had become unsteady. Tiny hallucinations flickered at the corners of his eyes, and once again his mouth was dry. He stepped inside Lucian's room, successfully avoided a pair of slippers then quietly snatched the aspirin.

What do you think you're doing? asked Lucian from the shadowed side of his double bed.

Michael jumped, tripped over the slippers and stumbled back to the door. Sorry, he whispered as he regained his balance and held up the box. Just needed some aspirin. Getting a cold again.

Oh what are you complaining about?

I'm not complaining. Go back to sleep.

This is everything you've ever wanted. The shortcut you've always dreamed about finding.

There's no need to get upset. Just go back to sleep.

No struggle. No sacrifice. No risk. Especially not to your precious pay cheque. It's just a promotion for you, isn't it? I've done this, I've done that. I know, next I'll become a writer. Just like putting on a hat. Ridiculous. You're going to have to stop thinking that by documenting an author's life you can learn what it means to be a writer. That's psychology, not literature. Is that why they call it literary analysis? Well it couldn't be further from the truth. Being an artist is not something you can think into existence. You either are or you aren't. It is or it isn't. And no amount of study will alter the situation. You can't buy your way in. You've got to earn it. Take the gamble. Fail. Lose friends. Lose everything. Accept the consequences. How else will you know if it's in you? *Really* in you. An imperative to your existence. So much so that success becomes irrelevant. By all means publish a book. Publish two. But it won't necessarily make you a writer. You have to forget everything you know. Or think you know. And start to feel around for it. Listen. Smell. They're not meant to be just words on the page. They're meant to be whispers. Shouts. Songs. Remember? Why anyone would want to...

Michael opened the bedroom door wider and saw Lucian sitting up in bed with his eyes closed. He was dreaming. Prattling on in his sleep. Flabbergasted with his secretary even in his subconscious. The tirade continued as Michael pulled the door to. He then hurried to the bathroom and washed down a double dose of aspirin.

96.

It was only 4pm. Why wasn't the general store open? There was smoke rising from the chimney. Maybe Carl was in the bathroom. Michael peered through the front windows and tried the door handle for a third time. Still locked. He knocked again. Waited in case Carl was doing something upstairs, or was on the phone. He looked around. Saw Matthew sitting on the bench outside the pub, reading. Maybe Carl was having a drink, or talking with Paul. Michael found the pub empty except for the regulars at the bar. No one was eating lunch at this late stage in the day. He waved to Paul manning the taps then stepped back outside.

Waiting for your mum to finish work?

Matthew nodded and continued to inspect the Lego catalogue that had been included with his latest purchase.

She doesn't usually work this late, does she?

Some pensioners came up in a bus to see the aqueduct, then stayed for lunch.

Oh, right. Michael turned back to the general store. You haven't seen Carl around have you?

I think he's gone into town.

Any idea when he might be back?

Matthew looked up from his catalogue. You shouldn't buy things from Carl, you know. It isn't right.

Really? Why do you say that?

You just shouldn't, Matthew whispered. He isn't very nice. He gets angry all the time.

Michael had little experience of talking with children, and quickly searched for an appropriate response. You know sometimes grown ups can have a lot on their minds and forget to be polite, he said as he sat beside Matthew to avoid appearing like an authority figure. Maybe you just caught Carl on a bad day. Try to give him another chance. I'm sure you'll find he isn't angry *all* the time.

Oh he isn't angry with me. He's nice to me. It's Paul he's angry with.

I see. Did Paul mention this to you?

No, Mum did. She says Carl isn't always a good friend, but Paul keeps forgiving him.

Maybe your mum is just trying to make sure that Paul takes care of himself.

Like sitting on his stool behind the bar?

Exactly.

But Paul won't do it anymore.

What do you mean?

He put it in the storeroom. He says that sitting on a stool all day makes him fat. But standing up all the time makes Paul's legs swell up and hurt.

Michael realised that Matthew was just repeating what Penny had said in the privacy of their home. I don't think you need to worry about Paul. He's a grown-up. He can take care of himself.

But Mum says we need to take care of each other. We take care of Paul and Paul takes care of us.

Well she's right, of course, but you shouldn't say those things about Carl to anyone else. If he heard you say them it might hurt his feelings.

That's what Mum said as well. She told me not to tell anyone.

Okay, well, good. Do as your mum says.

But I tell everyone I can.

Michael waited for Matthew to look up and see the seriousness of his expression. Well from now on I don't think you should, okay?

The nine year old shrugged and returned to the pages of his catalogue.

Michael stood up to leave, but was reluctant to end their conversation on such a serious note. Sorry I haven't been down for a Lego date yet. I've been busy trying to finish off some work. But when I see your mum next I'll arrange a time so when we can get stuck into it. Okay?

Matthew looked up with a puzzled expression. You want to play Lego?

Of course I do. Remember, we said that we were going to build something together.

Matthew still looked perplexed. All right. But make sure you bring Michael as well, okay?

97.

It must have been the beard, thought Michael. Had Matthew seen only the hairy face and automatically decided he was speaking to Lucian? Recently there had been no time to trim it back. He had been too busy writing his book. Researching Lucian's life. Changing Lucian's sheets. Assisting him to the bathroom. Cooking his meals. Rolling his spliffs. Of course it was the beard, otherwise there was no strong resemblance. How could there be? Michael stared at the bathroom mirror. All right, he would admit his face had changed a little. But surely not enough to be confused with Lucian. Hopefully he did not look *that* old yet. His whiskers had definitely grown more grey. And two blood vessels seemed to have recently broken across the bridge of his nose. But it was hardly enough to account for such a mistake in identity. Michael's heart began to race, and he started to search for a mirror small enough to hold in his hand. When the house failed to produce one, he attempted to improvise. However the blade of a carving knife was too small. The curve of a ladle distorted his face. And the lids of Lucian's pots were so old and worn that they offered only a blurred reflection of his head. But would a CD work?

Michael opened the bedroom door and checked that Lucian was asleep. A strong wind blowing across the peak of Mount Wellington was moving clouds fast enough to allow the last of the day's sunlight to flood the room intermittently. From the reading chair Michael examined Lucian's face, then compared it with the nose, skin, ears and eyebrows he saw in the CD's reflective surface. The image was far from perfect. Michael's features were sharp, but appeared to be covered by a film of mistiness and a shifting rainbow of refracted light. His forehead seemed too large, suggesting a degree of distortion, and the finger poking through the CD's centre hole certainly didn't help. After a while Michael decided that he could assess nothing with any certainty. His brain felt too flummoxed by the idea that Matthew could make such an error. Had he and Lucian been living together too closely? Were they like an old couple who were no longer distinguishable as individuals? But didn't that require thirty or forty years of marriage? Perhaps it was like those dog owners who looked like their pets. Or was it the pets who looked like their owners? Michael could never decide which one it was, and instead considered whether Matthew had merely got their names confused. It sometimes happened to children. Michael checked his face in the CD again. There might be a few rudimentary similarities. The hairline: shape of the jaw. But Lucian looked so much older. Michael conceded he no longer appeared as spry as he once had, but a haircut and a few hours in the sun would rectify that. Maybe he should shave the beard. It had definitely aged him. But it also helped to keep his face warm.

What's that you've got there? asked Lucian as he opened his eyes.

Huh?

The CD. Who's it by?

Michael turned over the object in his hand and realised he had no idea what it was. He had just grabbed a random CD from the nearest shelf. Kawabata Makoto – *Hosanna Mantra*, he read from the cardboard sleeve.

Well that's certainly a cosmic record. Are you going to put it on?

Sure, said Michael. I was just waiting for you to wake up.

98.

Lucian sat up in bed with a towel draped across his chest and felt Michael guide a razor down the length of his neck. It might have been morning. It might not. Lucian slept so much these days that his body clock had become disconnected with notions of night and day, morning and afternoon.

Oh god sorry. Michael reached for the corner of the towel.

What for?

I just cut your neck.

Didn't feel a thing! No need to worry. This is all rather pleasant.

Michael pressed the edge of the towel to the tiny cut, and dipped the razor in the bowl of warm water sitting on the bedside table.

What's this music you're playing? asked Lucian. It's quite beautiful.

DJ Sprinkles, *Midtown 120 Blues*.

One of yours or mine?

It's the other new record I bought at the same time as Oval.

Lucian nodded. I remember now. It has a painting of a laughing face on the cover.

That's right.

For a while there I thought its beat was a little too repetitive. But now I'm inside of it I can hear all sorts of ideas at work. It's very romantic, isn't it?

I thought it would appeal to you. It's all about rhythm, right? Michael pressed a thumb under Lucian's chin and started to shave the far side of the author's neck.

Lucian noticed that Michael's index finger was stained with ink. You've been working hard I see. How's the book coming along? You must be close to finishing it by now. Or have I been taking up too much of your time?

It's almost there, I think. A few more weeks and hopefully I should have a first draft.

Well done. Congratulations. I bet that's a relief.

When I'm finished it will be.

Will you promise to do me a favour when you think it's ready?

Of course. Anything.

I want you to send it to my agent in London. I'm sure you've come across her name and details amongst my papers. You're to tell her I'm recommending you.

That's very kind of you. But don't you want to read it first?

Lucian shook his head ever so slightly. Not necessary. I saw the opening chapters. I'm confident it's going to be an excellent piece of work.

Michael dried Lucian's neck and soothed it with moisturising cream. Would you like to lie back down?

No thank you. I think I'll keep looking out the window for a while and watch the weather change.

You think it's going to cloud over?

This is Tasmania, my boy. The weather is always about to change.

Lucian watched Michael open the curtains as wide as possible, then carry away the bowl and razor. From down the hall he could hear the kettle being filled for tea, and assumed it would accompany a soft-boiled egg. Fifteen minutes later the meagre meal appeared on a tray. Lucian had no appetite, and couldn't really taste anything anymore, but still accepted the morsels of egg Michael spooned into his mouth in the knowledge that it was necessary for him to stay strong for as long as possible.

You were adopted, weren't you? he asked in the hope of delaying another serving being inserted between his lips.

Michael paused, surprised that he had identified a feature of himself he thought was kept well hidden.

How did you know?

It wasn't so hard. I was as well.

But I thought you...

And so was the one before me. We all were. And we're all from Tasmania as well.

Michael endeavoured to steer the conversation back towards reality. I think you'll find I was born in Queensland. It says so on my birth certificate.

But where were you conceived? And who was your mother? Where did she grow up? Who was your father? None of us know for certain. But I can guarantee you that at least one of your parents was born somewhere on this island. It's why we always return. Like salmon smelling their way upstream. It's home for us and always will be. Every time we land back here we know it's exactly where we're supposed to live. Nowhere else in the world like it. The scent of the air. Sassafras and Needle Bush: sandstone and moss. It's cold and wet, but it's also crisp and clear. You can think down here. I don't know how anyone north of Melbourne gets any thinking done. I wasted a lot of time trying to live somewhere else, but eventually we all return here. Just like you have. So now we need to start getting in supplies. You'll have to stay hidden for a little while. I don't remember how long exactly. That period is always a little bit patchy. It's far from an exact science this whole process. You'd think that by the third time we'd know some things for certain, but it seems none of us has ever bothered to write anything down. I'd say food for at least four weeks should be enough. There's money under the rug in the hall. I guess there's no need to tell you where things are. You probably already know. And if not, you will soon enough.

I have absolutely no idea what you're talking about.

Yes you do. Deep down inside you do. Remember the last time this happened? In 1992? Just after *Foxtrot* came out? It was in this very room. And before that in 1972? Not long after Lucian got back from Vietnam. The house might have been less furnished then, but I'm sure it was the same layout.

How do you expect me to remember something from 1972? I wasn't even born then.

Born? You're not born even now, my boy. Not really. But you soon will be. That's why we're here. That's why we all come back to Tasmania. To this house and this mountain.

To build a cocoon. Every twenty years. That's what all this is for. Lucian moved his eyes around the room. To make a cocoon.

Michael tired of trying to make Lucian talk sense and decided to play along. You're planning on changing into a butterfly?

Me? No, there's little chance of that occurring. This body of mine is too weak and old to be transformed for a second time. The cocoon is not for me. The cocoon is for you.

99.

Jesus it's cold, Carl grumbled to himself as he walked around the store. He had forgotten to get in wood and kindling the day before, and it had rained while he slept, so the fire in the pot-bellied stove was refusing to stay alight. He heard Maureen's voice inside his head, explaining why he should do things and when, but it appeared so frequently throughout his day that Carl had stopped listening. He pulled back the bolts on the front door, which hardly seemed necessary in a place like Wood Green – South Africa, now there's a place where you need security – and noticed he was standing on a piece of paper. An envelope containing money and a shopping list had been slipped beneath the door during the night. As he read the numbers beside the items, Carl assumed that Michael and Lucian were giving a party. He had not received an invitation but that was hardly surprising. Beyond Paul, he had made no friends in Wood Green. Penny was civil enough, although her son had a surly manner about him. And the rest of the community, well they could manage a good morning or a good afternoon if they needed a loaf of bread. But as for saying hello in the street, how are you, is the business doing well, anything you need to know just ask, would you like to come to dinner as a welcome to Wood Green – you could forget it. He had put an end to home deliveries. Petrol was too expensive, no one tipped, and if you got something wrong in the order then watch out because the whole world was about to collapse, and it was *all your fault*. But he was willing to make an exception for an order this large. No one could be expected to carry home so much shopping. And Maureen had explained that neither Lucian nor Michael knew how to drive. Which to Carl seemed insane. Like a self-imposed exile, he thought as he reread the list. It was going to use up nearly all of the shop's fresh stock, and a good portion of its dried goods as well. Maybe he should take the opportunity, before he reordered, to close the place up and have a couple weeks off. To get his head straight. Figure out what exactly he wanted from Tasmania. From life. Though he checked his phone and computer every day, he still had seen no mention of his name in the newspapers back home. And increasingly it occurred to Carl that perhaps hiding was unnecessary. Of course returning to Johannesburg was out of the question. But there was a big world out there, bigger than Wood Green, and he still had his old passport. He could use some time away from Paul as well. There had been too many arguments of late. Carl knew he had a temper and that he could be impatient, but everything up here moved so slowly! Maybe it would be better if he just slipped away. Left a note on the shop's front door. He could cancel his regular deliveries with a few phone calls. And it was not as if he was going to be losing much money. Carl suspected that closing for a couple of weeks might even make good business sense. And after that, well, who knew what he might do. The desire to sell the business continued to pester him no matter how many times he rationalised it as imprudent to both his getaway and his capital. But a loss of funds was inevitable whether he stayed or quit. Carl also knew there were degrees of loss, and time after time reminded himself of the things in life more important than money: conversation; cafés; nightclubs; clothes shopping; meeting new men; being able to use his phone beyond the range of his home wi-fi. And let's face it, Paul and him were never going to make it. The pub owner was too passive for Carl's taste, and a little too soft. Sure they had fun together, but it was not as if either of them believed it was true love. No one was playing that silly game. So why hang around? Carl began to go through the items on Lucian's shopping list. Bread. Apples. Cheese. Biscuits. Flour. Meat. It was going to fill seven or eight boxes at least. If he did everything first – called the suppliers, threw away the remaining perishables, closed the upstairs windows – he could load the car, lock the front door, drive the boxes to Lucian's house, then head straight off. Why not? He hankered to feel free. Liberated from Wood Green. And here was his chance. The fire in the stove had gone out again, but Carl decided he could put up with the cold for a few more hours. After that who knew where he might be. Maybe even someplace warm.

100.

Michael lay on a couch in the sunroom sipping soup. It was all his digestive system could tolerate, and was no doubt why Lucian had instructed him to cook great vats of the stuff when the supplies from the general store had appeared on the verandah. In the two weeks since then Michael could hardly remember a single moment when his body had not felt like it was being broken apart and reassembled beneath his skin. He had hung a towel over the bathroom mirror. Inadvertent glimpses of his reflection while stepping out of the shower had become too distressing. The face he had seen was like a boxer's after a title fight – bruised, swollen, slack, broken. Maybe the pot was playing tricks with him. Though he took aspirin with breakfast, aspirin with morning tea, aspirin with lunch, aspirin all fucking day long, it needed to be supplemented with large doses of marijuana. This made the task of writing problematic. When he woke in the morning his head was languid and foggy – his ideas colourless and unintelligible. Only walking outside, in the cold air, around the house, through the forest, with Sadie by his side, for at least thirty minutes, could awaken and sharpen his mind sufficiently to begin the day's work. Michael left his office door open in case Lucian needed anything, and so he could hear the sound of a typewriter even as he slept. But by early afternoon the pain became too distracting and he would have to abandon his desk for his first spliff of the day. He would then sit in front of the open fire, or lie on a couch trying to ignore the strange bubbling in his stomach, the pulse throbbing in the side of his neck, his cracking joints, random nerve spasms, and the involuntary twitching of his muscles. Occasionally he threw up. Other times he wanted to but couldn't. Twice a day Michael also had to apply moisturising cream to Lucian's arms, legs and torso to prevent his skin from splitting. Keeping the old man hydrated with just drinking water was impossible. He was awake for only a few minutes each day, and even though Michael dedicated the entire time to encouraging liquid down Lucian's throat, it appeared his body was drying out. By around 8pm Michael was exhausted, and would fall into bed praying for the painkillers to endure until morning. Yet even if such a wish were granted it was no guarantee of a restful night's slumber. Just an opportunity to dream more confusing, terrifying, occasionally pornographic images from Lucian's past. Sometimes to the accompaniment of typing and shouting from across the hall. On particularly dark nights, when the wind blew strong enough to tug at the roof and make the surrounding trees sacrifice branches to avoid being uprooted; when the rain hammered against the front door and found its way down the length of the chimney to hiss in the fireplace, Michael would dream that Lucian was calling out all manner of rogue phrases and dissonant ramblings. Lucian! Lucian! Free as a bird. That's why the books are so different. You won't fly scared anymore. Price to pay. Something about the biology. Not an exact science. No children. Far from an exact science. Metal in your thigh. Dark days ahead. I already see the resemblance. For you and me. Home again. Brought it back from Vietnam. To be. To be. Lucian at last. Book number five. Show Maureen. I can see it now. Don't be shy. Get 'em out. Get 'em out. You're a lucky man. Give it a good name. Don't inhale. Aches when it's going to snow. A faultless barometer. The land. The sky. The sea. I'm taking it all. An apple isle. Beautiful Sadie. I'm not leaving. Time gentlemen. I'm not leaving. Rest with the others. I make three. Lucian makes four. Lucian the fourth! Lucian the fourth!

Sometimes when Michael woke he found himself standing in the hall with Sadie at his side. The typewriter silent and Lucian in bed, asleep, illuminated by lightning flashing across the mountain. Mornings after such nights he would feel even worse than usual, yet he always made it to his desk on time. The book was almost done. All it needed was another week, two at most. Michael felt drained by its creation, but as he lay on the couch, sipping soup, it also seemed as if writing the novel was the only thing holding him together.

101.

Maureen knocked softly on the screen door at the back of the kitchen. Can I get fries with that?

It's you! Penny quickly wiped her hands on her apron and opened the door. What a lovely surprise. Come here and give me a kiss. You look wonderful. How have you been? *Where* have you been? Oh, hold on a second and let me finish these orders.

Sorry. I thought the lunch trade would be done by now.

It usually is, but there's a retirement village in Hobart that's discovered what a great pub this is, so now we're getting a busload of pensioners three times a week. Penny plated two slices of lemon tart, then spooned a dollop of mascarpone beside them. I'll be right back, she said and carried the desserts into the pub.

You're waiting as well?

Penny shrugged. It's the last order for the day. And Paul's busy serving.

He must be pleased with the extra business. I'm surprised he hasn't hired someone to give you a hand.

We're definitely considering it. I can't keep doing all this by myself for much longer. Matthew will be on holidays in a couple of weeks, but he's still too young to go near anything hot.

How's he doing?

Great. Taller every day.

Tell him I said hi, will you?

You're not staying? He'll be home in an hour. I'm sure he'd love to see you.

I just popped in to say hello. I don't want to get in your way.

Don't be silly. I can pack up and talk at the same time. I suppose you've seen our news.

Yeah, where's Carl gone? The sign on the door says he'll be back in two weeks. Tim and I never took holidays like that. But maybe that was the problem.

That sign has been up for over a month. Penny carried the rest of the lemon tart back into the cool room.

You mean he just ran away? Maureen began loading plates into a dishwasher tray.

Certainly looks that way. Bet it won't be long before we see a For Sale sign going up.

But what happened? He can't have gone broke that quickly. Did something go wrong?

Penny almost told Maureen to stop what she was doing, but then remembered that Matthew had soccer practice this afternoon and there was still prep to do for tomorrow. No one knows. Maybe he just decided he didn't like it up here. Too cold perhaps. You certainly managed to avoid one hell of a winter.

You mean it's been colder than this?

Today is a summer's day compared to what we've been through. The roads have been closed four or five times since you and Tim left.

I'm kind of sorry to have missed that. It must have looked beautiful.

Penny stopped and smiled. Yeah, it did.

Maureen slid the tray into the dishwasher and pressed the start button. So what has everyone been doing for bread and milk?

Paul has set up a little emergency service until either Carl returns or someone else buys the shop. Don't suppose you want to take it over again? I imagine it's going for less than what you sold it.

No thanks. Done that. Still, I'm surprised it went so bad for Carl so quickly.

I'm not. He wasn't the sharpest tool in the box. Or the nicest for that matter.

I did get that impression. How's Paul taking it?

There were a couple of bumpy days to begin with. And every once in a while he still gets upset. But it's hard to think fondly of someone who just leaves without saying goodbye.

You're kidding.

Can you believe it? How mean is that? Just shot through without a word. Between you and me I'm glad to see the back of him. Paul is his old self again, sitting on his stool, and the pub has never done so well. But that's enough about our dramas. I want to hear about what you've been up to.

Nothing half as exciting. After Tim and I finalised everything I just went driving around Tasmania.

And it took you that long?

There wasn't any reason to rush. Most of my time in Tasmania had been spent up here, so I wanted to see some more of the state. Did a few bushwalks. Climbed a mountain or two. Read a lot. Ate a lot. Slept a lot.

Well it suits you. You look great.

Thanks. So do you.

Penny snapped lids onto the plastic containers arranged around the counter. I look the same as I always do. Any word from Tim?

Yeah, he's fine. Already has himself a girlfriend. Says they're going to open up a frozen yoghurt shop in the city.

Not Hobart?

No. Melbourne.

Thank God. I hate those things. So what are your plans?

I don't have any at the moment. I'd like to stay in Tasmania if I can, but I'll need to find some work eventually. I'd prefer just to sit at home and read books, but I've checked the papers and there was nothing advertised.

Yeah, not many jobs like that around I suspect. You could always come and work with me for a while if you've got nothing better to do.

Maureen glanced about the kitchen and smelled fennel, salad dressing and the oil in the fryer. You're serious?

Of course I am. I know you can cook. And you're sane... sort of. Penny carried her plastic containers into the cool room.

But I've never worked in a proper kitchen before. I've always just done my own thing in my own house.

I can show you how it works. It's not very hard. This was my first commercial kitchen as well, you know.

But wouldn't it seem weird for me to come back after leaving so recently?

Penny began to wipe down the benches. More like you've made an intelligent decision. I wouldn't leave Wood Green for the world. And I bet Paul would love the idea. You could rent one of his rooms upstairs. Or stay with me and Matthew. We've got a spare bedroom. And you already know everybody in town. Why wouldn't you do it? It's not as if it's going to be a lot of work. You won't get rich. But I can guarantee there'll be plenty of time for you to read.

Maureen stared out the screen door. I'm not sure everyone would be glad about me coming back.

Don't worry about Lucian. He never comes in here for lunch anyway. I haven't seen him in ages.

Maureen was surprised that Penny knew about her affair, but when she thought about it for a moment longer it made sense that other people would know.

He's probably finishing his latest book. I was going to drop by and say hello. We never really said a proper goodbye to each other. But it sounds as though he's busy. Maybe I shouldn't disturb him.

Of course you should. It'll give me time to have a word with Paul. The two of us working together is a fantastic idea. We could make this place great. Maybe even open up for dinner. You watch. Together we'll put this pub on the map.

102.

Michael woke struggling for air, as if something or someone had been sitting on his chest while he slept. He raised himself up, coughed clear his throat, reached for the box of aspirin on the floor beside the daybed, and was about to wash down his morning dose when he realised he was not in pain. For a moment he refused to trust the message his body was giving. Ache and discomfort had been present so long that their absence seemed false. And Michael braced himself for the hurt to suddenly emerge with a brutal vengeance. But when it remained absent for one minute, two, and then five, he raised himself out of bed and started to attend to Lucian.

Michael was able to stay at his desk all day. Working on his novel so deeply that at times it felt as if he was nothing more than a conduit for ideas to be conveyed onto the page. There was a cramp in his hand but he could not stop it from moving. His back ached but he refused to stand up from his chair. Hunger could be attended to later. His bladder would just have to wait. Michael had acquired a momentum that he would allow nothing to impede. He felt the influence of his circumstances guiding his thoughts. The story of the young writer's life as a husband, father and successful author had taken over the majority of the narrative, while the menace of the established writer lurked in the background, as if waiting for the perfect opportunity to reveal the coup de grâce of his betrayal. Except nothing was going to happen. The novel was almost done and the moment had arrived for its readers to understand that the established author's encouragement for a life beyond monastic clichés was the most altruistic guidance he could have given the aspiring writer. And that the only ulterior motives had been those brought by the readers themselves.

Michael's pen hovered over the page. He had thought there was more to do; more to say. But as he reread his last sentence he recognised it as the most fitting place for the story to end. He leaned back in his chair and felt a grief invade his heart. Unlike the completion of an essay or thesis, this was a deliberate severing with characters he had brought to life. Grown to know and love. And it involved a sense of bereavement. A lament for the world he was closing a door on. The feeling persisted over the next hour as Michael typed the final pages of his manuscript. All it needed now was a title. He had hoped that one would appear once the story was complete, but as he placed a blank sheet of paper on top of page one his imagination felt insubstantial. What it suggested seemed either too modest or too consciously obtuse. He wanted distinction, but quiet distinction.

He stood in Lucian's bedroom doorway holding his novel against his chest. It's finished, he said. The first draft at least. The body in the bed remained silent. Asleep. Its expression fixed. A chest barely rising with each intake of breath. Michael placed his manuscript on the reading chair so he could moisten a cloth and press it inside Lucian's mouth. Previously the body had made an instinctual sucking response, but this time there was none. Today, thought Michael. Maybe tomorrow. All excitement at reaching the end of his book evaporated in a desire for things to be as they once were. Michael knocking on the front door at 1pm. Lucian stirring risotto while extolling the virtues of Christina Stead or John Hawkes. A night spent sitting on the couches, immersed in pot, conversation and music.

Michael searched the shelves of vinyl for Roland Kirk's *The Inflated Tear*. Lucian had been right of course. What was the use of choosing music you were never going to hear? He turned up the volume so every detail would reach the bedroom at the front of the house, and by the time the first side was complete he was weeping. As side two began he returned down the hall and found Lucian awake. For an instant his heart filled with excitement at the prospect of sharing another moment together. But then he realised Lucian's eyes were no longer blinking.

103.

Michael removed the towel from the bathroom mirror and saw Lucian staring back. The shock and surprise that should have accompanied such a moment however did not materialise. Instead fascination triumphed as Michael calmly examined the details of his transformation. He winked. Poked out his tongue. Turned sideways to inspect his new profile. Every feature he remembered from Lucian's face appeared to be the same. He stepped back and took off his shirt. Found new freckles. A reconfiguration of chest hair. There were the scars from the knife wounds he had suffered in Italy. Michael opened his mouth. Two molars had disappeared from the back of his jaw. Had he swallowed them in his sleep? His neck seemed longer. His nose thinner. Michael unbuckled his belt. Just as he had thought. Circumcised. He leaned towards the mirror. Even the colour of his eyes had changed from brown to grey.

With a knapsack on his back Michael stood at Lucian's bedside and decided it was only right to include the old dressing gown. He pulled the covers away, gently sat the body up, and threaded Lucian's arms through the garment's sleeves. The author seemed smaller, stiffer, as Michael laid him back down and shimmied the dressing gown behind his legs. He then wrapped Lucian tightly in a sheet and found him light enough to lift off the bed with just one arm. As the body settled on his shoulder it made a crackling sound like a cicada husk. He carried Lucian to the backyard and grabbed the rusted shovel from the side of the house. The morning was cold and clear, and still so new that sunlight was yet to make its way to the forest floor.

Five hours later Michael reached the clearing where he and Lucian had first taken mushrooms together. He was exhausted, damp with perspiration, and an ache was throbbing in his shoulder where Lucian had grown steadily heavier. The shrouded body lay on the ground, in the shade, as Michael drank water, munched a handful of nuts, then slept with his face in a splinter of midday sun. He woke after an hour and began his search for a place to dig. The centre of the clearing was not an option in case someone stumbled upon the site by accident. Nor did Michael wish to accidentally disturb the graves of the two other Lucians whom he suspected were decomposing somewhere in the same location. He wondered if the mushrooms he had eaten had grown on top of a grave that had been dug twenty years before. It certainly seemed like the type of thing that Lucian would do. So he searched for a comparable site – out of the sun, near a fallen tree, with earth that was moist and soft, yet free from any fungi growing nearby.

The sun was almost behind Mount Wellington by the time Michael carried Lucian to the edge of the hole.

As delicately as possible he slid the body down into the six-foot grave. The white sheet looked stark against the black soil, and while Michael tried to catch his breath he searched for a prayer or sentiment to encapsulate all he felt. Except it was difficult to accept that Lucian was truly dead, as he had seen him earlier that day staring back in the bathroom mirror. The person he felt he was really burying was Michael. Along with all his fears. Lack of purpose. Guilt. The persistent sensation of never knowing who he was and where he stood within the world. He began to methodically shovel soil back into the hole, and after an hour all that remained was a short mound camouflaged with leaves and twigs and any other forest litter that had been close to hand.

With aching arms and legs Michael stumbled down a swiftly darkening mountainside. The sky was clear so the temperature plunged, chilling his face and lungs as he hurried towards the boundary of Wood Green. A rising moon outlined the trees and their branches and eventually the back of the house. Michael returned the shovel to its former position, kicked off his muddied boots, poured dried food into Sadie's bowl, drank a glass of water, then dropped onto a couch in the sunroom. His clothes were filthy and he needed a bath, but first he wanted to sit and wait for his heart to stop pounding, and acclimatise to the recognition that what he had just done was conceal the evidence.

104.

Michael felt Sadie lick his face, and opened an eye to see that it was morning. Sounds of popping and unsticking then erupted into the room as he pried his muddy clothes off the black leather cushions. Eyes bleary, he shuffled into the bathroom to set a bath running, relieve his bladder, and discard every item of clothing. While the water ran Michael raided the refrigerator for milk and cheese and breathed heavily though his nose as he masticated great mouthfuls of food. When the bath was ready he selected *Arthur Verocai*, for no other reason than it was a reliable record for every mood. Though after he had lowered his body into the hot water he questioned how he knew such a thing. He had never heard Arthur Verocai before. With Sadie's chin resting on the side of the tub, Michael lay still and listened to himself think. Was he losing his mind, or did his internal voice sound different? Breathier. Slower. And could he feel it reaching conclusions with greater speed and precision? As if skipping two or three steps in each deliberation? He also realised he was aware of more details in everything he saw. From the long whiskers extending from Sadie's eyebrows, to the bathroom tiles turning a different shade of green under the glare of the ceiling light. Michael felt a rush of horror. He had not expected the transformation to penetrate *that* deep, and frantically tried to hold on to ideas about himself that he had always known. But like the bathwater he sat in, each characteristic slipped through his fingers, until eventually he could not even remember what type of information he was trying to retain.

After making a selection from Lucian's wardrobe, Michael noticed his manuscript sitting on the reading chair; its cover page still awaiting a title. One would come he told himself as he gathered together the cups and plates in the room and carried them back into the kitchen. He then pulled off all the bedclothes, flipped the mattress, shook the pillows, and threw open the window to let in fresh air. He swept the floor, wiped the bedside table, put on Lucian's wristwatch, and remade the bed with fresh sheets and blankets. Next he went through the office, put the old typewriter back in the closet, unplugged the lamp, gathered together the various papers scattered around the room, and haphazardly piled them into boxes that he then kicked into a corner. Anything he did not recognise as belonging to Lucian – satchel, suitcase, mobile phone, laptop – he carried to the garbage bin at the side of the house. He put on another album – *Exuma* – then set to work tidying the sunroom. A hearty stew was defrosting in the kitchen sink, and he found a small crystal vase for a bunch of wildflowers picked from the backyard. Michael hung out washing, put on a second load, cleaned the mud off the couch, then passed through the house looking for his next job to do. Sadie followed him into Lucian's room, where he stood in front of the wall covered with photographs and identified the people within them. There was Tom Andrews in New York. Celia Porter from the weekend they had stolen together in Edinburgh. Raymond Cass from London. And Phillip Unsworth puffing out his chest on Kingston Beach. Remembering such old friends transported him through space and time, and only when he returned to the present did he finally notice the manuscript on Lucian's desk. It was thinner than he had expected, but a clear-sighted novella of heartbreaking beauty was not a bad way to end a career. He sat down and began to read, except the words on the page appeared out of focus. Michael tried on Lucian's reading glasses and his eyes grew wide with disbelief. He started to scan the pages; check for details; jump ahead; hold his breath. The story was almost exactly the same as his own novel, except Lucian's version seemed to be more of an outline. Descriptions to raise the work into a piece of crafted writing had not been included. And there were connections in the story that appeared to have missed. Dramatic opportunities not fully exploited. Michael could see the point at which Lucian's mind had begun to fragment, and wondered if it had occurred before his plane had landed in Tasmania, or some time after. For a moment he considered mining the pages for ideas or phrases that might improve his own version of the novel, yet with his next breath he decided against it. He opened the front door, lifted the lid to the wood box, and piled half a dozen logs into the crook of his arm. He waited for the fire in the sitting room to establish itself, then fed the pages of Lucian's manuscript into the flames. Like the body, there could be no evidence. As he watched the papers burn he decided that the only thing he would take from Lucian's version was its title. As a parting gift, and a way of saying thank you for everything he had been given. He returned to the bedroom, lifted his manuscript off the reading chair, and sat at Lucian's desk to write *The Hollow Tree* on the cover page. Underneath he signed Lucian Clarke. At first it shocked him to see his hand automatically create the name in the unfamiliar cursive. But a voice inside his head reassured him that there was nothing unusual about it. It was all perfectly natural.

Lucian fanned the pages of his manuscript and basked in the delight of having completed another book. Tomorrow he would begin revising, then maybe reward himself with a good dinner in Hobart. He set about tidying his desk. Replaced the ribbon in his typewriter; replenished his stock of blank paper, and gathered together the notes he had scribbled during the process of composition. As was his custom, he poured them into a yellow envelope, sealed it shut, and threw it into a box of unrelated materials somewhere in the junk room. On his way back across the hall a knock sounded at the front door. A final flicker of fear passed through Lucian's mind, but what was there to be scared of? He opened the door and saw Maureen standing on the verandah. Her hair tied loosely, and her cheeks bright with the effort of walking up the road from Wood Green.

It appears I can't stay away, she said with a tentative smile.

Good, said Lucian as he reached for her hand. Because I don't want you to any more.

Acknowledgements

Michelle Richardson, for generously sharing her house and enabling me to feel like Hobart is still my home. Also for her local knowledge, which was invaluable when I began writing this book.

Julie-Anne Ford, for expanding my knowledge of literature immeasurably, and knowing this would one day happen. Miss you.

John Tydeman, for persistent encouragement and calling me a writer from the very beginning.

Catherine Simpson, for asking (twice) to read my book, and actually reading it.

Alice Grundy and Ivor Indyk, for inviting *Wood Green* to be a part of Giramondo. I am more than proud to be in such company, and forever grateful for their intelligent, sensitive editing.

Sam Mills, Thom Cuell and Alex Spears, for giving me the opportunity to be a part of Dodo Ink from the beginning. I feel an enormous sense of excitement and privilege. Thank you.

Jessica Craig, whose fierce loyalty is all I could want in an agent. Her role in getting *Wood Green* published has been pivotal, and I feel like the luckiest writer to have such a dignified agent in my corner. Endless thanks to you, and everyone at Pontas Agency.

Francesca Ford, who has read everything I have written and always believed and backed and offered advice and argued and spoken the truth whether I liked it or not. Epic is the only way to describe her help in getting me to this point. Rare and precious is such a wife.

Dodo Ink would like to thank the following supporters, without whom this book would not have been possible...

Stephen Wright
Jim Spears
Jonathan Ruppin
Jenny Bullen
The Zebra
Beulah Maud Devaney
Tessa Brechin
Duncan Proudfoot
Françoise Harvey
Marc Owen Jones
Henrik Dahl Jensen
Helen Barrell
Maris Kreizman
Shanshan Xu
Miriam Miller
Victoria Connelly
Sharon Kivland
Blair Rose
ACHUKA
Ian McMillan
Shelley Bowdler
Olivia Bays
Paddy Reynolds
Paul Flieshman
James Miller
Caroline Goldsmith
Aki Schilz
Joseph Bain

Kit Preston Be
Hilary Freeman
James Wise
Kit Caless
Fiona McGlade
Zoe Hayes
Emma Jane Unsworth
Lynda Tahri
Sarah Jones
Andrey Zagoruyko
Tristan Rogers
RP Weston
Alison Ragsdale
Robin and Alison Jones
Dan Martin and Candice Lazarus
David Meller
Chris Williams
Sarah Harkness
Amy Clarke
Andrew Cook
Kat Smith
Ben Pattison-Gordon
Wendy Morrison
Nina Allan
Marion Grace Woolley
Louise Bach
Gabriel Vogt
Rachel Darling
Dixe Wills
Virginia Klein
A J. Ashworth

Sandra James
Jon Day
Thor-Einar Henriksen
Anders Eskemyr
Jennie Gillions
Clive Morrison
Sarah Bradley
Rachel Case
Jacques Testard
Charlie Hill
Jasmin Kirkbride
Hernan Toro
Sarah Wood
Nedda Tichi
Georgina Wright
Francesca R Zerenghi
Emily Sheehan
Jane Greig
Matthew Elizabeth Bryant
Jaimie Batchan
Sofie Blombäck
Alex Herod
Ben Stern
Brendon Warren
David Hebblethwaite
Claire Laurens
Marcus Gipps
Kirstin Lamb
Alice Furse
Philip Berridge
Luke Bartholomew

Dan Coxon
Ana Fletcher
Alison Whittaker
Annabel Gaskell
Naomi Hackett
Marion Kenyon Jones
Tania Hershman
Ben Howkins
Hannah Riches
Arno Vos
Elizabeth Aaron
Susan Osborne
Geoffrey Rabe
Tamara Craiu
Cat Rushmore
Mike Scott Thomson
Helen Swain
Graham Allen
Woody
Brian
James and Paula Wilson
Natalie Marshall
Efford-Eliraz
Nigel Parker
Paul Brindley
Katie Ley
Harriet Devine
Matthew Battle
@Not_James_Brown
Anne Marie Reilly
Adam Banks

Naomi Frisby
Maccewill J.D. Yip
Faaez Samadi
Francesca Ford
Richard Sheehan
Suzanne Kavanagh
Melissa Aho
Literary Kitchen
Ben Fergusson
David Troxler
Matthew Francis
Robert W Archambault
Anonymous
T Hill
Jo Bellamy
Alex Burton-Keeble
Anthony Trevelyan
Stephen Walker
Jayne White
Joanna Robinson
Tze-Wen Chao
Cathryn Steele
Nicholas
Julie Murray (Drynan)
Leesha Gaffney and David Evans
Thomas Sheridan
Irreverence Inc.
Nick Walden
Neil McNally
Jonathan Jones
Lucy Beresford

Anthony Brown
Amanda Jennings
Jim and Celia Spears
Damian Fuller
Kate Williams
Maureen Cuell
Benjamin Spears
Russell Heath

About Dodo Ink

At Dodo Ink, we're book lovers first and foremost. From finding a great manuscript to the moment it hits the bookshop shelves, that's how we approach the publishing process at every stage: excited about giving you something we hope you'll love. Good books aren't extinct, and we want to seek out the best literary fiction to bring to you. A great story shouldn't be kept from readers because it's considered difficult to sell or can't be put in a category. When a reader falls in love with something, they tell another reader, and that reader tells another. We think that's the best way of selling a book there is.

Dodo Ink was founded by book lovers, because we believe that it's time for publishing to pull itself back from the brink of extinction and get back to basics: by finding the best literary fiction for people who love to read. Books shouldn't be thought of in terms of sales figures, and neither should you. We approach every step of the process thinking of how we would want a book to be, as a reader, and give it the attention it deserves. When you see our Dodo logo, we'd like you to think of our books as recommendations from one book lover to another. After all, aren't those the ones that we take the greatest pleasure in?

At Dodo Ink, we know that true book lovers are interested in stories regardless of genre or categorisation. That's how we think a publishing company should work, too: by giving the reader what they want to read, not what the industry thinks they should. We look for literary fiction that excites, challenges, and makes us want to share it with the world. From finding a manuscript to designing the cover, Dodo Ink books reflect our passion for reading. We hope that when you pick up one of our titles, you get the same thrill—that's the best thank you we can think of.

www.dodoink.com